BEHIND CLOSED DOORS

JJ MARSH

TRISKELE BOOKS

Cover design and typesetting: JD Smith.

Published by Prewett Publishing.
All enquiries to admin@beatrice-stubbs.com

First printing, 2012.

ISBN 978-3-9523970-0-8

For Bonnie and Clive – wish you were here

Chapter 1

Utrecht 2007

"Howzit? You got here, then?"

"Yes, Joop. I got here. At last."

"Uh oh. Delays?"

"Right now I'm in a taxi from the airport. Not only did we leave Jo'burg three hours late, but I missed the transfer in Frankfurt and now we've just circled Schiphol for forty-five minutes, waiting for a slot."

Only an asshole like Joop would think it a good idea to whistle into a cell phone.

"Joop, listen. I need to take a shower and eat something. After that, I want to crash."

"Shit, man. That's all you want to do? Friday night is jol night, but if you're creamed…?"

Creamed? Where the hell had this guy learnt his English?

"There's just one other thing I need."

"No sweat. An SMS is on its way with the number of that agency I mentioned. It's not cheap but you can feel the quality."

"I appreciate that. Meet me in the foyer at ten on Monday, OK?"

"Don't wanna do anything tomorrow?"

"I got plans, Joop."

"See you Monday then. Sweet dreams."
Asshole.

He watched the scenery, such as it was. Grey, flat and bleak, with the occasional windmill to make sure you were paying attention. The hotel was a pleasant surprise. The first of the day. Street noise left behind, he glanced up at what looked like some sort of institution in its own grounds. Classy and quiet. His kind of place.

"*Goede avond en onthaal.* Welcome to Utrecht, Sir. We have good news for you. You have an upgrade today, to one of our Empire Suites. Please follow the porter."

A second pleasant surprise. Plenty of space, working area, two TVs, and most importantly, a vast bed. He palmed the kid a coin, who left him to explore the room in peace. Throwing off his coat, he sat on the bed. Heavy linen, an excess of pillows and a firm mattress, which would be seeing some action in the next twenty-four hours, if Joop wasn't exaggerating about that agency. The bathroom was massive, well-furnished with towels and little bottles of wife-pleasing potions. He made a mental note to throw some into his case. And a wall of mirrors behind the bath. Better and better. His mood started to lift. There was a message on the flat screen at the foot of the bed.

Mr van der Veld

Welcome to Grand Hotel Karel V

We hope you enjoy your stay.

Flicking to Bloomberg, he started to undress, while checking the screen for any significant currency movements. As he kicked off his shoes, he noticed the ice bucket and chilled Krug Grande Cuvée. There was a card.

With compliments of D'Arcy Roth.

That explained the upgrade. Nice touch. Unnecessary, as there was no one else in the running, but it certainly put their potential client in the right frame of mind. So, a shower, a glass of

Krug, order room service and put a call through to this agency. All needs met.

As he unzipped his case to find his toiletries bag, he heard a discreet knock at the door. He frowned. Unexpected visitors, including hotel employees who wanted to 'turn down' his bed, were not welcome. He yanked open the door and his frown lifted. The neat grey suit, official clipboard and pulled-back sleek blonde hair told him she was a hotel employee. The pale skin drawn over fine bones and a high forehead, grey-blue eyes and cherub lips told him she was more than welcome. He checked the name badge. *Annelise Visser.*

"Good evening, Mr van der Veld. My name is Frau Visser and I …"

"Good evening, Annelise. Nice to meet you." He offered his hand. A momentary flush before she recovered herself to shake it. He was well aware that conventions in the Netherlands dictate that one should use surnames in formal situations. He didn't give a shit.

"I am the Senior Hospitality Director, sir. I am here to check that your suite is satisfactory."

"The suite seems fine, Annelise, but I do have one concern."

The smooth dome of her forehead contracted.

"A concern? What would that be, sir?"

"The champagne." He pushed back the door and indicated the ice bucket. "Can I be sure this is top quality? You see, I'm used to drinking the best."

"Sir, the champagne is a Krug Grande Cuvée, and was specifically selected by your company …" a glance at her clipboard. "D'Arcy Roth."

"They are not yet my company, Annelise. They want me as their client. But if you'll consent to taste the champagne with me, I guess we can agree that the suite is satisfactory."

A proper blush now. He loved a blush on a blonde. Pink cheeks, creamy skin reddened with warmth. He wanted to turn her over, pull down those panties and spank her right there.

Raise some heat in *those* cheeks.

"Sir, I thank you, but I am on duty right now. Drinking alcohol would be inappropriate."

"This is the hotel that 'exceeds your expectations', right?"

"Yes, but …" She laughed. "OK, I will taste the champagne. But then I am afraid I must go. I have to consider the needs of other guests."

He didn't reply, but gestured to the sofa. She sat, knees together, the grey skirt riding up slightly. The lamp behind her created a halo effect. An angel. He smiled as he twisted the cork. She was going nowhere. As the cork popped, he caught the overflow in a flute, with a loaded glance at her to see if she picked up on the image. She returned his smile, politely. He slid beside her and handed her a glass. Before he could propose a toast, she set her glass on the table.

"I'm sorry, sir. Champagne always gives me the hiccups. Would you mind if I take some water? I can get it."

He placed a hand on her knee. "Sit still. You're my guest."

She jumped at the touch of his hand. And he still hadn't made skin contact, as she wore pantyhose. He hated pantyhose.

In the mini-bar, there was an array of different waters. He grabbed a bottle of Evian and showed it to her. She nodded. Returning to his seat, he placed the water in front of her and raised his flute.

"To a very pleasant stay in Utrecht."

She tipped her glass to his and looked at him. "To a pleasant stay in Utrecht." She sipped at the fizz and closed her eyes. "Mmm. I don't wish to prejudice your opinion, but in my view, that's lovely."

Her voice was soft, intimate and breathy. He wanted to hear her say those words again. *Mmm, that's lovely.* Preferably as she drew her fingernails down his back. He hadn't even registered the taste, but his glass was two-thirds empty.

"I don't know, Annelise, the jury's still out. Maybe the second glass will clinch it." He refilled his and she didn't stop him replacing the tiny sip she had taken. A good sign.

"Now, what time do you finish tonight, Annelise?" His tongue felt thick and his speech sounded slow.

She swallowed some water and caught a stray droplet with the tip of her tongue. Shit, he wasn't sure if he could wait till later.

She avoided the question. "Why are you in Utrecht, Mr van der Veld? Is it just business, or pleasure?"

He took another slug and leaned towards her. He felt hot, horny and even a little drunk.

"Until five minutes ago, strictly business. But now, I'm not so sore."

That struck him as funny, because he wasn't sore at all. But he was as sure as he'd ever be. He started to laugh, but her eyes were looking into his, with intent. Was it too soon to …?

She smiled and reached for the bottle, refilling both glasses. Her voice was low, full of suggestion. He watched her lips.

"Have I satisfied your concerns regarding the champagne, sir?"

That was flirting. No doubt at all. His body felt warm and heavy and soft, with the exception of his cock, which hardened as she placed her hand on his thigh. She lifted the flute to his lips.

"Satisfy my champagne yet." His lips buzzed and he seemed to be slurring. It didn't bother him. He felt euphoric, completely relaxed. This was turning out to be quite a hotel. Who needed an agency when room service was laid on? She dropped her gaze to his crotch and up to his eyes. Pupils dilated. She wanted him.

"I guess you wanted to freshen up before I arrived?"

He nodded, and managed to mumble the word, "Shower."

"How about I run you a bath? More fun."

No mistaking that. She moved to the wardrobe and opened the door. He tried to tell her the bathroom was behind the other door, but she'd already found it. He laughed again. You'd think the staff... He reached for his glass, barely able to lift it to his lips.

His arms were leaden as hell and he felt fantastic. No idea if he'd be able to perform.

Here she comes. Pulling him to his feet, helping him undress, just like a nurse, what with the gloves and all. Easing him into the bath. Beautiful; soft hands, warm water. He sinks up to his chin, smiling. He can't recall feeling better in his life.

She's smiling too. And singing. He recognises the tune and tries to join in. He wants to touch her face but he can't move. He's happy, stroked and caressed by this beautiful woman.

The patterns are hypnotic. Crimson clouds twisting and swirling in the water. He watches as clear water loses the battle, dominated by red. She reaches for his other arm and turns his wrist, as if she's trying to see what he has hidden in his hand. It's funny and it makes him laugh. She's not laughing. Her face is sharp with concentration as she draws the razor blade along his vein, from wrist to elbow. More red joins the fray, and the clear water doesn't stand a chance. Now she smiles and puts the blade in his right hand. He can't hold it and it falls into the redness. He watches it fall, helpless. He heaves his head up to look at her reflection in the mirror and attempts a smile.

It's not working. He looks like an old dog with wind.

Chapter 2

London 2012

As the theme tune faded, Beatrice was not surprised to hear the doorbell ring. Family and friends knew that little couldn't wait until after *The Archers*. So her bright greeting into the intercom was in expectation of a welcome, familiar voice.

"Hel-lo?"

"Stubbs?" The voice was familiar, but as welcome as gout.

"Yes, sir."

"Need a word."

"Yes, sir." She buzzed him in. Hamilton visiting her at home? There were several explanations, and none was positive.

"Evening, Stubbs." He came straight into the flat and sat at the dining table.

"Good evening sir. Can I get you anything? Cup of tea? Glass of wine?"

Eyeing her half-empty glass of Chablis, he shook his head. "I never drink alcohol during the week. Now, I want to discuss a possible project for you. Highly confidential, see, hence my decision to come all the way out here."

Beatrice smiled. One would think that Hamilton had struggled through hail and wind to a remote Hebridean island rather than enjoying a chauffeured drive from Westminster to

Shoreditch. Although it *was* raining, to be fair.

"I see. Must be something difficult in that case, sir."

"Look here, Stubbs, would you be prepared to leave home for a while? Work on a secondment sort of thing?"

"Without knowing the exact terms of 'for a while' and 'secondment sort of thing', I'd have to say no, sir."

"Right. Good. So if the terms suit, you'll do it."

Beatrice did not respond.

"Need to identify someone to leave London in a week or so, possibly to remain in another location for some months. In addition, must be able to lead an international team, deal with a complex cross-border case, and crucially, remain discreet. I thought you might fit the bill."

"Thank you for considering me, sir, but ..."

"I will have that tea, thank you. Wouldn't say no to a biscuit, either. Nothing fancy."

Sacrificing her last three ginger nuts, Beatrice placed the tea tray in front of her boss. He made her wait; he always did. Round and round the roses. She gazed out at the rain. Rush hour over, Boot Street enjoyed the lull before people headed out to the pubs, the galleries and the attractions of Hoxton. Warm lights in windows opposite reminded her of Edward Hopper paintings. Glimpses of other lives.

Hamilton sniffed, before taking a cautious sip of tea. His large nose and side-swipes of grey hair evoked an American eagle. He was ready to speak.

"Thing is, a series of cases may, or may not, be related. Remember Brian Edwards?"

Beatrice scanned all her mental filing systems for a match. A classic Hamilton technique. No clue as to whether the name was a colleague, criminal, or hurricane. She shook her head, allowing Hamilton's grin to spread.

"Sorry, sir, I don't think I do. Not unless you mean the Brian Edwards of Watermark, committed suicide in France, 2009?"

Hamilton's smile dissolved.

"2010. And the suicide part is suspect. No note, you know."

"Is there a connection between Edwards and this sensitive case?"

"Possibly none whatsoever. Fact is, Stubbs, we need to know if the evidence of the Swiss police has any bearing on the Edwards incident. Your job is to establish whether there's a case to open."

"The Swiss police, sir?"

Hamilton ate a biscuit. "Indeed. The Swiss police have worked closely with the force in Liechtenstein on the death of Jack Ryman."

This one Beatrice recognised immediately, but Hamilton got in first.

"American banker. Plastic bag ... oh, you *do* remember. Given the chap's position, the investigation was jolly thorough. Some DNA found at the site could indicate that his death was not accidental."

Beatrice considered.

Hamilton continued. "Search of Switzerland's DNA database threw up a connection. You may recall the Australian newspaper magnate who froze to death in St Moritz?"

"Dougie Thompson. Of course. The 'death by misadventure' hoo-ha. A major news item and much controversy over the coroner's verdict."

Hamilton sipped more tea and sniffed. "And rightly so. Not only in my view but that of the Swiss police. Foreign DNA on his flask, you know."

"They kept *that* out of the papers. Two deaths in a similar region, the chances of the same DNA ..." Beatrice muttered.

Hamilton nodded, and polished off the second ginger nut. Only one left.

"The combined opinions of the Swiss and Liechtenstein forces saw it as an unusual link, so they put it through Interpol."

"And the DNA was registered?" Beatrice asked. "Not with the Brian Edwards case?"

Hamilton swallowed some tea. "Not only Edwards, but a

South African diamond dealer, name of van der Veld, who topped himself in a Dutch hotel. The key issue, see, is that all these deaths were apparently self-inflicted. Yet no suicide notes and now the same DNA at each incident? Bottom line, Stubbs, Interpol want to open a non-investigation. They're putting together a team, based in Zürich, to find out if this leads anywhere. Discretion is essential. As far as anyone else knows, we're simply tidying up loose ends."

"I see. Hence the foreign job you mentioned. Can I ask, sir, why you described this as a secondment?"

"Fair enough, good question. Situation here is, you'll be on loan. Answerable to the General Secretariat in Lyon. This is not one of ours."

"And the time-frame is presumably as precise as the case itself."

"Quite. Well put. My rider was that we can spare you no longer than a six-month. If you've got nowhere by then, you might as well come home."

"May I have some time to consider, sir? I have various ongoing projects I would like to assess before deciding."

"Regarding your work assignments, all bases are covered. As for your personal life, that's up to you."

Typically, he didn't meet her eyes. Both points skirted dangerously close to a topic which made him most uncomfortable. Naturally her work was covered; she'd had nothing more than light administrative duties for the past eight months. That reference to her personal life was clear. He wanted reassurance she was stable enough to take this on. There was a certain irony to the situation. Less than a year after she'd attempted to take her own life, her first major investigation would revolve around a series of suicides. Offering her such a case was a sign Hamilton trusted her once more, and he wanted confirmation of her capability. She remained silent, unsure of the answer herself.

Hamilton spoke. "Very well, Stubbs, think it over for the weekend, but Interpol want someone top notch, and if you really feel you can't step up to the crease, you'd better have some damned good ideas of who can."

Beatrice nodded once, aware of both compliment and threat.

"I'll get back to you first thing on Monday, sir."

"Make sure you do. And you are aware that one can listen to Radio Four anywhere in the world these days?"

Any suggestion of a smile was hidden as he swallowed the final biscuit.

"Good evening to you, Stubbs."

"Same to you, sir."

"By the way, those ginger nuts were stale."

Beatrice checked her watch before dialling Matthew's number. On Thursday afternoons he usually had a faculty meeting on campus, which could drag on into the evening. Academia was notorious, he'd told her, for enjoying the sound of its own voice.

Thankfully he was home and she launched into her explanation without preliminaries. Predictably, he did not react at all how Beatrice might have expected.

"What a marvellous opportunity. Not only will you take on a fascinating case, but what a location in which to do it! You can climb mountains, boat round lakes, visit chocolate factories and the Swiss have some impressive collections of art, you know. In Gruyère, there's the H.R. Giger museum. Gave me nightmares for weeks. You'd love it."

"Thank you. That would be worth a trip. But I'd be going there to work, Matthew. My chief concern, rather than how I might spend my weekends, is whether I'm up to the job."

"Yes, of course, naturally. Hamilton is notorious for selecting utter incompetents to represent Britain in European investigations."

"Sarcasm is lazy."

"Insecurity is boring. So, do you intend to swot up the entire weekend, or are you coming down? I would understand perfectly if the former held greater appeal."

He really could try and sound as if he would miss her. No need to gush, but ...

Beatrice made up her mind. "Swotting can be done on the train. And seeing as I have no idea when I am likely to see you again, you may meet me from the eight-fifteen tomorrow evening."

"Ooh, you sound awfully Celia Johnson."

"Not quite yet, darling. Not quite yet. Will your girls be there?"

"Not this weekend, we're on our own. Regarding dinner, would sausage and mash suit?"

"Oh definitely. With red onion gravy?"

Matthew chuckled. "I thought so."

"Perfect. We'll eat sausage and mash, drink red wine and light a fire. And on Saturday, we'll walk, and buy scallops from that stall by the beach. Eat them flash-fried, with home-made chips. On Sunday, let's read the paper and have a pint at The Toad, before I catch an afternoon train back. That should give me some ballast to weather the week ahead."

"Sign me up for all of the above. Have you spoken to James?" he asked.

"Not this week. I only see him every fortnight now. Why?"

"Just wondered how you'll manage the dogs while you're away."

"The dogs are under control. Don't worry. Meet me at quarter past eight tomorrow. If you forget again, my revenge will be hot and furious. Do you want me to bring anything?"

"A smile?"

"See you then."

"Can't wait. Don't forget your wellies."

Chapter 3

Zürich 2012

The taxi emerged from another tunnel into dazzling sunshine. Looking up from her notes, Beatrice absorbed her first view of the city. To her right, a river ran beside the street, with a park beyond. Bright clumps of snowdrops and primulas dotted around the green space made her smile. Tall apartment buildings in shades of sober grey rose to her left, whose austere architecture was softened by scarlet geranuims on the balconies. Zürich presented itself with discretion and charm. The city's spires ahead stood out sharply against blue sky and distant mountains.

Like a film set, she thought. Odd how the power of Nature at its most impressive could only be compared to its imitator. None of the people striding along the streets seemed to notice the awe-inspiring backdrop. Business people, tourists, roller-bladers, students, and lots of dogs. The taxi driver, who had answered her initial German enquiry in English, looked in the mirror.

"This is the *Hauptbahnhof*. The main train station, late-night shopping, emergency doctors. But be careful, keep your wallet safe, huh?"

"I will. Thank you. How far is the apartment from here?"

"Only two minutes. But the street is one direction, so we make a loop."

They turned away from the station with its enormous rack of bicycles to drive alongside another river. Beatrice liked the look of this. Lots of greenery, water and a compact city centre. As they stopped at the traffic lights, a blue and white tram clattered past at surprising speed. A cheerful bell rang out. The feeling of a clean, efficient, friendly place calmed her nerves as they pulled up in front of the pale yellow building housing the *Apartments Züri*.

The apartment was twice the size of her own flat. It had a living area complete with balcony, a kitchenette with a proper coffee machine and a huge bedroom, with enormous amounts of storage space. Beatrice cautioned herself against becoming over-excited. Instead, she washed her face and brushed her hair and stared into the bathroom mirror, going over it once again. The intranet photograph was clear in her mind. Dark hair, thick moustache and bright blue eyes. The man looked like one of the Gypsy Kings' grandfathers. She knew this speech by heart.

"Good morning, Herr Kälin. I apologise for my early arrival. I know the team are not due to meet until lunchtime. But the truth is that I wanted to meet you first. A thorough reading of my notes tells me that this whole investigation arose out of your own work. I respect that. I also respect that the Kantonspolizei cannot release you to work solely on this investigation. But I wanted to come here to say that I have a great deal of admiration for what you and your team have achieved. Therefore, I would like very much to lean on your expertise, up until the point where it encroaches on your daily responsibilities. Herr Kälin, I have been given a role. Which is to lead this team. I am here to ask you to help me to do that, as I fear I will be less effective alone."

Grab the goat by the horns. All unpleasantness washed, aired and dried. And if she wanted to catch him before the meeting, it would be wise to leave now.

"*Grüezi?*"

A serious young woman sat behind the reception desk at the Zeughausstrasse police building.

"*Grüezi*. My name is Beatrice Stubbs, from Scotland Yard, London and I am here to meet Herr Kälin."

The woman did not answer, but turned to her computer screen. After some tapping, she nodded.

"Yes, Frau Stubbs. You have an appointment at 12.30. You are too early."

"That's true. But I hoped to speak to Herr Kälin before the meeting. Would that be possible?"

The girl looked dubious. "I can check. Please sit yourself."

Beatrice smiled her thanks and manoeuvred her little wheelie case beside her. She studied the various posters on the walls, attempting approximate translations. In such a country, the graphics naturally spoke louder than words. Translating each hard-hitting slogan into three or even four languages would strain the most creative ad-man. The woman tapped on her glass window.

"Frau Stubbs, Herr Kälin is at lunch. Do you wish his assistant?"

"Lunch? Already? Oh. I suppose I could talk to his assistant, yes. Thanks."

Lunch at half past eleven? Or was this a deliberate rebuff? Don't be so negative and suspicious, she reprimanded herself. Positive, co-operative and effective, remember? And it's your own fault for not calling first.

"Frau Stubbs? My name is Xavier Racine. I am joining your team, I hope."

Beatrice's spirits lifted. Well dressed, with strawberry blonde hair and an open, enquiring look. And freckles. Beatrice liked freckles.

"Nice to meet you, Mr Racine. I'm sorry to disturb you. I had hoped to meet Herr Kälin for a preliminary chat. But it seems he's already gone to lunch."

A blush. All the proof she needed this was indeed a snub.

"Oh, yes, of course. Herr Kälin wanted to have an early lunch in order that he is ready for you."

But Beatrice was tenacious, and would say her piece, whatever it took. "How very thoughtful. Tell me, Mr Racine, is he in the police canteen? Perhaps we might join him there? I would very much like to speak to him before the briefing."

"No, no, Frau Stubbs. He always eats in one of the local restaurants. I cannot say exactly. He changes every day. I am sorry. Maybe you would like to have lunch here? I can arrange it."

Don't get at him, he's only the messenger. "Thank you. But it's a little early for me. Do you think we could have a cup of coffee and then you could show me the briefing room? I would like to set up before the others arrive."

"It is a pleasure."

Nice lad. Even bought the coffees. As Xavier departed to get some food, Beatrice paced the briefing room. It was a setback, but a minor one. So she would do the briefing first and talk to Kälin later. The important thing now was to be prepared. She opened her wheelie case and withdrew her materials.

By 12.35, no one had turned up. The projector hummed quietly, the first slide glowed blue and every chair stood empty. Heat began to rise up Beatrice's throat. This was not Swiss. She'd read all about the cultural habits of this country, and in particular, this region. Lateness was extremely rude. But why all of them? Kälin may have wanted to make a point, but all four of the others? Including Xavier Racine? She stood up, furious, and dug in her bag for her mobile.

"Frau Stubbs!" Xavier burst through the door. "This is the wrong room. Everyone waits for you upstairs."

"But … you showed me this room. I thought …?"

"Yes, I am sorry. Herr Kälin changed the room. He thought it would be better if we meet in our working room on the top floor.

He sent me an SMS and left a notice at reception for everyone else. I just realised you would not see it. You are here since 11.30. I'm sorry. But we have to go. Everyone waits."

Lugging her wheelie case up the stairs, Beatrice felt wrong-footed and harassed. She intended to speak to Herr Kälin about this. It was most unprofessional and if she didn't know better, she would suspect him of doing it deliberately to unsettle her. Xavier, carrying all her handouts and charts, tripped on the top step and scattered her presentation across the landing. Her breathing was laboured as they collected everything, especially as she had to repeatedly assure Xavier it didn't matter.

Xavier opened the door to silence. Feeling itchy, warm and out of breath, Beatrice entered to face her new team. Two women, two men. The black woman with the erect bearing and deep blue suit would be Interpol's forensic DNA scientist. The relaxed long-limbed individual to her right must be the Dutch chap, information technology genius. So the psychologist had to be the delicate blonde in the white shirt. So young! Stony faced and sitting apart from the team was Herr Karl Kälin. Beatrice's image of him evaporated. The sparkle in his eyes she'd seen in the photograph was absent, replaced by a cold antipathy.

She heaved a deep breath to apologise, but he spoke.

"Ms Stubbs. It is unfortunate that you did not get the message intended for the team. All the others received the information without difficulty. And it is always a good idea to make an appointment when you expect to meet someone. I would like to make one thing quite clear. I am not a member of this team. I am a consultant, advising on any case that might arise. I have many other responsibilities in terms of my daily police work. So I would appreciate it if you treated my time with respect."

An awkward silence hung in the room, amplifying Beatrice's heavy breathing.

Chapter 4

St Moritz 2008

"M'sieur? Bad weather comes. It can be dangerous. Maybe you prefer to wait for tomorrow?"

Dougie found the chair lift attendant presumptuous. "Maybe I prefer to go now. Cheers all the same."

He pulled the bar down over his hips, lifting his skis clear as the chair moved upward. The attendant shrugged and turned to the other couple behind him. Dougie twisted over his shoulder and saw the gloom-monger had persuaded the others to turn back. One girl gesticulated at his own ascending form in enquiry.

"Why me? Good question. Because I can."

He threw back his head and laughed, out to the open sky. The idea of tackling the run alone, with no amateurs to limit his manoeuvres, shot adrenaline into his system. The weather was a stroke of fortune. A rare opportunity to pit his skills against a hostile environment. And Dougie took every opportunity, in nature as in life. He smiled, recognising the bad habit of writing his own epitaph.

Of course, he shouldn't waste time. As that lumpen idiot had observed, it could be dangerous. The mountainside rushed up at him, as his poles and skis dangled below. The sharp edges, the blacks and whites, the geographical clarity challenged him, and he began to twitch like a hyperactive child. Going off piste accounted for only a part of his excitement. After almost a week of persuasion, Ana-Maria had finally agreed to a date. In fact, it was she who suggested this run; '*only advisable for the truly talented*'. They had arranged to meet at the tree-line; it would not do to be seen leaving together. Opportunities, yes; risks, no. The reservation at the lodge was made in her name. After they'd checked in, he would send a text message to his wife. Julia would understand his decision not to take on the storm, and accept his stay in a mountain lodge as an example of her husband's good judgement. Win-win.

The car ratcheted up to the platform and Dougie disembarked with grace. Another jobsworth advised him against taking the run; 'one must respect the weather', but Dougie dismissed him with a look. The scene was undoubtedly dramatic. The valley below reflected late-afternoon sunshine, while the blue sky and various pointed roofs completed a ridiculously cute Alpine village setting. Yet behind him, the remainder of the mountain sat; dark, huge, and unassailable. Grey, violet and yellow clouds – the colours of a bruise – moved to obscure the white tip, and a flash of fear stopped him. He had nothing to prove; his prowess as an expert, all-terrain skier was established. There was no need to take on millennia of ice, stone and snow. A second's decision would take him back down to Julia and the kids. He knew Rui and Katia would be ecstatic. They could have a raclette, play some games and he could do this run in the morning with fresh snow. The girl could wait. He hesitated.

No.

Dougie Thompson never backed down in the face of a challenge. He checked his boots, surveyed the piste, and with a glance back at the threatening storm, took off.

The snow was firm to hard. After adjusting to the terrain, his first few slopes were pure pleasure. *Only advisable for the truly talented.* She was right. He would never have known about this run had she not let him into the secret. The luck of the devil, his mother used to say, while his brothers called him a jammy bastard.

As he approached the trees, his route became less evident and he slowed to assess each stage. The sky darkened and the landscape became monochrome. It was an increasing challenge and he balanced pace with diligence. A mistake would be unacceptable, possibly lethal. A previous skier's trail indicated a sharp turn toward the edge of the forest. He followed, his pulse a bass-line in his ears. Something lay under the tree. The ski-suit was white, with blue and pink flashes; Ana-Maria. Prone, skis detached, surely not a fall? She was an instructor, for God's sake!

Dougie slowed and drew up beside the body. Her goggles covered half her face and a ski-mask took care of the rest. He crouched and watched her chest. No movement. He removed his gloves and lifted her goggles. Her eyes were closed. Convinced she was already dead, he reached his right hand to her neck for a pulse. Her eyes opened and he jumped.

"Hello. I've been waiting for you."

He exhaled, fear turning to irritation. "That was a damn silly thing to do."

"Sorry. I didn't mean to scare you. It was a joke."

"I wasn't scared. And I'm not laughing."

Sitting up, she reached for her rucksack. "Don't sulk. I brought us some *Kaffee Fertig* to warm us."

"Café what?"

"*Kaffee Fertig.* It means 'fixed coffee'. The Swiss version of *Kaffee Schnapps.*"

"No thanks." He pulled on his gloves. "We should move on. The weather's getting worse. Get up. Let's go."

She didn't argue and put the flask away. Dougie waited impatiently, surveying the slope through swirling flakes of snow. Silly bitch. If she thought that was funny, she had a bloody weird sense of humour. A shadow crossed his vision and as he turned, her hand hit his neck. A sharp prickle pierced his ski-mask in addition to the blow. He stumbled sideways, snatching at the place she'd struck him. She ran off into the trees, leaving her rucksack behind. Christ! Another stupid game? What the hell was she playing at? He attempted to chase her, before tripping over his skis. Releasing both clips, he lurched after the girl. The snow was hard-packed and as firm as concrete. But his legs seemed to think they were in deep wet slush. One of the fittest men in his empire, with a sportsman's thighs, he could move no faster than a turtle. He stopped and fell backwards, onto his arse. As he stared into the shadowy forest, he saw her emerge. She waved. Dougie's attempt to wave back toppled him onto his back.

The figure in the white suit worked at speed. After heaving him across the snow, she propped his back against the trunk of the tree where he'd stopped to 'rescue' her. His head fell back, and she tipped a little of the liquid from the thermos flask into his mouth. He swallowed. Unzipping his jacket, she struggled to pull his arms free. Between giving him sips of liquid, she removed all his outer clothing, folding it in a neat pile beside him. The flask empty, she replaced the stopper and retrieved the lid from a plastic bag in her rucksack. She set it beside the pile and crouched to stare at his face. Nothing.

She glanced upwards. The sky loomed lower and blacker, as if it disapproved. Snow flew across her goggles. But the pastel-trimmed figure took several risky minutes to explore his mobile phone, before switching it off and placing it on top of his clothes.

Large white flakes floated onto the body and settled on his eyelashes, his hair and his cheeks as the figure replaced her skis. She smiled at him and whispered, "It's all in the public interest, you know." With one last glance at the scene, she skied with great caution down the mountain, her pale suit disappearing into the landscape like winter ermine.

Chapter 5

Zürich 2012

Placing her bag at her feet, Beatrice allowed herself a slow scan of the room while she regained her breath. The two women appeared bemused and looked to her for a reaction. The Dutchman raised his eyebrows with a small grin of sympathy. Xavier did not meet her eyes, but his high colour gave away his discomfort. Only one way to go, she decided. A cold stillness settled on her and she walked directly to Herr Kälin, extending her hand.

"Beatrice Stubbs, Scotland Yard. Pleased to meet you."

His face hardened still further, yet he stood and gave her hand one brisk shake.

"Detective Kälin, Swiss Federal Criminal Police."

Beatrice smiled as if she had received a polite welcome and turned to the team.

"I apologise for having kept you. I'd like to thank Herr Kälin for that reminder on how important it is that we use our time efficiently. So rather than my using more valuable time by restarting my presentation, perhaps we can kill two birds with one blow. I would like you to introduce yourselves, tell us why you were seconded to the team and give us your thoughts on this case." Kälin was looking out of the window. "You all received a briefing pack, and I have no doubt you have read it with care.

From what you have read, does anything strike you?"

The uncertain silence of a new team stretched out. Beatrice let it continue.

The tall man spoke. "OK, I'll go first. Detective Chris Keese, Europol, The Hague. I specialise in e-crime and IT forensics." He leaned back in his chair. "The obvious thing is what these guys have in common. We don't need to bother with the question *Did they have any enemies*? but instead we should be asking, *Did they have any friends*?"

Beatrice acknowledged the comment with a smile. The Dutchman's attitude was relaxed to the point of indolence and she was aware of the contrast he demonstrated to the rest of the team.

"You're right, Mr Keese. All the men in question had either made highly unpopular decisions, or were involved in morally dubious business. Identifying those who may wish to harm them would be time-consuming and, in my view, unlikely to prove fruitful. If we are talking about homicide rather than suicide, suspects will be legion. I am inclined to agree with Mr Keese. We need to be searching for the links between these individuals. Who indeed were their friends? This is certainly one line I would like to pursue. Any … yes, Ms Tikkenen?"

The three men in the room took full advantage of the opportunity to stare at the speaker. Cheekbones as sharp as ski jumps, white-blonde hair and strong eyebrows arching outward, she reminded Beatrice of a Russian model. A lovely creature; just the type who might cause all sorts of unnecessary tension.

"Sabine Tikkenen. Central Criminal Police, Tallinn, Estonia. I am a crime analyst. I agree that we have some background to research, but we already have the most concrete lead to finding out how these men died. My question is this – how far can we go with the DNA?"

Beatrice was puzzled. "I'm not sure what you mean. We will exploit any available information we can glean from the samples we have."

"Yes, that I already know. But can we test this DNA for features that are not standard? For example, where does he come from? Does EU protocol allow us to find out everything we can about this person?"

"No, Ms Tikkenen, it does not." If Sabine Tikkenen drew all eyes, this voice commanded all ears. The lightness of a Portuguese accent coupled with West African gravitas, the black woman spoke with a voice you could never interrupt.

"European law dictates that ethnic group profiling could be counter-productive on several counts. We can only assume so much from these samples."

Sabine frowned. "That is disappointing. Having some information on this person's cultural background could make a psychological profile much more informed. But as the Interpol representative, you are telling us that we have the same investigative powers as the local officers; which is to say, none."

Kälin stared at the young woman in evident disbelief, but said nothing.

"Ms Tikkenen, I must explain. My name is Conceição Pereira da Silva."

Beatrice allowed a sigh of relief to escape. Now she knew how to pronounce the woman's first name; Con-say-sow. Rhymes with cats-say-miaow.

"I am a junior DNA advisor, supervised by MEG, and have no authority in this situation. My contribution could be on the side of how to extract all the information we can from a strand of DNA. And to consult on the legal issues relating to such a case. If we were to identify a suspect through legally questionable processes, we would be wasting our time. And I want to clarify: I am not an Interpol mole. We're all simply advisors here."

Beatrice spoke. "Thank you, Ms Pereira da Silva. Your attention to correct procedure whilst handling forensic evidence of this kind is essential. Ms Tikkenen, I appreciate that the more information you have, the better criminal profile you will create. I hope we will be able to contribute much more evidence to assist you. Personally, I would like to add that it is of overriding importance we follow the letter of the law, particularly now. The harsh truth is this. Despite the fact you are each a brilliant asset to this team – otherwise you would not be here – our job is going to entail a lot of dull, everyday police legwork. And we must be beyond reproach. Herr Racine?"

"Thank you. My name is Xavier Racine. Herr Kälin and I are both members of the Federal Criminal Police. Herr Kälin is our main Zürich investigative officer. I am on loan from Task Force TIGRIS, a specialist operations unit. My opinion on this case is we may only scratch the surface, with what we know. I believe it would be worthwhile checking any other similar 'suicides'. High-profile men who left no explanation or indication as to why they chose to end their lives. We may find a bigger pattern."

"Fair enough." Chris Keese replied. "Makes sense. So how are we going to start on this?"

"By playing to our strengths. I suggest that you, Mr Keese …"

"Ms Stubbs? I don't mean to tread on any toes, but I'd feel a whole lot better if you called me Chris."

Beatrice winced internally, in the sure knowledge Kälin would hate the idea.

"I see. Does everyone else feel comfortable using first names? It's quite usual in Britain. But I can understand other countries find that rather informal."

"For me, it is no problem." Ms Tikkenen raised her shoulders in a tiny shrug. "You can call me Sabine. We will have to work closely together, so we can be relaxed with names."

"How do you feel, Herr Racine? Ms Pereira da Silva?"

The young Swiss officer gestured toward his colleague to go first. She smiled.

"I have a feeling that although Conceição will be harder for people to pronounce, it is the right approach. I'm happy with first names."

"Me too. You can call me Xavier. It is the modern way." His

smile spread more slowly than his blush.

Kälin shook his head. "No. I'm afraid that's completely unacceptable to me. Herr Racine and I work together on a professional basis. We use formal address. This team is operating in Switzerland, and Swiss prefer formality. Not because we are old-fashioned, but to indicate respect. We are forced to speak English as it is the only common language. However, I fail to see why you should impose your cultural habits on us."

Beatrice took a deep breath. "So, Chris, it seems you have your wish. First names are fine with everyone except Herr Kälin. My first name is Beatrice. However, equally acceptable forms of address would be Boss, Ma'am and Your Ladyship."

Chris led the laughter and Beatrice had a feeling the chap could well prove to be the team glue.

"Now let's get to work. As I understand it, the Kantonspolizei have given us equipment and space on this floor, in preference to downstairs. Is that right, Herr Kälin?"

"I have my own office. You can work downstairs or up here. I don't care."

Xavier jumped in, face aflame. "I think Herr Kälin means he doesn't mind. We often make this mistake in English."

Kälin turned his scowl on his colleague. "Herr Racine, my English may be inadequate. But I will not accept corrections from a non-native speaking junior officer. As I said, Frau Stubbs, I don't care where you work."

Beatrice moved on to spare Xavier's embarrassment.

"So upstairs it is. All those stairs might help keep me fit. Xavier, I'd like you to work with Chris on looking for links. We need to know if there was anything at all which might connect these men. Did they use the same bank, airline or masseuse? Who were their golf buddies? Was there any connection between their wives? Did the companies have any dealings with one another? Had these chaps ever met? Fine toothcomb, cross-referencing, your sort of thing, Chris.

"Sabine, here are all the at-the-scene details. You may wish to liaise with Chris and Xavier on details of the deceased. Your task is to profile the kind of person who could and would want to perform such efficient disposals.

"Conceição, all the forensic equipment you need is provided. You will need to check all the samples and ensure there's no possibility of error. I'd like us to be thorough. No stone unturned. But first, Xavier, could you show everyone where the canteen is located? I would like a word with Herr Kälin."

The room emptied surprisingly fast.

Beatrice closed the door and fighting her instinct to put the briefing table between them, took a seat beside him. She half turned to him and opened her palms.

"Herr Kälin. I had a speech prepared for you. I arrived an hour early so I could say my piece and clear the air between us. My plan did not work and it seems we got out of bed on the wrong foot. Would you like to tell me why you are so angry?"

"Ms Stubbs, if we are to have any kind of working relationship, I must ask you not to patronise me. This is not a conciliation meeting with a badly behaved junior. I am the Fedpol senior detective here. The case, such as it is, arose out of my report. From the work of my officers. However, Interpol find it appropriate to use me only as a 'consultant' and to bring in a foreign woman to lead this investigative team. A woman who seems to have little respect for the demands on my time."

"I see. If I understand you correctly, you are unhappy about the fact you are not in charge of the team, because your work has led us this far. You are displeased with me because I did not go through the correct channels in terms of arranging a pre-meeting with you. Is that right, or have I forgotten something? Are the words 'foreign' and 'woman' in any way relevant?"

He stared at her for a beat, then glanced down at his watch.

"Is there anything else, Ms Stubbs? Because I cannot see us making any progress."

"Nor can I, Herr Kälin. You'd better go."

He wrenched open the door and left, his footsteps thumping down the stairs. Beatrice closed her eyes and tried to stop shaking. She repeated the mantra James had taught her: Convert defeat into opportunity. Every failure carries the seed of success. Kill negativity.

She dwelt awhile on the last.

Chapter 6

Utrecht 2012

Flight LX 728 to Amsterdam began its descent to Schiphol airport at 13.45. Chris skimmed his notes once more.

Jens van der Veld, (57). South African (Afrikaner) based in Kimberley, South Africa. Married to Antjie Heese (34), two sons Uys (5), Henk (3). Active in South Africa, Europe and the US.

Business interests: breweries, real estate, and diamond dealing.

Died in Utrecht, Feb 2007, suicide. Slit wrists in bath.

Forensic assessment: Victim unclothed in bath. No evidence of struggle or forced entry. In main room, two champagne flutes, one with victim's fingerprints and DNA. The other with no fingerprints and unidentified DNA. Do Not Disturb *sign on door, thus body undiscovered until Monday.*

Mobile call log as follows:

Friday 27 Feb

21.50: Outgoing call. Amsterdam. Call traced to Joop Kneppers, associate and colleague. (duration, 2 mins)

21.56: Incoming SMS. Amsterdam. Business card from Kneppers, with tel. no. of escort agency.

22.59: Incoming SMS. Kimberley, RSA. Message from wife, checking victim's safe arrival.

Van der Veld had confirmed meetings for the Monday

morning, and according to colleagues, expected to finalise two significant deals in the Netherlands.

Kneppers came to hotel for a pre-arranged meeting at 10.00 Monday, and raised concerns when van der Veld could not be reached.

No visitors registered at reception.

Chris folded the papers into his briefcase and tucked it under the seat in front. So van der Veld drank champagne with someone before getting naked into the bath, and slitting his wrists. The champagne drinker. Someone he knew? Or wanted to know? Was it possible his visitor had provoked such an almighty attack of conscience? Wheels hit tarmac, and a powerful reverse thrust tilted him forward. He looked at his companion. Absorbed in *The Financial Times*, she gave no reaction to their landing.

"I checked out the meaning of your name, you know," he announced.

Conceição folded the paper. "Really? I didn't check yours. How rude of me."

He laughed, pleased she had a quick wit. Yet her face was unchanged.

"The meaning of Chris? I'll tell you myself, one of these days. But I've never met someone called Conceição before. I'm naturally nosy."

"Well, if you checked the name Conceição, you only know half the story. My full name is Maria do Conceição Pereira da Silva. Now what does that tell you?"

"You come from a Catholic country which likes long names."

"I can see why you became a detective."

She rose from her seat and reached for the overhead locker. As they exited the aircraft, a cool breeze caused Chris to hunch his shoulders.

Conceição. Weird name. Conception. Weird female. Seemed

intent on slapping him down every chance she got. With some relief, Chris left her at Paardenveld-Kroonstraat police station, and wove a path through the crowds of shoppers on Catherijnebaan. As he walked, he replayed each curt conversation in his head. Had he overstepped the mark at all? He couldn't recall. She had no need to be so hostile, when they were both chasing the same goal. Yet he sensed a faint tone of disapproval from the whole bunch. Beatrice seemed to appreciate his humour and gestures of friendship, but even she was pretty uptight. Maybe it was a language thing. A local cop attitude. What would be the best way to handle it? Change nothing. Do your job, be yourself, and to hell with the rest of it.

Hotel Grand Karel V sat back from the street, in expansive grounds. To claim this much land in the heart of the city, it had to be something special. Entering the magnificent lobby, Chris managed his expectations. The incident he was here to investigate was over five years old. The staff would be worse than the Utrecht police; no one wanted this dragged up again. The chances of his finding anything useful were as likely as his cracking Conception. Still, go through the motions and you never know.

"Milk or lemon?"

"I'll take a little milk, please, Ms Zajac."

The housekeeper was an unexpected surprise. Her thin, steel-coloured hair was drawn back in a tight bun and the black frames of her glasses added to the severe image, but her face folded into a homely smile. She went out of her way to make him feel comfortable. Pouring a touch of milk into the tea, she continued.

"Back then, I was assistant. Now I am Head Housekeeper. I arrange all cleaning, laundry and maintenance." The grey uniform underlined her serious tone. "I found body of Mr van der Veld. The police came and took all they wanted. After that, we cleaned. Surprising, but it was not too bad. The bath needed work, but for a suicide, he was quite tidy. I have seen worse." Her dark brows dropped into a frown.

"You have?"

"Not here. When I was housekeeper in very good hotel in Rotterdam. We had two suicides. One with gun. That room – oh! It took us weeks to clean all blood, little pieces of bone, hair. Very bad."

Her reproach seemed directed at the inconsiderate shooter.

"And the other?"

"Pills. Terrible smell, difficult stains and some vomit. But if I compare to way some guests leave rooms, not so bad."

"So Mr van der Veld had a relatively neat death."

"Death in hotel is always problem. Police come, staff try to keep quiet, and we need extra cleaning."

"Of course. Ms Zajac, was there anything else unusual about that weekend? The Saturday in particular?"

"I have day book. We make notes in day book. Guests to be careful, staff problems, maintenance update, like diary. Like diary of hotel."

"You still have the day book from 2007?" Chris sat up in anticipation.

"Yes, I say already. I have here. 2007. Mr van der Veld died in February, no?" She flicked through her pages.

"That's right. Around the 27th February. Any notes about guests, or anything unusual for the week before?"

"Wait please. Yes, here. February 24th; two porters reprimanded for smoking in sight of guests. Fire alarm control. February 26th; complaint – Room 670 regarding noise from Room 671. One special request for upgrade to Empire Suite. Note van der Veld as VIP. Also, good bottle champagne required. 27th; Ballroom out of bounds for perfume convention. Two complaints – Room 670 and 672 about noise in Room 671 – occupants: Mr and Mrs Schmidt. Manager suggested room change. Offer refused, guests promised to be quiet. 29th; Visser given verbal warning. Police called – body in Empire Suite. I think you know the rest, Mr Keese."

"Yes, I'd say I do. Can you go back there, Ms Zajac? The fire alarm check – was that scheduled?"

She didn't need to check her ledger. "We always have control, February and November. Same company for last nine years."

"OK. Is Room 671 anywhere near the Empire Suite?"

"Different building."

"Hmm." Chris scanned his shorthand. "Visser? One of the smoking porters?"

"No. Receptionist. Let me look. Yes, on 23rd February, Annelise Visser reported uniform missing. She was told find or replace. She failed. So verbal warning. One hundred forty people attended perfume convention for launch of new fragrance, *Wish*. Horrible smell."

Chris smiled at her wrinkled nose. "And no one saw or heard Jens van der Veld until Monday morning?"

"He had *Do Not Disturb* sign. So we did not disturb. His friend arrived on Monday, and insisted checking room. And we found him, in bath."

"You said you found him, Ms Zajac?"

"Yes. I authorise opening rooms when guest is absent. I checked living room, bed and bathroom. I saw him in bath. Dead, no question. Up to his neck in blood."

"You worked the weekend?"

"No. I work Monday to Friday. Is enough."

"Who requested the upgrade for Mr van der Veld?"

"One moment." She flicked back a page. "His company, D'Arcy Roth. They booked room, not him. The porter told he was mean. Tipped only two Euros."

"Does that porter still work here?"

"No, no. Aard only worked here during studies. He left since two years."

"Is there any chance you could get me a list of guests who stayed here that weekend, Ms Zajac?"

"I think is possible. I ask."

"And does Ms Visser still work here?"

"Yes. Senior Receptionist. You want to speak with her?"

"That would be great."

"Mr Keese? Annelise Visser."

Chris stood to shake her hand. Her open and confident smile gave her a vague air of amusement. Her dyed-black hair was cropped short, gelled into perky spikes and her grey eyes were heavily made-up.

"Sorry to disturb you, Ms Visser. I'll only keep you a moment. Just a question or two. I'm here to clear up any details relating to the death of Mr van der Veld, February 2007."

"Yeah, I know. The suicide."

"Did you meet him at all?"

"No. At that time I didn't work weekends. So I knew nothing until his colleague arrived on Monday. He was impatient and rude, and insisted we check the room."

"You lost your uniform that week, is that right?"

"That's right. I change my uniform once a week. On Monday evenings, I always take the dirty one to the dry cleaner's and pick it up on Thursdays. I left it on the coat rack in the staff room on Thursday morning. When I went to pick up my things that evening, it had gone."

"What do you think happened?"

"I guess someone took it home, thinking it was theirs. I didn't worry too much; I thought they'd bring it back. It had my name badge on it, so they had to know it was mine."

"Did you get it back?"

She rolled her eyes. "No. I got a verbal warning for losing hotel property, and had to replace it. I learned a lesson. Now everything goes into my locker."

"And just out of interest, where were you that weekend? Do you remember?"

She smiled. "I remember. Same place as every weekend. I used to be a DJ in Rotterdam. So I left here on Friday evening, did my set till 5am, slept all day, did it again on Saturday night and slept on Sunday till it was time to come home."

"You're not DJing anymore?"

She shook her head. "Too old."

Chris raised his eyebrows at this sharp, articulate girl. "Oh God. If you're too old, what does that make me?"

Her grin widened. "Way too old?"

Chris laughed at her cheek. "Thanks Ms Visser. You've made my day."

"You're welcome." She rose, still grinning and slipped out the door. Chris headed back to his hotel, unsure as to whether he'd got anything more than a reminder of how much time had passed.

Entering the hotel dining-room, Chris noted he was not the only admirer of Conceição's posture. The woman held herself upright and moved with a hip-rolling gait which caught the attention of several diners. The waiter led them to a window table where they could observe the passers-by. She ordered sparkling water and he asked for a beer.

"Strange to arrange a hotel for us. I am sure there would have been flights back to Zürich tonight," she said.

"You're probably right. But maybe if we chat things over this evening, we might find something we need to take a look at before we leave tomorrow."

"Such as?" Her cold look expressed disbelief.

"I have no idea."

She picked up the menu and read in silence. Chris scanned the specials and made up his mind to try one of the classic Dutch sausages. With fries. To hell with it. If he had to sit opposite Sniper of the Year, he could at least look forward to his food.

A waitress arrived. "Two gin tonic?"

"I think that must be for someone else. We ordered one beer and one sparkling water."

"Oh. Sorry." The kid looked stressed.

"It's no problem." Chris gave her a friendly grin and returned to the choice of sausages.

Conceição folded her menu and met his eyes. "Chris, I should apologise. I have been most unfriendly to you and I think it is undeserved."

A waiter arrived with the right drinks and Chris's mind hurried to catch up. He had no idea why she'd changed tactic. But if she wanted to stop with the sour stuff, it suited him fine. Her speech seemed over, so he raised his glass.

"OK, so let's toast. A positive working relationship."

She hesitated, before raising her water to him. "A positive working relationship." She sipped. He slugged. Nothing else was forthcoming. Chris stopped trying to second guess the woman.

"Tell me about the *politie*," he said.

"Well, you were right. They were not pleased to see me."

"But they gave you what you needed, did they?"

"Yes. I spoke to the attending officers and the coroner. The DNA sample was taken from a champagne glass. Perfect procedure, so I can see no way it could have been contaminated."

"Good news for us. Isn't it?"

"Yes, I suppose it is. The body gave little away. The time elapsing between Friday evening and Monday morning meant that testing for substances was almost worthless."

Chris sighed. "Found in the bath with a razor blade, slit wrists, and he had no plans to meet anyone till thirty-six hours later. A verdict of suicide seems like the only possible choice the coroner had. Can't blame the guy."

"The coroner is a woman. Did you make much progress at the hotel?"

The judgemental tone returned. Maybe that was it. Did she have a chromosome chip on her shoulder?

"Yes and no. They were helpful all right. But I don't think I found anything significant. He checked in, tipped the porter and that was the last anyone heard."

After delivering their order to the waiter, Conceição leant

forward. "Chris? What do you think is going on here?"

He stared back into her huge earnest eyes. Candlelight flickered across the planes of her forehead, cheeks and jaw, illuminating the tones of her skin. He cleared his throat.

"The way I see it, there'll be a simple answer. Like in the case of *Die Frau ohne Gesicht*. The woman without a face. Series of crimes across Germany. Turns out the DNA samples were all taken with a certain kind of cotton bud, contaminated by the factory worker who packed them. Or, much less likely, the same person was present at the suicides of four powerful men. The truth is, Conceição, I think we're probably on a wild goose chase. What about you?"

"Interesting. You think this case is pointless, but you still want to turn all the stones."

"If in doubt, stone-turning is all I've got."

"You might be right. There could be a prosaic explanation. Yet for me, there is something more. This man was a father, a husband. He was successful. His business was suspect, but it had never bothered his conscience before. Why would he end his life just then? My instinct tells me there is something wrong."

"Right. In the face of all the evidence, you're going on instinct?" Chris knew he sounded sarcastic.

"If in doubt, instinct's all I've got."

"I can see why you became a detective."

A smile broke across her face, revealing startlingly white teeth, and she began to laugh. Chris smiled back, feeling an odd swell of warmth towards this prickly peach.

Chapter 7

Brno 2009

Belanov closed one eye as he looked through the Schmidt & Bender sight of the TRG-42. The Mil-dots in the cross-hairs enabled him to calculate range and height precisely, so that the man in the blue suit could be determined as just under two metres tall. The rifle was designed for accuracy at 1400 metres. The suit was less than 100 metres from his perch. Wouldn't stand a chance. He stroked the trigger and with a satisfied smile, removed the gun from his shoulder.

"Beautiful."

State-of-the-art design, and easily customised to the end user's purposes. It had .338 Lapua Magnum chambering, which could be adapted with a 254mm twist rate for the heavier stuff. He raised it once more to look at the people milling around the stands below. The black stock was two kilos lighter than the camouflaged version and had detachable muzzle brakes. A sniper's dream weapon. He played with the variable magnification as he swept the dull greys, blues and blacks of the crowd. Some colour caught his eye.

The redhead from yesterday. He trained the sights on her, placing her trade fair badge in the centre of the cross hairs. She stood in front of the chemical warfare protective clothing display, her head bent as she read some brochures. He calculated her height as 1.6 metres using the telescopic sight as a guide. A slim figure, with average tits and boyish hips. Her vibrant hair stood out against a pale green trouser suit, with a dark stain on the left shoulder. He returned the sight to her face and jolted as he realised she was looking right at him. Her head tilted and she raised her eyebrows. He removed the weapon, placed his hand on his chest and mouthed the word, 'Sorry'. She waved a hand as if to dismiss the apology and turned into the crowd.

It took him under three minutes to find her, in front of IDET's orientation board and map of the site.

"*Mluvíte cesky? Ukrajinśkoju?* English?"

She looked at him over her shoulder, suspicious. "I speak English."

"I wish to apologise. That was me, up there." Belanov indicated the gallery. "I was trying out the sights of a rifle. But I should not have pointed it at you."

Her face cleared and she turned to face him. "Oh I see. It's OK. There's just something weird, you know, about having a gun trained on you. Demo model or not."

"Of course, I understand. I guess I got carried away with such a piece. I am sorry if I alarmed you." On closer inspection, her tits were a little above average.

"No, no. Not at all." She hitched her handbag strap up her shoulder.

"I noticed your jacket. Did you have an accident?"

"Oh yeah. It certainly wasn't accidental. The protestors outside? They were throwing eggs at the attendees. One of them was a pretty good shot. I had to wash it off in the bathroom."

"They threw an egg at you? That's very bad. Yes, they have the right to express their opinions, but using missiles? No. That is dangerous. The police should stop this. You could have been hurt."

"Well, you know, it was only an egg." She looked around, obviously planning to leave.

"Even eggs can do damage. My name is Symon Belanov." He offered his hand.

She took it. "Caroline McKendrick. Nice to meet you."

"Are you exhibiting, Ms McKendrick?"

"No, no. Just browsing. And you?"

"Likewise. These kinds of things fascinate me. I am like a little boy in a sweet shop. But I was going to take a break for a beverage. I would be pleased if you consented to join me."

"Well, just a quick coffee. I have a meeting at five."

Belanov acknowledged her point and guided her towards the café.

"So what do you do, Mr Belanov?"

"My profession is much less exciting than what we see here. I sell used cars."

"You work in Brno?" She pronounced it 'Ber-know'.

"No, I'm based in Ukraine. But I do business in the Czech Republic, Slovakia, Poland, everywhere." She stirred her cappuccino, looking completely uninterested in his answer.

"And you?"

"I'm from Montreal. My company sent me here with a shopping list."

"And did you find what you wanted?"

"Not really. You're right, this place is quite a candy store. But what I'm looking for is a little different; handmade specialty chocolates, if you like."

"Perhaps you are looking in the wrong place?" He did not meet her eyes, observing the other customers.

"Well, yes and no. I won't get what I want right over the counter, that's true. But I was lucky enough to meet someone here yesterday who might be able to point me in the right direction. That's why I have to leave at four. I'm going to meet him in the city centre to talk it over."

"Be careful, Ms McKendrick. I hope your meeting is arranged in a public place."

"Sure. I'm not stupid, Mr Belanov." She flicked a glance at him and put down her cup.

"I apologise. I had no intention of suggesting you were in any way naïve. Yet I know many of these 'helpful' people, and therefore I have concerns for your safety. Is this man a reputable dealer?"

"I don't know if he's reputable. I only met him yesterday. And he's not a dealer. He described himself as a 'fixer', someone who can introduce me to the dealers. It's important to get a personal recommendation with those people, you know."

Belanov sipped his tea, watching her as he mulled it over. She drained her coffee and glanced at her watch.

"Ms McKendrick, may I make a suggestion? Call your contact and tell him you have already made personal contact with one of 'those people', so you have no need of his services. Then you and I can have dinner somewhere, you can tell me exactly what you're looking for. And if I can't help you, I will certainly know someone who can."

She stilled and looked into his eyes for the first time. He gave a small nod.

"Used cars?" she asked.

"And sundry other items. Shall we go?"

Pressing the fob, Belanov registered her expression as the Porsche Cayenne Turbo S flashed into life with a beep. The basalt metallic black beast sat in the spring sunshine, exuding class. His stomach still thrilled each time he saw it come to life at his fingertips. Sometimes, he had the same feeling while shaving. Running the blade across his jaw, watching the shape of his lips, exploring the planes of his face, he knew he was good looking. Coupled with his self-made wealth, there were times when he felt omnipotent. This was one such moment. He helped her in, before taking his seat. Her eyes took in the leather seats, the black interior and olive silk-wood steering wheel.

"This is not what I'd call a used car." Her smile flashed

appreciation.

He gunned the gas, and sat back as the engine gave its big cat growl.

"A man should treat himself, sometimes." He drove out of the exhibition area, itching to get on open road and show her what 550 horsepower could do.

"Mr Belanov, where are we going?"

"That's up to you. You're staying in the city centre, I suppose?"

"I'm at the Holiday Inn. But I'd be happy to have dinner downtown."

"That's a possibility. Or, I have rented a small cabin in the forest. It is useful for me to have a place to entertain clients. I would be happy to cook dinner for us, and drive you to your hotel later this evening."

"I appreciate the offer, Mr Belanov, but as you said earlier, a woman in my position should be careful. If it's all right with you, I'd prefer to eat in public. And I haven't yet gotten the opportunity to see the sights of Brno."

"Of course, and you are quite right. To tell you the truth, I have very little food in my cabin, so eating out is a much better idea." He gave her a wide smile and could see her relief. Such fine bones, she was a pleasure to observe.

"However, I would like to collect some printed material in order to better demonstrate what I can offer. Would it bother you if we drove by my place quickly for me to pick up a few things? You can stay in the car, if you feel safer that way."

She laughed. "That's fine with me. And I get to see a little of the countryside."

The Porsche thundered through the trees. Belanov steered with his left hand, allowing his right, complete with TAG Heuer, to rest on the gearstick. Her colour was high and he could sense her exhilaration. He allowed the vehicle a four-wheel slide as they arrived at the cabin.

"OK, Ms McKendrick. I'll be five minutes. Would you like me to leave the music on for you?"

"You know what? I think I might be safe enough to come in while you get your stuff. Apart from anything else, I could use the bathroom."

Belanov repressed a grin and bowed like a gentleman as he opened the passenger door and offered his arm. He ran through his list. White wine and snacks in fridge, vodka in freezer. Fire laid, clean sheets, camera charged. And in the bedside drawer, a high-quality twist of cocaine. Czech.

After shoving a selection of brochures into his briefcase, he returned to the living room. She leant back on the sofa, arms behind her head.

"Cosy."

"Can I offer you anything while I prepare myself?" He maintained the pretence that they would be leaving soon. Maintained his style.

"I guess. What do you guys drink as a pre-dinner aperitif, Mr Belanov?"

"'Us guys' enjoy vodka, before, after and even during dinner."

He had no objection to playing to the stereotype, so long as she played into his hands.

"But can I ask you to call me Symon? In Ukraine, a good working relationship is based on friendship."

"No problem. I like that. And you gotta call me Caroline."

Like taking candy from a baby. In the tiny kitchen, he selected two shot glasses and poured a decent measure into each. The sound of whistling reached him, but he brushed off his discomfort. How could a Canadian be expected to know it was bad luck? He chose to focus on the moment rather than outdated superstition and headed back to the living room. She still wore her coat.

"Are you cold, Caroline? I can light a fire."

"No, we won't be here all that long, will we? This is such a cute cabin, Symon."

"For me, it is perfect. I am not the businessman to sit in public bars talking loudly. I prefer discretion and privacy. So do my clients. Now, *na zdorovia*!"

He threw back the vodka and felt a sense of achievement as she did the same.

"*Na zdorovoia*!" Her eyes widened and she coughed as the liquor hit her throat. She pressed a napkin to her mouth.

"Strong stuff, huh?" she wheezed.

"A Ukrainian special. It works well with small fish snacks. Would you prefer to go to the city directly, or shall we have another, accompanied by an *amuse bouche*?"

"Why not? Let's go local."

He poured another good measure in each glass.

She touched his arm. "And you know what? I think a lighting a fire might work pretty well right now."

It was sealed. No woman, not one, had ever drunk his vodka, sat with him in front of a crackling fireplace and left. He placed a match to the kindling in the grate and watched the flames grow. As he turned, she slid forward to hand him his glass.

"*Na zdorovoia*!" she smiled. They both threw back the vodka and locked eyes. Belanov was struggling. It would be wise to get the business settled before the inevitable, but he didn't want to appear rude.

"Caroline? Do you still prefer to go to the city or would …"

She moved onto her knees, pulled his head towards her and kissed him. Her tongue slipped into his mouth and touched his. His hands reached for her, but she pressed her palms to his upper arms, pushing them behind his back. His dick danced and twitched as she confidently drew his tongue into her mouth. She moved forward, kissing him, nibbling his lower lip, pressing her body until he relented and lay back on the hearth rug. She straddled him and sat up, grinding her pelvis over the swelling in his trousers. Her blue-grey eyes, dark with lust, never left his as she reached for his groin.

He stretched his arms above his head and let her get on with it. She surprised him, unbuckling his belt, whipping it loose from the loops, and fastening it around his wrists. Just the kind of dirty slut he liked. This could be a lot of fun. She tied the end of his belt around the leg of the armchair. He yanked at the leather to see if it would give, but he was trussed like a hog. His thighs spread as she undid his flies. He grunted and pushed his hips towards her. Suck it. Take it in your mouth. Do it.

She stopped moving and he realised he'd spoken aloud. His vision was blurred, but he could see her intense eyes focused on him and the only sound was his laboured breathing. She stood up and walked away.

"Caroline! Come back! I didn't want to …"

She was back. Out of focus, but she was back. She laid something on the sofa, and slid both hands up his thighs, meeting in the middle. His dick pulsed and strained to get at her. She clasped him and he groaned. Smooth, soft hands, rhythmic upward jerks. His eyes rolled backwards in his head. He was going to come, right there. She let go and spoke.

"Suck it. Take it in your mouth. Do it."

He couldn't even see what she was forcing between his lips. But it was cold, hard and had a familiar smell.

Something went off.

Chapter 8

Zürich 2012

"Beatrice, can I interrupt you?"

"Of course, Xavier. Take a seat. Have you found something?"

"Maybe it is nothing. But I wanted to discuss about it."

The team had quickly adopted a routine, guided by Xavier's diffident insights into how the Kantonspolizei worked. So they started between 07.30 and 08.00, and worked till at least 18.00. Lunch was early and they usually ate together. Beatrice found these sessions an excellent way of discovering more about her team. In the first few days, a rapport grew which seemed strengthened rather than shaken by the occasional unpleasant appearance of Herr Kälin. He attended the daily update at eight with almost theatrical impatience, before disappearing into his own office, only communicating by email. Suited Beatrice just fine.

"Sorry." Xavier picked up the files he'd knocked from Beatrice's desk.

"It's no problem. Sit down, Xavier. It's safest."

He shrugged. "Sorry. I'm a ... how do you say that ... *ein Tollpatsch*?"

"Accident-prone, I imagine. Or failing that, clumsy."

"Clumsy, yes. It drives Herr Kälin crazy. I wanted to speak with you about the business connections between the dead men. Something keeps coming up. D'Arcy Roth."

Beatrice recognised the name. "The auditors?"

"Yes. They offer all kinds of financial services and consulting. One of the Big Five. Each man had a connection. The meetings van der Veld planned for the Monday after he died. One of them was with D'Arcy Roth. He was looking for a firm to handle his compliance issues."

"That's one of the best euphemisms for money-laundering I've heard yet, Xavier."

He grinned, and a hint of pink warmed his freckles. "I'm learning to be diplomatic, Beatrice. Now, Thompson and Edwards were also clients of the same company, but were a little more than average customers. They were personal friends of Antonella D'Arcy, the CEO."

"Mmm. That is interesting. You said all the men had a connection. Was Ryman a client too?"

"No. And this was the one that really made me think. Ryman's bank didn't use D'Arcy Roth at all. But the day he died, he was on his way to a polo tournament in Switzerland. To play against a team from Zürich, which included Antonella D'Arcy. They knew each other through the polo circuit and had previously played one another on several occasions."

"That is curious, you're right. So what do we know about this woman?"

"I already prepared a file. Details on her company, clients, and perception in the media. Also, information on her own background, hobbies and connections. This is not comprehensive, but I thought it would be helpful as an introduction."

"You're several steps ahead. I am grateful for all this. Perhaps I should go and have a chat with this lady."

"Good luck. She does not have a nice reputation. Nor does the company."

"Oh?"

"D'Arcy Roth are known informally in the business world as having the slogan; 'No such thing as dirty money'. Apparently, they deal with anyone; dictators, pirates, drug cartels. All that matters is that you have the cash to pay their bill. People also say that she …" He puffed out his cheeks.

"What do people say?"

"They say she has balls, Beatrice. Balls of steel."

"Really? That would be unusual. Yes, I think it's best if I check."

Xavier looked uncertain. "Do you want me to come with you? She speaks English, but you know, if you need me …"

"No, I don't think that will be necessary. I appreciate your bringing this to my attention and doing so much groundwork. But I believe the best person to assist me in interviewing a woman with steel balls would be Herr Kälin. Don't you agree?"

A wide, guilty smile of complicity spread across the young man's face.

As the BMW accelerated, Beatrice gazed at the late afternoon sunshine playing on the water. She wanted to look at the properties overlooking the lake, all leafy gardens and imposing architecture, but that would involve looking past Herr Kälin. She settled for an interesting enough view of the *Zürisee*.

"The 'Gold Coast'. So called because of the wealth?" she asked.

"Money, yes. And sunshine. The sun sets on the other side of the lake, so this coast gets the last of the light." He seemed slightly more forthcoming once out of the police buildings.

"I see." The BMW cruised past high walls and security gates, allowing glimpses of green lawns, French windows and occasional sculptures.

"These places must cost the earth," she said.

"They do. Similar to a town house in Kensington, I imagine. But in the area of Zürichberg, above the city, property costs even more."

"Good grief."

They sat in silence for several minutes, Beatrice absorbing the sense of privilege around them.

"How do you want to play this, Herr Kälin? Shall we do interviewer and observer, or would it be more effective to work as an interview team?"

"You're the boss."

"I am aware of that. But it doesn't answer my question."

He was quiet for a long time. He slowed to allow a dog walker to clear a zebra crossing. The retriever was dripping wet and carried a Frisbee in its mouth. It occurred to Beatrice that seeing as the road markings were yellow and black, a *zebra* crossing was rather a misnomer. A wasp crossing?

"She's a Swiss-American. Bilingual. I think it would be better if you ask the questions and I watch. Good cop, bad cop. I will add something if necessary," he said, eyes fixed on the road.

"I agree. That should have the right effect." Herr Kälin's skill as glowering, malevolent presence was beyond doubt. She hoped it was powerful enough to rattle steel balls.

The security guard examined their IDs and waved them through. The drive led up to a huge pink villa, sun reflecting from every window. The terraced gardens were well tended, with neat paths winding through blazes of yellow forsythia. Before Kälin had even switched off the ignition, the front door opened and a young woman waited to greet them. Beatrice observed the black high-collared dress, the court shoes and the serious face. The girl's hair was neatly tied back in a bun. How marvellously old school.

"*Grüezi mitenand. Mein Name ist Dina, Sekretärin und Tochter von Frau D'Arcy.*" She stood back to allow them in.

"Did she say she was the secretary and the doctor?" Beatrice whispered to Kälin.

"Secretary and daughter." His tone was dismissive, although

he too was whispering. Beatrice attempted a friendly smile, but the girl's gaze remained fixed on the floor. She offered to take their coats, giving them a moment to assess their surroundings. It reeked of money. The floor was mosaic and probably depicted some dramatic image which could not be seen while standing on it. The optimum viewing point would be the landing of the grand curving staircase which arced upwards, from right to left. Despite most of the doors leading off the hallway being closed, light poured onto a variety of thriving giant plants from a cupola far above. A chaise longue upholstered in green leather sat beneath the staircase.

"*Frau D'Arcy wartet im Wintergarten. Bitte, kommen sie,*" the girl mumbled and led the way through an elegant reception room. The décor was gold and green, with a fireplace and grand piano, wooden parquet flooring and several oil-paintings clearly chosen for their colours. Few photographs, Beatrice noted. More like a hotel lobby than a family room. Beyond the piano, French windows opened into a conservatory, filled with fig trees, succulents and indoor palms.

"Herr Kälin, Frau Stubbs," the PA-daughter announced.

Antonella D'Arcy rose to meet them. Black hair swung over her shoulders like watered silk. Her grey cashmere dress managed to convey sobriety and professionalism while making you want to reach out and touch its softness. Her face had that barely there make-up which took hours to achieve, highlighting her strong bones, dark-blue eyes and wide smile. The hand she offered was pale, manicured and free of adornment, apart from the silver Patek Philippe wristwatch.

"Ms Stubbs. Herr Kälin. I am happy to welcome you to my home. Please, take a seat and allow me to offer some refreshment." Her eyes, still smiling, flicked over Beatrice. "Ms Stubbs, it is a foolish hobby of mine to try to guess a person's nationality. I am often wrong, but I flatter myself I am improving. My first guess would be that you are British, more specifically English. Am I terribly wide of the mark?"

In a second, Beatrice became aware of her own hands. Whilst clean and tidy, they were also dry, wrinkled, and her fingernails echoed her name. The Marks and Spencer suit seemed provincial and style-free. Her shoes needed a polish.

"Correct first time, Ms D'Arcy. Well done."

The smile widened. Her teeth were perfect, reflecting light with as much sparkle as the diamond at her throat. "Thank you. Dina, bring tea. I presume that you are also a tea-drinker, Ms Stubbs? Or is that as much of a cliché as the Americans surviving on burgers? Herr Kälin, is tea acceptable to you?"

He nodded and Beatrice realised she was not required to answer. The girl left the room without a sound.

Antonella indicated the well-cushioned chairs and sat. "I must express my gratitude to you both. It was very kind of you to agree to meet me here rather than my office. I'm sure you realise that financial markets are immensely sensitive, and even the faintest breath of police interest in a company could sound the death knell. So I am genuinely appreciative of your taking the time to come out here. From what your officer explained on the phone, I understand your enquiry concerns the suicides of some high-profile men."

Kälin gazed around the room while Beatrice responded. "And we want to thank you for meeting us. We are simply tying up loose ends in these cases of suicide. All these men had significant enemies. We are trying to establish if they did indeed choose to end their own lives."

"Really? I am shocked. You don't think someone else was involved, surely?" D'Arcy's concerned expression seemed synthetic, like that of a wealthy politician extending sympathies towards victims of a poor nation's catastrophe.

"At this stage, we cannot say. We're investigating exactly what happened. Obviously, we need to explore any links between the individuals concerned. It seems one of those connections is you."

"Excellent police work. To find a connection between all

these individuals to me is quite remarkable. However, perhaps we should make a distinction, just for clarity. There is Antonella D'Arcy, the woman, and D'Arcy Roth, the company. Now, the woman has been successful, and therefore mixes in certain circles. The company provides services to forty-three countries and every kind of business under the sun. It is natural that in one guise or another, I have crossed paths with most of the biggest animals in the jungle."

"Of course. And we are here for two reasons. Firstly, to eliminate you from our enquiries. That will be quite simple. If you can tell us where you were on those key dates, we can move on. Secondly, we hope to achieve some insight into the men who died. As someone who knew them professionally, or socially, your views could be most helpful."

A clinking of crockery announced the arrival of tea. D'Arcy's daughter placed the tray on the table and began distributing cups and saucers. Beatrice noted how the girl's awkwardness grew under their silent observation.

"Thank you, Dina. That's all right. I can be mother." D'Arcy flicked her eyes at the girl and at the door. It was the briefest gesture, but no doubt a curt dismissal. Dina fled, apparently grateful to get away.

D'Arcy's voice, however, was light and pleasant. "Ms Stubbs, how do you take your tea? Herr Kälin?"

As the woman observed the niceties, Beatrice observed her. She was a player. Smooth, urbane and polished, not only in appearance, but in small talk. She had prepared for their visit; Beatrice noted the laptop, Blackberry and desk diary on the table beside her. She devoted all her attention to Beatrice, barely giving Kälin a glance. She knew who held the power and how to get at it. Small wonder she had done so well. It would take a specialist kind of arrow to pierce this finely wrought armour.

"And here is the sugar. I serve it in lumps, the British way. I hope you approve, Ms Stubbs. These are Luxemburgerli, by the way. Similar to macaroons. But they may not appeal unless you have a sweet tooth."

Beatrice accepted one, but was urged to take two. The shiny little thing looked like a Disney hamburger. Pastel-coloured halves of meringue sandwiched together with matching cream, and small enough to fit between finger and thumb. It was delicious, dangerously so. Kälin refused the cakes, but added several sugar lumps to his teacup and stirred vigorously. He gave D'Arcy a humourless stare, as she took a pink cake and popped it into her mouth, wiping sugary fingers on a napkin.

"Oh dear. I just cannot resist Luxemburgerli. An extra twenty minutes in the gym tomorrow for me. Now, you asked about my diary. Would you like to give me the dates and we can check?"

Kälin detailed the days in question and D'Arcy found the relevant pages or screens while making pleasant small talk with Beatrice.

27 February 2007: ski weekend in Davos. Six companions. Left Friday morning, returned Sunday evening.

Did Beatrice live in central London, or further outside?

21 March 2008: Brunch with friends in Feusisberg. 10.00 to 13.00. Then they took a walk around Einsiedeln, the monastery.

Had Beatrice been there yet? It was an absolute must. The home of the Black Madonna.

Home at 16.00.

D'Arcy had done her MBA through the London School of Economics and used the opportunity to improve her British accent. She aspired to speak cut-glass British English.

Beatrice nodded. "R.P."

"I'm not familiar with that term."

"What they call 'BBC English'. It stands for Received Pronunciation." Beatrice felt a childish delight in scoring a point.

12 September 2010: Flight back from New York. Attended a remembrance service for victims of 9/11. Twenty eight D'Arcy Roth employees had perished in their World Trade Centre office. Very sad.

Last time she visited London, she'd found a Swiss restaurant, had Beatrice ever seen it? Wardour Street, or somewhere near there?

"I live in the East End, Ms D'Arcy, so I tend to eat closer to home."

"The East End! Good decision. It is a growth area; the Olympic investments have made this highly desirable in terms of real estate. You made a wise choice."

Beatrice smiled. "You credit me with excessive foresight. I bought my little flat in 1982. I would like to get back to Herr Kälin's point. Jack Ryman. You played polo together?"

"Not quite correct. I played opposite Ryman. Let me top you up. Herr Kälin? Do you know anything about polo, Ms Stubbs? No? Well, I'll assume you have enough intelligence and research capability to appreciate what I say. I usually play number one in our team. Ryman played number four in his. We met often on the field and were direct aggressors. Nevertheless, with my track record, he had more reason to wish me dead than the other way around."

"Would you say Mr Ryman was a popular man in his social circle? I know he was disliked by the media," Beatrice asked.

"The media dislike anyone who takes tough decisions. Ryman was respected by those who understood his business. They are fewer than you think."

"That is becoming apparent. Most people who invested in these debt obligations seem to have found themselves holding a piece of worthless paper. Or are you referring to his company's so-called 'vulture funds'? The ones where the rich get richer by trading on Third World misery. I find it surprising you consider Ryman's strategy to be 'tough decision-making'. I am not a financier, Ms D'Arcy, but it looks like the man lacked any kind of moral compass and was selling hot air at a premium."

"If you can sell hot air at a premium and financial regulators see nothing wrong with that, you sell hot air at the best price you can get. That's what Ryman did, and he did it very well. Hence his impressive bonuses and profits. I actually admire someone who plays the game to win."

"Despite the disproportionate amount of losers?"

Kälin shifted slightly and Beatrice sensed it was a signal. She reminded herself of the reason for their visit and decided not to wait for a reply.

"Let's talk about van der Veld."

"There, I'm afraid I will not be able to help you. I never met the man. He was a potential client, but it seems he changed his mind."

"Did you know anything about his business, Ms D'Arcy? About the provenance of his diamonds?"

"He had a range of interests besides diamonds and needed some help with staying on the right side of the law. It is not my job to investigate the ethics behind his money. I am a professional, Ms Stubbs, which requires me to be neutral and unbiased. Anyone has the right to be a client of mine, if they can afford it."

"So I hear. But you did know Dougie Thompson and Brian Edwards personally, didn't you?"

"I knew them as social acquaintances, yes."

"And despite their unprincipled activities, you retained them as friends. That didn't bother you?"

D'Arcy folded her hands together and gave Beatrice a kind smile.

"I can see you feel quite strongly about certain issues, Ms Stubbs. And I admire you for it, I really do. However, it appears we see the world differently, so let's leave it at that. As far as I'm aware, it's not my ethical perspective which is under investigation, is it?"

Kälin's voice rumbled into the silence.

"The fact remains, Ms D'Arcy, you knew all these men. Why do *you* think they died?"

She turned to face him for the first time. "Do you think it possible they may have discovered a conscience?"

Beatrice cocked her head. "That's certainly possible. In which case, when you discover yours, will you do the same?"

Kälin's spoon stopped stirring.

D'Arcy's face smoothed. "It seems that we have gone past enquiry and into judgement. Is there anything more I can help you with, officers, or would you like to beat the traffic back into the city?"

The girl fetched their coats.

Beatrice's view of the lakeside buildings was unimpeded. Cyclists, joggers, picnickers, couples, groups of friends wandered through the spring sunshine towards the water. An inspiring evening, into which she carried her own little rain cloud.

Kälin kept checking her with sideways glances. "Where do you want to go?"

"It's late. Let's de-brief on Monday. I'd prefer to go home."

If only she could. A wild thought grabbed her. If she checked the flights as soon as she got in, it might be possible to fly to Exeter tonight, spend a weekend in Matthew's calming company, allow him to fuss over her and puncture her paranoia ... Or not. Or she could stay here and work. After her outburst, jetting off for a weekend with her lover seemed to lack gravitas.

Traffic on Bürkliplatz held them up. She watched the tourists; he kept his eyes on the road.

"Herr Kälin, I am sorry I handled that so badly. Purely through my own aggressive attitude, I turned a friendly witness hostile. Maybe we should have worked as a team after all."

He didn't answer. Beatrice watched the west coast darken, while the sun's rays continued to bless the golden east. The weekend stretched ahead, full of nothing but shadows. The dogs were restless.

Kälin stopped in front of her apartment block but did not turn off the ignition. He turned to look at her as he spoke. "We did work as a team. My mistake was to think *I* was playing the bad cop. I wish you a good weekend, Frau Stubbs."

"Same to you, Herr Kälin."

His moustache lifted in an unfamiliar way. If Beatrice hadn't known better, it could have been a smile.

Chapter 9

Zürich 2012

"So what would you like to achieve from today's call, Beatrice?"

"The usual, I suppose. To explain how I'm feeling, and check with you that I'm still on course."

"OK, good. I'd be interested to hear how you're feeling. And when you say, 'still on course', what do you mean exactly?"

"That I'm still going in the right direction. I felt we'd made a lot of progress before I left London, but here, I feel more wobbly."

"Right, I see. Should we start with 'wobbly'? Is that the word which best describes how you're feeling?"

"Yes. What I mean is that I have very little self-confidence. Sometimes. I'm afraid I'm out of my depth. I ballsed up an interview yesterday because I let my temper get the better of me. And I did it in front of the Senior Detective here. He doesn't have much belief in me anyway, and now his respect has reached rock bottom. The thing is, James, I'm not at all sure I'm up to this. Maybe it's too soon."

"That's a possibility. But only one of many. I'd like to hear a bit more about what happened."

Beatrice explained, trying to rein in her urge to exaggerate D'Arcy into a monster and paint Kälin as a pantomime villain.

"So, you're saying you may have created hostility with the

detective by being judgemental with that interviewee?"

"Exactly. I upset her, and him by behaving badly."

"Funny you should use the word 'bad.' Didn't you just tell me you had agreed to play 'good cop, bad cop'? How should a bad cop behave?"

"Oh, you know. Intimidating, aggressive, maybe showing obvious dislike of the witness. Come on, James, you've seen *Life on Mars*."

"I have. And isn't that exactly what you did? So I'm puzzled by why you think your behaviour upset your colleague. Tell me again what he said in response to your apology?"

"He said that we had worked as a team, and he just hadn't realised I was the bad cop. But he was being sarcastic."

"How did this sarcasm manifest itself? Did he say anything else?"

"No. Apart from wishing me a good weekend. You think I'm exaggerating."

"What I'm hearing may be a magnification of a negative moment, yes. What are the other factors that make you say you're not up to it?"

"It's a complicated case, the team are very young and whizzy, Kälin thinks he should be in charge and I'm homesick." Heat rose in her face, as she felt tears tickling her nose. She sniffed, her sudden self-pity followed by sympathy for James. How many times had the poor man sat listening to her grizzles?

"Sorry, James."

"I believe we had an agreement by which you did not apologise for your feelings?"

"Yes, you're right. I'm not sorry then. But it has been bloody tough."

"That I don't doubt. And I'll come back to that in a second. But first I'd like you to remind me of some of the recurring patterns we identified when you are under stress."

Beatrice sighed deeply. "I am selective. I remember events with a focus on the negative. And I magnify the bad things, so they become far larger than the good. I also tend to nurse a grievance, so that I feel hard-done-by for longer and more often than is necessary."

"You mentioned how tough you find your circumstances. Have you noticed any of these thought patterns happening as a result?"

"A bit. Yes. But I have been trying to make something positive out of it."

"Can I ask for an example?"

Beatrice considered. "By not showing myself to be rattled by Kälin, I think I'm earning more respect from the team. And even, perversely, from him."

"So his level of respect is actually increasing, you think?"

"It may have been until yesterday."

"Is there any chance you are projecting your own frustrations with your performance onto this man?"

"Possibly. But he can be quite horrible, James. I'm not making this up."

"I know that. Just remember that quotation; 'no one can make you feel inferior without your permission'. You are in control of how you feel. If you feel you made a mistake, it's fine to be angry at yourself. Let's remove this one step. If one of your 'young and whizzy' team had lost their temper with a witness, how would you feel? I'd like you to think about a specific individual, please."

"I would feel annoyed at his lack of professionalism. But if he recognised the mistake, apologised and learnt from it, I would forgive and forget."

"Good. Might your colleague do the same for you?"

"He might, I suppose. I did apologise."

"People make mistakes, Beatrice. It's how we deal with our mistakes that takes us forward. Now, a couple of practical questions ..."

"Yes, and yes. I am taking the Depakote without fail. And I have kept a diary. Not religiously, but noting any low symptoms."

"Good news. That'll be useful for charting lows, highs, and middle bits, so I'd like it if you made a daily note of your general outlook. Now, shall we turn to the positive things that have happened since our last call?"

After a session with James, Beatrice always needed time to digest and test her recalibrated outlook. She felt like someone who'd just discovered the reason why walking hurt was because she had her shoes on the wrong feet. A stroll by the river did wonders, especially as she watched people cycling, jogging, playing football and enjoying themselves. Wandering as far as the Allmend playing fields, she realised her feet now hurt because she'd walked so far and made up her mind to take the train back into the city. But first she stopped at a little cabin-café in the park and spent half an hour watching dogs and replaying James's words. Wagging tails, the sunshine and a good idea for a jaunt the next day lifted her into almost glad to be alive.

The S-Bahn delivered her back to the city and she returned to her extensive, empty quarters. She'd just put the kettle on when the phone rang. She skipped to answer it, keen to talk to Matthew.

"Hel-lo?"

"Good afternoon, Frau Stubbs. This is Herr Koch at reception. I'm sorry to disturb you. A young man just handed in a mobile phone. He found it outside in the street. I checked through the address book and I have the impression it might belong to you."

"I don't think so. One moment." Beatrice rooted through her bag. Her phone was indeed missing.

"Herr Koch? It seems you're right. I had no idea I'd lost it. I'll come down now."

"There's no need, Frau Stubbs. I'll send someone up to your room."

"That's very kind of you. I'll be more careful in future. Have a nice afternoon."

"Thank you. I wish the same for you. Goodbye."

People in this country were so nice, so honest. Very civilised.

"Zürich calling. How's the weather in Devon?"

"Outdoors, fine with a light breeze. Super washday weather. However, indoors we have thunder, lightning, black clouds and the strong possibility of torrential rain."

"Oh dear. Is Luke having a tantrum?"

"No, no. He's right here in front of the television. We're watching something rather sinister called *Teletubbies*. His mother, on the other hand, is prising open the yawning pit of Tartarus with a nail file. An alimony payment has failed to arrive."

"Poor Tanya. Send her my love, and sympathy. How's Marianne?"

"The second of the Eumenides is winging her way here as we speak. From Crediton. It may be wise to take young Luke out for a pint tonight. Too much female vitriol can put a chap off his food."

Beatrice laughed. "There may come a time to share advice and ale with your grandson, but you cannot take a baby to the pub. And your local hostelry is quite strict about under-eighteens," she said, envisaging the mismatched pair in a corner of the snug.

"Yet no laws exist on under-ones accompanying me to the shed for a pint of home-brew, as far as I know."

"True. Wrap him up warm and give him a kiss from me."

"Enough of my domestic low pressure system. How's the high life?"

"Nothing to write home about. I lost my temper yesterday and have been in a fug ever since."

"A fug?" She could hear his disguised concern.

"It's perfectly all right, Matthew. I should expect these insecurities, everyone has them. And I've just talked it through with James. I confess to having more perspective now."

"I'm happy to hear that. Would it help if I were to visit for a couple of days? I should very much like to see you."

Beatrice's smile broadened, but she hesitated.

"And I'd like to see you. Can we discuss this later in the week? I just feel a need to ... manage. Does that make sense?"

"Absolutely. I said exactly the same thing to my father. Three days in a row I came home with bloodied knees, raw elbows and grazed hands. He offered to put the stabilisers back on my bike, but I stood tall in my short trousers, looked him in the eye, and said, 'Thank you, Father, I can manage.' So manage away, my dear one, but if you need an extra wheel, you may summon me at a moment's notice."

"Thank you. It's good to know my stabilisers are in the cupboard under the stairs. It's peculiar, you know. I always rely on systems at work. They are there to make sure I don't miss anything, that I follow best practice, to keep me on the straight and narrow. Where work is concerned, I know I am fallible, so I adhere to my systems, my stabilisers. Now I have to learn to do that in my private life."

"We all have them, Old Thing. And some of those systems, which I prefer to see as habits, can become obsolete, outdated and counter-productive. Your life has just had an overhaul, and you're in the adaptation phase. A few scabby knees are part of the learning process."

"I know. But I'm an awful old dog to be learning new bicycle tricks."

"Had anyone else referred to you as an 'awful old dog', I would have offered him outside. Talking of tricks, when you come back, I thought we might try learning to juggle with that circus group in Totnes. Learning new skills keeps you young, so they say. Oh Good God!"

"What is it?"

"The television programme is over and the sun has gone down. It had a baby's face, and as it sank below the horizon, it gurgled. That is one of the most disturbing images I have seen since *Chucky*. Right, I am taking Luke to the shed and shall read to him from Rudyard Kipling, which will soothe us both."

"Excellent idea. Off you go. Just don't read him astray."

His laughter was rich, like gravy. "Was that deliberate, or one of your Bea-lines?"

"I rarely manage to be so apt by accident. Your turn to call me tomorrow."

"It will be the highlight of my Sunday. Apart from *Antiques Roadshow*. Enjoy your Saturday, my love."

"Matthew? After you refused your father's offer of stabilisers, did you stop falling off?"

"Yes, eventually. Although the day after that conversation, I broke my nose."

Smiling, Beatrice dug her laptop out of her bag and typed the word *Chucky* into a search engine. Sometimes, her contemporary cultural knowledge had the most appalling gaps.

Chapter 10

Zürich 2012

An unusual level of excitement hummed through the top-floor room. Sabine set up her laptop and projector, apparently oblivious to the louder-than-usual banter from her colleagues. Even Kälin's arrival failed to bring the buzz down. Sabine picked up the remote control and looked to Beatrice for permission to begin. It was 07.58.

"OK, folks. Sabine's ready so I'd like to get started. Just a reminder, this session is likely to generate some significant steps forward. So today's meeting is scheduled to run till eleven. It may not last that long, but if it does, I hope you'll understand why." Beatrice made eye contact with each individual, lingering no longer on Kälin than anyone else. Despite the fact that everyone in the room knew whom she was addressing.

"Sabine, over to you."

"Thank you, Beatrice. And thanks to all of you for being so patient. I have taken quite some time over this profile and demanded much of your attention and time with my questions. Cases reported as suicide tend to involve less evidence than homicides. So there were a limited amount of photographs, crime scene reports and witness statements to analyse. In other words, I have been filling in the gaps.

"Slide One. My method. I am a fan of the deductive system

of profiling. That is to say, I want to find out everything I can about this individual before making comparison to statistical data. What do we know? For certain?"

The question was not rhetorical. Beatrice went first.

"The only thing we know with any certainty is that four men are dead. And that what appears to be the same DNA was found at each scene."

Conceição spoke. "In my view, we can drop the 'what appears to be' the same DNA. It's him. Since 1989, EDNAP – European DNA Profiling, and ENFSI – the European Network of Forensic Institutes have standardised procedures across the continent, setting the benchmark for short tandem repeat analysis. The vast majority of laboratories agree on STR testing for the European core loci. Some countries test for more, some for less, but all include the basic four. My checks show that the samples taken were large enough and handled with textbook care. It's the same guy."

Sabine nodded. "Thank you, Conceição. But even taking the DNA as a given, my point is we cannot be sure that these deaths were homicides. So let us work on premise one. These four men killed themselves and the same individual was present before, during or after the death. Could this person have triggered the desire to end their lives? If so, how? Blackmail? Coercion? That is an intriguing possibility. Yet something bothers me about this theory. These deaths were carefully orchestrated. Personally, I have a feeling these methods were purposely chosen. I will come back to this in a moment or two."

"Frau Tikkenenn. Is much of your presentation today likely to be based on your 'feelings', or do you plan to provide us with something of concrete value?"

"Herr Kälin, do you mind if we leave questions to the end? As I think you will see, my work is to a professional standard."

Beatrice froze at the girl's curt dismissal of a senior officer and steeled herself for the slamming of a door. Kälin didn't move. But no one dared look at his face.

"Premise two. If these events were intentional killings, serious questions are raised. The perpetrator is a serial killer. These were organised, meticulously planned and perfectly executed crimes. To leave a trace of DNA looks a little clumsy. Was it done on purpose? I'll come back to that, too. Let us focus on motive and method.

"Motive: Why kill these men, and in this way? This is where Chris and Xavier's research proved very useful. All the dead men had a reputation for a lack of ethics.

"Van der Veld's wares came from mines known to violate working practice codes, and three out of these five mines were in litigation for abuse, inhumane treatment and corruption.

"Dougie Thompson. Thompson and family owned mainly right-wing newspapers and television channels all over Australia and New Zealand. They had a majority stake in two key US TV networks, both of which represent the 'Real American Family'. Every broadcast contains some reference to the abuse of the American system, by foreigners, kids or Democrats. They also own several of the worse gossip tabloids. The ones which feature stars with cellulite or Photoshopped romances. In the UK, the approach was more subtle. They claimed the middle ground."

Chris nodded. "The middle ground of Middle England."

"Yes. His papers laid claim to the morally righteous position, while whipping up anti-immigration, anti-gay, anti-intellectual, anti-teenager sentiments. Their trademark was exposing the youth leader as drug-pusher, the pregnancy consultant as baby-killer, the asylum-seeker as cynical sponger and so on. Every week, the front page 'exposed' some liberal or humanitarian cause as waste of the good taxpayer's money."

Beatrice twitched. "Sabine, can I ask you to stick to the factual side? Your personal bias is distracting, to be honest."

Sabine acknowledged the point with a twist of her head.

"Brian Edwards, whose company, Watermark, was found guilty of contaminating the water supply of a large area in the Peak District of Britain. Edwards resigned, accepting a four million pound pay-off. Lawyers are still seeking reparation for over three hundred brain-damaged babies and several hundred infertile women.

"Jack Ryman, used to be key client-manager for Mendoza and Schwanhof, investment bankers. Sold collateralised debt obligations at inflated prices, thus bankrupting the company, and dragging down several others. Fortunately for him, he saw it coming and jumped ship with his enormous bonus, mid 2008. Set up RAM, Ryman Asset Management, which specialised in buying up debts in war-torn countries. After those countries made peace, RAM sued for repayment. So rather than rebuild their infrastructure, they were legally obliged to hand over anything they had to investment vultures like Ryman."

"Sabine," cautioned Beatrice.

The girl sighed. "Sorry, Beatrice. I shouldn't get carried away. Although do keep in mind this is how these stories were reported and could therefore influence public perception."

"Carry on."

"In the years they died, these names were in the top ten of everyone's most hated. International press reported their deaths with a sense of justice. This, I believe, is our first pointer. Very few serial killers, or spree killers, continue to pursue this activity without an eye on their own 'fifteen minutes' of fame. I suggest the person responsible did this either because he felt it was the right thing to do, or that it was seen to be the right thing to do."

Chris offered his uncensored opinion. "So an extreme left-winger? Anti-capitalist who sees it as his duty to shoot fat cats?"

Sabine clicked to the next slide, which showed a pie chart of statistics. "This is where comparisons to similar cases can help. The vast majority of serial and spree killers tend to have more political affiliations with the right. That is not to say a left-wing vigilante is impossible. Simply unusual."

Kälin pressed his fingers to his forehead and looked down. Either he was crying or laughing. Beatrice attempted to give

Sabine a sharp indication to continue and ignore his theatrics, but there was no need.

"Modus operandi. He made each death look like suicide. As Chris points out, one can see why. He assumes the role of their absent conscience. Our man is performing a 'cull' of those seen as malignant to society. Murder motivated by a political agenda? This is not unheard of, but as I say, rare for left-wing causes."

Xavier raised a finger. "Sabine, you said something about methods being specifically chosen. I know you were talking about your 'assisted' suicide idea, but I wonder what you meant?"

"This is not relevant at this point, and I did ask if we could keep questions until later."

Beatrice intervened. "That is usually the way I prefer to present, too, Sabine. However, we should be flexible to interruption and diversion, especially in an international team. Not all our thought processes work the same way. Answering Xavier's question may well make him better prepared for the remainder of your input."

"That's fair enough. Sorry, Xavier. It's just because my slides will now be mixed up."

"No problem. I can wait." The poor lad's complexion gave everything away.

"No, I will answer." She clicked forward to a table detailing how the victims died. "The first death. Van der Veld. Apparently slit his wrists in the bath. Found up to his neck in his own blood. Does the expression *blood diamonds* mean anything, anyone?

"Thompson froze to death, drunk on schnapps, while on a skiing holiday. The man who made his fortune by bugging cars, taking long-lens photographs and dragging his targets onto the front page, died of exposure. If I were a vigilante, I couldn't think of a more appropriate way to dispose of a media mogul."

Chris grinned. "Well, not unless he was hacked to death."

Sabine groaned but even she seemed to have difficulty suppressing a smile.

"Moving on, Edwards, poisoned by carbon dioxide in his car.

Are the parallels clear?"

"And Ryman?" Chris asked. "Bag over his head? How does that figure?"

Sabine rifled through her notes for a moment.

A deep voice spoke. "The man achieved his fortune by selling something that didn't really exist. Maybe someone forced him to inhale his own toxic assets."

Like the others, Beatrice turned to Kälin. He stared blandly back, giving no clue as to whether his comment was sarcastic or contributory.

Sabine gazed into the middle distance. "Yes, that actually makes sense. I focussed on the fact that the killer left the top of the car down and therefore the body open to the elements and nature's scavengers."

"Both interesting thoughts," Beatrice agreed. "However, I feel we have only just started exploiting what we know. Can we continue with that and return to hypotheses later?"

Sabine snapped back into efficiency. "Yes, of course. Personal risk. How far did the killer jeopardise himself? So far, the deaths were seen as suicide or misadventure, thus no one was hunted. But in order to know where, when and what was going on in these men's lives, this person must have done serious research. In each case, there are signs of acceptance, welcome and co-operation with the other individual. Why?"

Chris threw in an idea. "I'd make a guess at some kind of service provider, obviously under-the-counter. He's a rent boy. Perhaps we should examine the sexual preferences of these four individuals. Or he's a drug dealer, high class, only deals with the top brass. Maybe he decides that enough is enough and wastes them while they're wasted."

"Good ideas, with plenty to support them. Anyone else want to offer something?" Sabine asked.

Conceição spoke with deliberation, thinking aloud. "With what you have given us so far, Sabine, I have to lean towards a professional hit man. There is no motive, apart from cash. He murders to order, and is either instructed, or chooses to add the poetic justice element. He may have different employers. This guy knows how to gain access, knows how to subdue and kill, and to depart leaving no trace."

"Apart from the single sample of DNA," added Xavier.

"Exactly." Sabine gave a satisfied smile, like a cat. "Now I offer my picture from such data. This person is a professional. He knows where to find his victim and can do enough preparation to arrange an 'appropriate' death. I suggest the killer was in place before the arrival of the victim and arranged circumstances to suit. I will offer the following theories. Firstly, the dead men knew, or wanted to know, the person who orchestrated their deaths. He had access to the victim, he had knowledge of the victim's movements and he must have appeared benign to each individual.

"Conceição's forensics lead me to believe if these men were killed, as opposed to performing the act themselves, they must have been drugged. It is near impossible to take a healthy man, force him to sit in the bath and bleed him to death with no signs of struggle. Edwards sat peaceably in his vehicle and allowed the carbondioxide to poison his blood with no attempt to leave. Which leads me to the idea that our man has access to narcotics. Legal or otherwise. Conceição?"

"Taking the deaths chronologically, Van der Veld's coroner's report showed no suspicious substances. Thompson, same thing. Bear in mind they were found around thirty to thirty-six hours after death. Nothing there." Conceição raised a finger. "But Edwards's body was retrieved quickly. The autopsy showed traces of GHB, gamma hydroxybutyric acid, in his urine. GHB works much like Rohypnol, a benzodiazepine better-known as the date rape drug. You need add only a few drops to liquid, and the effects of muscle relaxation, sedation and a lack of anxiety can happen in less than twenty minutes. At which point, you are free to do whatever you want with that person for the next four to six hours. Another key factor is that GHB metabolises fast into carbondioxide and water. It's difficult to detect, but easy to make, if you have some knowledge of pharmaceuticals."

Chris looked up from his notes. "And Ryman?"

Conceição shook her head. "It was late April, but that weekend Swiss meteorologists recorded summer temperatures. His body had been out in the forest for three days in 28-degree heat. So that must have been one unpleasant, and fruitless, autopsy."

Sabine smiled. "Thanks for that, Conceição. So what can we tell about this person so far? He has a conscience, and a need for attention. So does half the human race. He knows details about these men, their movements and crucially, their preferences. Each scene shows all the elements of a professional hit. He is organised, prepared and very well researched. He is not in any way weak with blood, violence and death, but coldly professional. Just look at van der Veld."

"Why van der Veld in particular?" asked Chris.

"The killer slit his veins open. That is not an easy task. I know. I have killed chickens," Sabine assured them with great solemnity.

Beatrice caught her lip between her teeth to avert a smile. Kälin exhaled sharply and Beatrice saw his moustache twitch once more.

"So to profile. Gender we know," Sabine said.

Xavier shifted forward in his seat. "Do we? If the DNA is planted, it could be a woman."

Sabine managed her annoyance more smoothly this time. "Possible, but unlikely. A tiny percentage of serial killers are women. And those that do kill more than once usually have a personal reason, like vengeance."

Xavier cleared his throat. "Yes, I understand that. But in theory, we could be talking about a vengeful woman, who leaves traces of male DNA, possibly on purpose, to implicate someone?"

"In theory, Xavier. But you don't need to make this so complicated. Look at the statistics. He is most likely to be white. As for social class, I'm divided. He could be a working-class hero, maybe a drug dealer who serviced these men. Or a medic, someone they would meet socially, but who had access to debilitating drugs. As for age, that's a tricky one. Received wisdom is that serial killers tend to start their 'career' around the age of thirty-five. The first murder we know of was in 2007. And it was perfectly planned. Five years later, our killer is most likely early forties."

Chris picked up a marker pen and noted the details on the whiteboard.

"He is more than likely to live alone. He works in some kind of pharma-related industry. Or deals with less legal pharmaceuticals in his free time."

"Sabine?" Xavier had another question, while Chris added more data to the mind-map. "Why do you say he lives alone?"

Sabine sighed. "Most serial killers do. Or possibly with someone infirm or elderly, who cannot check up on them. I believe he prepared the ground for these killings in detail, which means being away from home for some time. So I cannot imagine he has an invalid at home whom he can abandon for days."

"Although if he did, that might explain access to sedating drugs," Xavier replied.

Sabine thought for a moment and nodded. "OK, I'll take that into account. Thanks, Xavier. Either way, this guy has an 'in'. He's a professional, someone respected, someone they want on their side.

"We can't test his DNA for any markers of ethnicity, but one thing we should note. These kinds of crimes usually start close to home, in an area the killer knows well. The incidents we know about occurred in the Netherlands, Switzerland, France and Liechtenstein. He may be Swiss, or a Dutchman living here."

"Have we checked *your* alibi?" Conceição looked sideways at Chris.

Chris feigned realisation. "Of course! It all seems so obvious now. Everyone knows the Dutch are all drug-crazed left-wing hippies. I think we should take me in for questioning."

Conceição released a deep laugh.

Chris continued. "But seriously, this profile does tend to point more towards some kind of businessman. The hotel in Utrecht is the sort of place where people stand out if they're not wealthy professionals."

Sabine nodded. "Exactly. This guy is a chameleon, fitting in easily to his environment. As for his psychological make-up, I'm still struggling to piece together the motivation. This kind of world view where he believes he alone can rescue society from, in this case, capitalism and greed, is not uncommon. He is an avenger, a righter of wrongs, and sees himself as a very intelligent person."

"Not forgetting a meticulous planner," added Chris.

Sabine agreed. "Definitely. From what I have assessed, I see this man. He works, or maybe used to work, in the world of pharmacology. There may be some moral indignation in his world view. His trajectory was thwarted somehow and he now resents the 'proper way' of doing things. He may have been disappointed by the law, or his career path. He wants to correct what he sees as wrongs. I would guess that he brewed these plans for many years, and as explained before, he's likely to be around forty to forty-five years old.

"And finally, the dates are significant. We know of four suspicious suicides; 2007, 2008, 2010, 2011. No connected death in 2009. Did something major happen to our man in that year, so he took a sabbatical? Or did we miss one? And as Xavier mentioned many weeks ago, can we be sure that the first 'suicide' was in 2007?"

Chris looked at Xavier. "You suggested this before. We have to do that trawl for any similar kinds of deaths in 2006 and 2009."

Xavier's eyes shone bright. "Got it."

Sabine continued. "He's unlikely to be any kind of team player, with a strong conviction in his own beliefs. If this person is operating this way, his confidence and belief in his own power is increasing proportionally. He will be very attentive to any investigation and potentially become involved, whether that is observing, or attempting to hide himself behind a witness. We must all be very aware of any external interest in this case."

The girl was rising like a hot air balloon in Beatrice's estimation. Her presentation crystallised so many vague thoughts which had bothered Beatrice since first reading Hamilton's notes. Sabine came to a close.

"My views are based on both this particular person, and any parallels he may have with a similar MO. And while his operational strategy is one thing, his calling card is another. The DNA is not a mistake. Judging by the meticulously clean scenes of crime, I believe this person quite deliberately leaves some saliva, or hair for the police. His own, or someone else's. I think he must know this DNA is not registered on any database. Why?"

Chapter 11

Zürich 2012

Kälin's suggestion that Chris might like to accompany him to a second interview with Antonella D'Arcy was casual to the point of indifference. It caught Chris on the back foot. On one hand, he definitely wanted a close-up of a platinum-coated rich bitch. On the other, he wondered why Kälin hadn't asked Beatrice. Curiosity overcame courtesy and he accepted the invitation.

The foyer of the D'Arcy Roth building, classy and intimidating, warned that herein moved serious money. Grey marble flooring surrounded the receptionists' island in the centre of the vast entrance hall, giving way to pale blue tiles the other side of the glass security doors. Chris was impressed. He was supposed to be.

Suits came and went, often throwing curious stares in their direction. Chris sat at one of the visitors' tables while Kälin paced. At first, Chris put it down to impatience; D'Arcy was still in a meeting. But then he observed the detective's behaviour more carefully. Mobile to his ear, rattling away in Swiss German, Kälin frequently pushed back his jacket and rested his hand on his hip. The gesture allowed glimpses of his holster and police weapon. Unmistakeably, Kälin was announcing to everyone he was a cop. D'Arcy would be delighted.

One of the identikit ponytailed receptionists called over. "Frau D'Arcy is between meetings and will see you for five minutes. Here are your security passes and board level is on the sixth floor."

Passing the glass doors, into the lift, through another set of security gates at board level and they were finally admitted to the inner sanctum. Visitors to senior management level enjoyed deep-blue plush carpeting, leather armchairs and a selection of soft drinks. D'Arcy kept them waiting another ten minutes before a secretary showed them to a meeting room, complete with golf and yachting magazines to browse. The woman liked to remind people of her status; that much was clear.

She entered the room, closing the door behind her and sat at the head of the table. Her eyes swept over Chris and fixed on Kälin. Her black hair pulled up into a knot complemented her displeased expression. She wore a white shirt with a sober navy skirt and looked just like the headmistress of a private girls' school.

"Frau D'Arcy, can I introduce Herr Keese, my colleague. Thank you for giving us a few moments of your time."

She didn't acknowledge Chris at all.

"You gave me very little choice. So let's get to the point. How can I help?"

"When we spoke last week, I omitted to ask you how long you'd known each of the men in these cases of suicide."

She gave a disbelieving laugh and shook her head. "What possible relevance does that have to your investigation?"

Kälin's expression was regretful. "I'm afraid I can't possibly divulge why we need to know, Frau D'Arcy. It would be unprofessional to share our approach with suspects."

She sat quite still, her voice dropping lower. "Are you telling me I'm a suspect, Herr Kälin? If so, perhaps I should contact my attorney."

"I think calling your attorney, or lawyer as they say in *British* English, is possibly premature. But of course, it's your decision."

Chris wasn't sure exactly how, but Kälin had got under her skin in a matter of seconds. D'Arcy's pinched expression and grim jaw was testimony to that.

Kälin must have seen it too. "Let's just say we have not yet eliminated you from our enquiries. So to my question."

"I'd be happy to provide you with all the dates, times and locations where I first encountered these people, but it will take me some time. And this afternoon, I'm flying to Kiev. Had you called ahead rather than just turning up, I could have prepared all the information and saved us both the inconvenience of your visit."

Kälin shook his head. "I always prefer the personal touch. Could you confirm the duration of your relationships with these men ..."

"More acquaintanceships, I think."

"... by tomorrow afternoon? It would be most helpful."

She didn't reply but stood and looked at Chris for the first time.

"So you've sacked that British woman already? I can understand why. Her interview technique was barbaric."

"Detective Inspector Stubbs, of the London Metropolitan Police, continues to lead our team most effectively. She's currently working closely with our psychological profiler and making impressive progress."

"Really." D'Arcy's voice exaggerated her lack of interest as she opened the door to leave.

"Yes, really. We're closing in on the perpetrators. It won't be long, Frau D'Arcy. The wheels of the justice may not turn quickly, but once in motion, they cannot be stopped. Rather like a train."

"A train?" She gave a dry laugh. "Yes, the image is apt. Slow, steaming and cumbersome, not to mention expensive to maintain."

Kälin sat back, a bland expression not quite disguising the sharpness in his eyes.

"I was thinking more of the modern Swiss railway system and its worldwide reputation for efficiency. As the slogan goes, you can count on us."

"I'm so pleased to hear it. So all of us who keep the economy ticking over, paying taxes to cover your salaries, can sleep safely in our beds. Please return your security passes as you leave."

She left the door open and disappeared down the corridor. As Chris turned to his colleague, he got quite a shock. He'd never seen Kälin smile before.

Chapter 12

St Germain du Bois 2010

Carp.

Ironically appropriate.

He slammed the door and trudged around to the boot. Just preparing his gear made him feel calmer. He would spend the day at his favourite swim and forget all about it. Push it all behind him. Unbelievable. She was perfectly happy to spend it before she got a crisis of conscience. It was a storm in a bloody teacup and would blow over in a couple of weeks. All they needed to do was to keep their heads down and let the lawyers deal with it. That, and avoid the press. The French retreat would have been perfect, but for her checking the news websites every day and relaying every hysterical accusation to him over dinner.

Forget about it. Unbelievable, really. The perfect loyal wife through the good times; well dressed, expensively groomed and a practised hostess. Now, at the first sign of trouble, she wants to leave. His retort this morning should shut her up. Tears, of course, and she'd threatened to go home. Well, up to her. One way or another he'd get some peace.

Rods, bait, landing net, waders, picnic, stool and blanket. He locked the car and headed toward the lake. A breeze blew through the forest, shaking free some leaves. Despite the reminder of autumn, the sun's warmth could be felt through his jacket and the sky was bright and clear. He was glad he had his sunglasses.

As he approached the swim, he focused his mind. Today, he wanted a big one. After all, he deserved it, the bullshit he'd had to take these last few weeks. Landing a thirty-kilo-plus carp would be just the thing to put a spring in his step.

He stepped onto the jetty and took the left arm of the T, setting himself up for maximum comfort. Bait, hooks and rod holder to the left. Book, flask and picnic to the right. He prepared his line, allowing his mood to settle in the peace of lake, forest and silence. No one around. Naturally. He'd paid his fees and this was his swim for the week. The heat was pleasant, and he took off his jacket, arranging it neatly under his stool.

He settled back on his chair and cast a line, taking a deep breath. Everybody has a chance. He has. The carp have. The odds might be stacked against the fish, but that is the nature of the game. You are in a pool, you take risks, you should be prepared to lose. You can't blame the winner. Some fish grow bigger than others and the British media were bewailing the one that got away.

A flash of white between the trees caught the corner of his eye. Someone making directly for him. No way was anyone sharing this location. All bought and paid for. Whoever this bloody chancer thought he was, he'd chosen the wrong bloke on the wrong day.

He waited till he heard footfalls on the wood and snapped round. "What do you want?"

The figure jumped and Brian realised his mistake. It was the artist, weighed down as usual with a heavy bag, sketch pad and collapsible stool. His attack had stopped her in her tracks. She wore a white shirt, jeans and a startled expression.

He apologised immediately. "Oh hello. Sorry, I didn't realise …"

She gave a relieved smile. "Hello again. You gave me quite a fright! Am I intruding?"

"No, no, not at all. I just thought you were another angler, trying to muscle in. I paid for this pitch, you see, for the week."

"I see. Well, I only came round to say hello before I set up my own pitch. I'm definitely not after your fish." She smiled again, teasing.

"Hey, look, it's OK. You can stay, if you like. There's plenty of room."

"No, no. Thank you, but no. When I paint, I must have silence. I really need to be alone. This is a big lake, there are many other places. I wish you a successful …" Shifting her load, she lost her grip on her pad and roll of brushes. The pad slipped onto the jetty, and the roll unfolded, spilling brushes at his feet. Two bounced into the water.

"Oh no, how clumsy of me!" She knelt, trying to collect all her equipment. He bent to help her, as a gentleman should. She looked at the brushes, floating below their feet.

"They were quite expensive. I need to get them back." She placed her bag down and started unbuckling her shoes.

"There's no need for that. Look!" He reached for his landing net and leant forward to scoop the two brushes out of the water. He could feel her eyes on his back. He was glad he'd removed his jacket, so she could see the muscle movement beneath his shirt. He drew the net closer and fished out the brushes.

Her face was flushed. "You see? You really don't need someone like me around to frighten your fish. Thanks so much for helping me. Have a good day. I hope they bite. Goodbye."

"Goodbye."

He debated asking her to meet for coffee later, but she'd already gone into the trees. Shame.

The Artist. He'd seen her around the lakes several times, and a couple of days ago, she'd joined him at an outside table of the *Café du Chat Noir*. They had a brief conversation about the weather. The Artist. From Alsace, quite bashful about her work, but she teased him lightly about his British tea-drinking. She drank an espresso. Her accent was sensual, throaty French and she was very easy on the eye. Fine features, milky-white skin and a ready smile topped by messy blonde curls falling out of a hairclip. He watched for occasional glimpses of white as she moved along the lake path, and shrugged. Women rarely enjoyed fishing, nearly always getting upset at the most exciting bit.

They didn't bite. All morning, nothing. He changed bait, from maize to halibut pellets. His mood grew murky along with the sky. The breeze was sharp without the benefit of the sun. He replaced his jacket and poured himself a cup of tea from the flask. At midday, he drank another. By one o'clock, he had no doubts. It was going to rain, he was going to catch nothing and he felt enormously tired. As the first fat drops spattered the wood, he began to pack up. Maybe he'd go to the café in the centre, drink a Ricard, and wait for the weather to clear. He would *not* go home. He couldn't face all that again. The rain fell hard and fast, so he donned his wide-brimmed hat. Heaving his gear up the path, the rain was unrelenting, flecking and splashing his glasses. He chose not to stop and wipe them, as he was almost at the car. A movement caught his eye and he saw the artist coming up the fork in the path. She was soaked, her shirt clinging to her like tissue paper. Her hair fell limply around her face, and she still carried her painting materials.

He shouted and beckoned to her. "This way! My car's just here. Let's get dry."

She hurried towards him, no coat, wet through. God knows what she would think of his ancient Volvo. But it would give him a close-up of that shirt.

"*Merde*!" She threw up her hands in a gesture of resignation as she placed the dripping sketch pad in the boot. There would be little worth saving in there, it was sodden.

He dumped his bag in the back seat and fishing gear in the boot, dragging off his jacket and retrieving the towels. She sheltered underneath the Volvo's hatch door, until he gestured for her to get into the passenger seat. She did so, placing her heavy bag in the foot well. He handed her a towel and as she patted the fabric to her face, he saw her small breasts press together. The blouse was totally transparent, and the bra she wore did not disguise her dark nipples. He shifted in his seat and after a brief rub of his hair, dropped his towel into his lap. She released her hairclip and patted herself dry, before arranging her towel around her shoulders.

"I'm sorry, already I made a mess of your car."

"Please, don't worry about it. This is what I call my 'fishing car'. Over twenty years old and purely functional. I keep it in France, because I can't bear to get rid of it. However, it does have a decent heater." He switched on the ignition, and twisted the dial. While his head was still fuzzy, his mood had improved no end.

"Oh! I can feel it already. Mmm, that's wonderful."

He swallowed, conscious of something he hadn't felt for some time. Desire, and opportunity. God, that accent was sexy.

"Now that we warm our outsides, I think we should do the same for our insides." She gave him a mischievous look from under her brows and reaching into her bag, pulled out a little hip flask.

"Irish whiskey. For emergencies like this."

She unscrewed the cap and poured a tiny shot. His eyes blinked, slowly. If he drank anything now, he'd fall asleep in seconds. He needed to keep his concentration.

"That's a clever idea. But I'm afraid I can't join you. Driving, you see. I'd better stick to tea." He reached behind him for his picnic bag, and his flask. Her eyes seemed to darken as he poured the steaming liquid. Surely she was not taking his rejection personally?

"OK, you know best." She raised the tiny cup. "Cheers! And thank you for rescuing me."

"Cheers. It was my pleasure."

She sipped and closed her eyes momentarily as she swallowed. He took a gulp of tea. Still hot, and sweet. Restorative.

"Did you land a good catch today?" she asked, her face open and pure as a daisy.

"Today was not a lucky day for me. I haven't hooked a single thing."

She gazed out at the lessening rain. "Well, you haven't hooked any fish." Facing forward, he couldn't confirm if that statement meant what he hoped. He drained his tea and agreed.

"As you say, a lucky day for the fish."

She turned to him, her pupils wide. She did not smile. The depth of her gaze embarrassed him.

"And you? Was your day more successful?" he asked, disliking the sound of his flat British voice.

"My day is going very well. Not the way I had imagined, but if one is prepared to be flexible, one can still achieve one's objectives." Her voice had dropped and even a gauche old fool like himself could see this woman had an agenda. It was hard enough to manage a flirtation after years of inactivity, without the fact that his mind seemed to be a complete muddle. She leant towards him and looked deeply into his eyes.

"Are you feeling well? You look sick."

She rested a cool, damp hand on his brow and his eyes closed. It was damned rude of him, but he didn't seem to be able to stop himself. She stretched across him and put his seatbelt on. That was kind of her. Feeling her presence over him, he forced his eyes open to apologise. She nodded.

"The best thing for you would be some more tea."

She picked up the cup and tilted the flask towards her. There was a price tag on the bottom. She placed it between her knees, and offered him the cup. Something bothered him. He swallowed obediently until it was finished, and she replaced the cup. The price tag. That was not possible. She stroked his forehead, and his lids fell. He'd had that flask for years. It was a little battered and scratched, and had been washed thousands of times. Someone turned the car off. The sound of rain on the roof had stopped. He'd rest his eyes for a few minutes and then drive back to the gîte. No arguments, just upstairs for a nap. And they could get chicken breasts out of the freezer. The Artist would have to wait. He felt a breeze. Doors slammed and he wondered where the fish were. Maybe they'd gone home. They said they might, if he carried on ignoring their feelings. That was not his flask. So why was she in his bag? The car started up again. Lovely breasts. He had to think, it was important. What was her name? God, he hoped she could drive, because he was in no fit state … warm, comfortable and so incredibly tired. Windows down, windows up. Who was doing that? Very nice. Chicken windows for dinner. Truth was, he was sick and tired of fish.

Chapter 13

Zürich 2012

The locker room in the Zürich Main Station was situated on the mezzanine level, which was huge, busy and perfect for the purpose. A figure left the escalator, took a key from a pocket and inserted it into locker 4149. The Jiffy bag was there, as promised, containing a phone. Seven minutes passed before it rang. The figure began walking, alert for eavesdroppers.

"Hello?"

The voice at the other end dispensed with pleasantries. *"Do you need anything else from me?"*

"No, everything's covered. All I need to decide is when. Circumstances should be perfect in the next two to three weeks."

"Complete this one as soon as possible. Because I have something else I want you to do."

The figure stopped. "Just a minute. You chose this one. And I want to hit the drugs trade next time. I already have a shortlist."

The voice did not reply.

"Not only that, but I don't want to do another short notice thing again. It's dangerous to be under-prepared. For all of us."

"You won't be under-prepared. I've already got plenty of background. I'll do the research now and you take care of the implementation. You don't have to travel far, either. It's right

here."

"In Switzerland?"

"*In Zürich.*"

The figure began pacing along the line of lockers. "I'm not sure. We've been far too close to home recently. The risks are beginning to ..."

"*Yes. Which brings me to our second point. Once these two are complete, we'll stop.*"

"Stop? What do you mean? For how long?"

"*For good. You can go back to Mozambique or whichever desperate region needs you most, and I will find myself another hobby.*"

"No. We can't stop now. There's so much left to do. What about my list?"

"*There are other ways of administering punishment to those on your list. Look, it couldn't last forever and the risks now outweigh the satisfaction. We've reached the end of the line. I want to deal with these last two cases, that's all.*"

The pause lasted for over a minute as the figure stared, unseeing, at the people borne upwards by the escalators.

"Who is the second one? Someone connected to the airline management?"

"*No, not the airline. A different branch of corrupt industry. The police. This is a detective. They're investigating some unusual suicides and think they've found a link.*"

"The police? But surely if they already think there might be a connection, acting against them would be almost ..."

"*... suicidal?*" The voice laughed, apparently amused. "*It would be if I didn't have our alibis all prepared. Plus, if you do this right, it will be impossible to prove it wasn't self-inflicted.*"

"How does a police detective fit with what we're trying to do? Or is this just a case of self-preservation?"

"*The role of the police is to fight crime and punish criminals. Not judge and condemn those who are doing good works while corruption and greed remain above the law. It will be our final statement.*"

"But ..."

"*But what?*"

"Nothing. Which way round do you want it done?"

"The lawyer goes first. Then immediately afterwards, the police detective ends it all, unable to bear the public humiliation and failure. It's practically poetic. I've already started the ball rolling."

The figure leant over the barrier and gazed down on the shoppers below. "How do you want it done?"

"I haven't made up my mind yet. Let me think about that. It must definitely be spectacular. It's our swansong, after all. But I've found enough detail for you need to start work and left it in the usual place. The other material you need will be sent to your home address, under the guise of a perfume sample. Keep your eyes open for a silver envelope advertising Homme Fatale."

"Right. I'll get started."

"Good luck. And ... this really must be the last time."

The figure didn't respond.

"I'm serious."

"I know."

Ending the call, the figure placed the phone in the Jiffy bag and went in search of a post-box to send it back.

Chapter 14

Zürich 2012

Reception at Zeughausstrasse Police Station was ridiculously busy for ten to eight in the morning. Beatrice stood in the open doorway, her route blocked by a shifting crowd of people carrying microphones and cameras.

A young man spotted her and addressed her in English.

"Are you Detective Stubbs, from London, working on the serial killer case?"

Attention switched to her and a sudden panic surged as the questions began.

"Sorry, no comment."

"*Entschuldigen Sie, bitte*! Excuse me! Frau Stubbs, this way." Xavier cleared a path through the group of journalists. She put her head down and bulldozed her way forward, a little surprised at the lack of resistance as she squeezed past. They continued to ask questions, she continued to say, 'No comment', but they didn't thrust their equipment in her face or block her path, even stepping back to give her room. It wouldn't happen like that in London.

She reached Xavier, who appeared redder than normal, but rapidly swiped them both through the security doors.

"How do they know?" she asked.

"Front page of the *Neue Zürcher Zeitung*. The phones are

ringing all the time and Kälin's not happy."

"For once, I feel the same way."

Everyone in the workroom seemed to be talking at once. Xavier immediately joined in. Beatrice stashed her bag in her office, collected a cup of water and stood at the briefing table, listening. She hoped her actions would convey the message she wasn't harassed. It also gave her chance to get her breath back. The room gradually quietened and Kälin spoke.

"We have a leak, Frau Stubbs."

The noise began again and Beatrice waited for some order before offering her opinion.

"Do we? Is that the only way the information could get out there? I haven't read the article, but I'd like to be sure before jumping to conclusions."

Sabine managed to make her voice heard over the wealth of opinions. "I've read it, Beatrice. And I believe Herr Kälin is right. The amount of detail in the report – the names of the men, the DNA connection, the fact that you're leading the investigation, the names of most of the team, except Conceição and me, although it mentions psychological profiling – this seems like an inside job. And to be honest, the article makes us look like a bunch of idiots."

Beatrice considered. Why would any member of her team leak confidential information? The potential damage could be fatal, stalling the investigation in its tracks, not to mention warning their target. Why would anyone in this room scupper the case? Her eyes rested on Kälin, who took it as his cue to speak.

"The most likely explanation is that this is not deliberate. Someone here has been talking to the wrong person. Think back over the past two weeks. Who have you talked to about this case? Did you share details with anyone? Journalists are experts at befriending people they think have a story. Think carefully."

Puzzled faces considered, eyes roamed the room and silence

settled like dust. But the only result was a series of shaking heads. Beatrice examined her own conduct. She never shared details with anyone she didn't wholly trust and generally kept her profession quiet. Of course, she always discussed latest developments with Matthew, but he was as likely to blab to the Swiss press as he was to abseil through the window.

Kälin lifted his brows. "Frau Stubbs, I suggest you and I prepare a press statement for later this morning. The rest of you, I recommend you say nothing to anyone, not even to your families. Then, perhaps, we can work this investigation in peace."

"Herr Kälin?" Chris spoke. "It could have been you."

Kälin's head joined all the others swivelling to stare at Chris.

"I don't mean you spilled to some bloke in the pub. But you did give a lot of information to Antonella D'Arcy, about Beatrice leading the team, about using a profiler and she already knew the names of the victims from your first interview."

No one spoke.

Kälin looked out of the window, his frown dark. "That is possible. D'Arcy had enough information to trigger a news story and the journalists could dig up the rest. It would work in her interests to sabotage our investigation and to direct attention away from D'Arcy Roth, no matter whether she is involved or not. And she would enjoy making us look stupid. It's possible the fault was mine, sharing too much with a suspect. I apologise, everyone. I should also remember to keep my mouth shut."

In the shocked speechlessness that followed, Beatrice decided something was definitely up. Kälin never accepted criticism, never admitted a mistake and certainly never apologised. He was right. If this investigation appeared clumsy and ineffective, it would certainly suit Antonella D'Arcy. But she wasn't the only one.

The press briefing was short and bland, as they accepted no questions. Beatrice found it relatively painless. Unlike London, not only were the press polite, but senior police officers weren't breathing down her neck. She decided to get a sandwich and go for a walk over lunch, to allow herself some thinking time. The leak was one issue, but her concerns regarding Kälin quite another. Or was it? Both boiled down to the same thing – could she trust her team? Up until now, she'd had no doubts. Surely even Kälin wouldn't cut off his nose to spite this case? On her return to the office, her mind was no clearer and her thoughts muddled. The news she received from the receptionist made things worse.

"Frau Stubbs? You have some visitors. Herr Fisher from Lyon and Herr Hamilton from London wait in your office."

Hell's bells. Not only an Interpol executive, but Scotland Yard yanking her choke chain. Just when the day was going so well.

Rounding the corner to her office, she came face to face with Hamilton's familiar craggy features. He jerked his head, unsmiling.

"Stubbs."

She jerked hers back. "Sir." She looked past him to Fisher.

"Beatrice! Terrific to see you again. Hope we haven't put you out too much, dropping in like this? Only we thought we'd pop by and get up to speed. See if you needed anything."

Fisher shook her hand with enthusiasm before gesturing to a chair. Interesting. Her office, her desk, her chair, and yet he invited her to sit. "Have you had lunch yet? We could take you out and treat you to something stodgy with cheese."

Absolutely charming man; solicitous, informative and helpful. She could not fault Fisher's behaviour. Therefore she really ought to consider why she found him so utterly odious. He laughed at his own brand of xenophobic humour and Beatrice stretched her lips to be polite. His mud-brown hair was slicked back with gel, so that each individual tooth of the comb had left its mark. Something about him rubbed her up the wrong way; the high forehead, sharp nose and peculiarly British mouth, while his eyes had all the colour and animation of a dishcloth. It looked as if he was having a similar effect on Hamilton.

"Good afternoon, gentlemen. I had no idea we were due a visit from Head Office. Perhaps I missed the email. Forgive me if I am a little unprepared. I've already eaten, thank you, but I can arrange some tea."

"Have you? Gosh, that's early. Very well, tea must suffice. And it's not exactly a visit from HQ, which is why we didn't email. It's just that two weeks into the project, we thought it might be time to see if we can offer any further support. Particularly now the media have got wind of this."

"How kind. To be truthful, I cannot think of anything further Interpol could offer, unless it were another pair of hands. We're at the dull, workaday stage, just making painstaking enquiries."

"Oh, I think any more hands on deck would raise a few questions in Lyon. There are already six full-time experts provided, not to mention a range of professionals at your disposal. It's rather an expensive exercise, Beatrice. And given the calibre of personnel you have, we're wondering when you might be likely to progress beyond enquiries."

"I'd be happy to update you, Mr Fisher. But I'd quite like a cup of tea while I do so." She picked up the phone, trying not to grind her teeth. "Frau Stettler? This is Frau Stubbs. Would you mind bringing three black teas? And milk and sugar? Thank you." Replacing the receiver, she turned to the immaculately dressed irritant and his brooding counterpart.

"I have, in point of fact, emailed Lyon on a regular basis, just so that you know what we're doing."

"Yes. We all read your updates, Beatrice. However, there is a growing concern in respect of progress. If I can summarise, you have revisited some of the scenes, checked the DNA and produced what we call a Picture of a Serial Killer." His laughter reminded Beatrice of someone clearing their nose.

Portrait, not picture, you Philistine. She dragged the corners of her mouth upwards.

A knock at the door heralded tea and Frau Stettler placed the tray on the desk with a polite, “Good afternoon, together”.

Fisher beamed. “Thank you so much. Oh, and biscuits as well? We don’t get this kind of service in Lyon. Thank you very much indeed and have a good day.”

Nice to the point of patronising to staff, observed Beatrice. Well-mannered, popular, and thoroughly unbearable.

“Let me recap,” Beatrice began, as she distributed tea. “My brief, as I understand it, is to ascertain whether we have a case to investigate. I and my team have done exactly that. We have double-checked the DNA samples for accurate gathering. We have revisited the scenes of each ‘incident’, to see if there is any information to be gleaned. We have cross-checked for connections between the deceased and Sabine Tikkenen has put forward an astute profile of the man who may be responsible. There is a case. And we are taking the first steps in trying to resolve it.”

“Mmm, yes. Good work. The concern, Beatrice, is not how hard you are working. I’m sure you’re all beavering away. It is just we had hoped to see some concrete results by now. Just thought we’d check if we’ve got the balance right in terms of personnel.”

Beatrice decoded and bristled. “By which you mean you want to change some members of my team?” She began to feel some sympathy for Kälin.

“Oh, good gracious! I couldn’t possibly say, not at this phase of the proceedings. The point is merely that we’d like to be certain that the mix is working. Are you with me?”

“Personnel modifications at this stage would be counter-productive. The case covers four different countries, and stretches back five years. We have taken some time to get up to speed, but now we’re working on several leads simultaneously. I am confident of making a breakthrough in the next month.”

Fisher nodded, his angled head and plastic expression all designed to convey understanding. Hamilton glared out of the window as if displeased with the scenery.

“No doubt that it’s complex, Beatrice. Bigger than we initially thought, in fact. That's why we want to check that we have tasked the appropriate people. One month. That *is* a concern. You really think it could take another month to bring this to heel?"

"I have no idea what that expression is supposed to mean. But to clarify, I said I expected to be able to show significant progress within the next four weeks."

"The powers-that-be would like to see something a touch earlier. Let's say that in a fortnight's time, we re-evaluate this project in the light of advancements made between now and then. How does that sound?"

Like management bullshit.

"In that case, Mr Fisher, I will deliver a full report to the General Secretariat by next Friday, with a copy to London. I am sure you appreciate investigating such a case does involve making diligent enquiries that would apply to any normal police procedure. We can only start running with the ball when we are convinced we have possession."

He gave his laugh once more.

"Rugby analogies, Beatrice? Had you down for more of a cricket widow. No, no one is accusing you of running with the ball. Particularly not at the pace you are progressing. You feel able to deliver a viability report by the end of next week? That will go down very well in Lyon. We shall look forward to reading it. Now, I really should meet the team, I think. Would you be so kind as to make the introductions? Thanks for the tea, it was jolly good, I have to say. And perhaps later this afternoon we might have a little chat about how the press got hold of such sensitive information. Rather awkward, that. Shall we?"

Hamilton cleared his throat. "While you explore, Fisher, I'll stay here. Want a word with Stubbs when she gets back."

Beatrice bit back a groan and opened her palm towards the doorway.

Fisher leapt to his feet, bestowing a full beam on her as he led the way out of the office. His odd behaviour reminded her of that magician fellow, David Whatzisname, who kept locking himself in peculiar places. She watched him depart, slick and sickly as molasses, discomfited by the fact that this bug-eyed buffoon probably knew more about her than most of her friends.

The main room was empty, but for one gingery head bent over a keyboard. Beatrice made the introductions.

"Xavier? Can I introduce our visitor from Interpol? Herr Racine, Mr Fisher."

Xavier scrambled to his feet as Fisher held out his hand.

"Hello Herr Racine. Heard lots of good things about you. Just a friendly visit to see if we can help at all. Are you all alone today?"

"Pleasure to meet you, Mr Fisher." He pumped Fisher's hand with enthusiasm. "At the moment, yes. Sabine is at the University Hospital and Chris and Conceição are exploring Langstrasse. Herr Kälin is in his own office."

"Ah, good. I hoped to meet Herr Kälin at some stage. Langstrasse? Now would I be mistaken in thinking that's Zürich's red-light district?" asked Fisher, with disingenuity.

Xavier nodded and pointed to the pin board. "Yes, it is. It's also the 'alternative' quarter, where we might contact anti-capitalists, political activists and so on. Sabine's profile shows that our killer could have a left-wing agitation agenda. So Beatrice sent them to investigate."

"Really?" Fisher gave a fake smile and slow nod, as if Xavier were a small child enthusing about Lego. "I have to say, it's so cosy the way you call your senior officer by her Christian name."

Beatrice took over. "Each team finds an appropriate way of operating, as you know. And Xavier's point is that we're trying to find out as much as we can about militant left-wing ..."

"Aaa-chi!" Xavier released an explosive sneeze, turning his head away and hitting his forehead against the felt board as he did so.

"Bless you!" offered Beatrice, finishing her explanation while leading Fisher away.

As the workroom door closed behind them, Fisher pulled down the corners of his mouth in sympathy.

"Is he the best Swiss police could do? Looks like a work experience boy."

A flash of petty temper provoked Beatrice but she kept her mouth shut, instead indicating the stairwell.

"So Mr Fisher, as you can see, most of the team are out on fieldwork. But you mentioned wanting to meet Herr Kälin. You'll find his office on the first floor, second door on the right. You might want to ask him for his view on the press leak. I must get back, my superior awaits. Lovely seeing you."

She strode back to her cubicle with an odd mixture of infuriation and curiosity. *Oh, to be a fly on the wall in that room.*

Hamilton stood at the window, arms folded, evidently still dissatisfied with the view.

"More tea, sir?"

"Stubbs, a frank answer, if you will. Exactly how much progress have you made?"

Beatrice sat in the 'visitor's chair'. Once again, Hamilton used his status to minimise hers.

"In my view, a great deal. I have faith in this team; we work well together. Now we're sifting evidence, tooth-combing, narrowing the net and building a solid case to prove this was a systematic series of pre-meditated murders."

Hamilton flared his nostrils and raised his eyes to the ceiling, affording Beatrice an unimpeded perspective up his nose.

"So there is a bloody case, after all?"

Beatrice grew irritable. "Yes sir, there is. You would have preferred us to chase our tails?"

With a glare at her and at the door, Hamilton picked up his briefcase.

"Come along, Stubbs. Show me the city and let's talk some sense."

Instinct guided Beatrice away from the shopping areas in the direction of Stockerstrasse; a street of merchant banks, insurance companies, art galleries and the Swiss Stock Exchange. The calm tone and sober environment worked its charm on Hamilton, his posture relaxing to merely stiff.

Taking a left towards the river tributary, they crossed the little pedestrian bridge of Bärenbrüggli. Office workers sat on benches beside the water, eating sandwiches, feeding swans and chatting in Swiss German. Hamilton stopped, peering over at the water rushing silently beneath.

"Fact is, Stubbs, they don't think you're up to it. The only personnel change they want to make is you. Seems you're not Interpol material."

A surge of heat inflamed her entire head, burning the tips of her ears and scalding her scalp. Grateful that Hamilton's focus remained on water birds, she thought his comment through.

"Can I ask why now, sir? Actually, I think I can answer that for myself. When it was a political exercise to tick paper boxes for European collaboration, any old fool would do. Now it appears a series of politically motivated murders exist, they want someone ... well, someone else."

The ducks gave up on them and bobbed back to the banks, where crumbs were more plentiful.

"Look here, Stubbs. Interpol asked for an experienced detective to lead an international investigation, which is precisely what I provided. Had I known this might degenerate into a facile game of draughts with greasy pole-climbers such as Fisher, I may just have kept out of the whole festering shebang. I've loaned them one of the best in my entire force and if they don't appreciate that, they can go service themselves."

Warmth crept over Beatrice again in recognition of Hamilton's bluff loyalty.

"Why drag you here in person, sir? To take me home on a lead? To break the news to me yourself?"

He exhaled sharply. "Buggered if I know. As yet, no news to break. You've got another two weeks, Stubbs. So for all our sakes, pull your bloody finger out."

At the end of a thoroughly disheartening day, Beatrice headed back to her apartment. As always, she made a detour to Talacker and *Big Ben*, the English tea shop. In addition to teas, cakes and groceries, they sold a range of British newspapers and magazines. It had become Beatrice's daily treat to stop in, drink a pot of Earl Grey and read *The Times*. And it seemed churlish not to have a hot buttered crumpet, or a scone with jam and cream at the same time. The sustenance was welcome, but her real attraction to the place was provided by Ken.

"Wotcha, Beatrice! Ooh, dear, don't like the look of your boat. Bad day? Let's get you a cuppa."

Ken. Born in Yugoslavia and carted off to London at the age of five, he spent his formative years in the East End. The family relocated again, leaving Britain when Ken was just shy of eighteen and he had lived the intervening forty plus years in Switzerland. His career: army officer, fitness instructor, private investigator and security guard proved him to be a fully paid-up member of Swiss society. But he had made a clear choice of identity. His heart remained in 1960s' London, a place that no longer existed. His cherished memories were of red Routemasters, mini-skirts and Minis, bobbies in Dixon of Dock Green helmets, and a feeling of being in the right place at the right time. He'd never been back. Beatrice hoped for his own sake that he never would. She sat at a rear table, grateful for the lack of clientele.

"One pot of Earl Grey, pot warmed, of course. Noemi's made a Victoria Sponge, if you're peckish, or there's some McVitie's Jamaica Ginger Cake, very moist."

"I won't today, thanks Ken. But I will take a copy of *The Times*."

"Up to you." He reached for the paper and looked at her. "Bad day at the office, dear?"

"Not good," she admitted.

"Right, I'll leave you in peace, but when you're ready, I'm having awful bother with 17 down."

She smiled, their routine all the more precious for the illusion of familiarity it provoked. Ken collected some cups and stopped to chat to the other customers, all of whom sat outside, enjoying the early spring sunshine. His Cockney tones drifted back to her as she tried to focus on the paper. *Vote of no confidence likely for new Treasury Minister.* She poured the tea and pushed away the vision of Jamaica Ginger Cake, very moist. The viability report. If they got no further in the next fortnight, in all likelihood, she'd be sent home. They'd bring in someone younger, more dynamic to lead the investigation and she would have failed in her first worthwhile job in almost two years.

What a stupid, unprofessional train of thought. This situation was not about her. She was leading this investigation the best way she knew how. It was far from spectacular, but it was thorough. A method that had always worked for her before now. She would spend the weekend going over the whole case again, just to be sure she had overlooked nothing. And anyway, why would she not want to be sent home? Back to Shoreditch, to Scotland Yard, to Matthew. She'd recently considered running away for a weekend. And now?

If she were honest, she had to make a good job of this. She wouldn't get another chance. Hamilton had taken a gamble on her, and if she failed, she would be letting him down. This circular misery wouldn't help; she couldn't allow herself one of the troughs. Not now.

A youngish blonde with Jackie O sunglasses settled herself two tables away, ordered tea and opened a copy of Tatler. Her clothes, her hair or maybe her teeth led Beatrice to assume she was American. It was a local species she recognised, flitting in and out of designer shops, occupying café tables, promenading up and down Bahnhofstrasse. How did they always manage to look so groomed? It would take her all day to present such a polished facade. She watched idly as Ken pottered behind the counter, humming something which sounded ominously like *Jerusalem*.

This situation was very much about her. Was she seriously up to this? Confidence was key, but if it was not backed up by ability, she was deceiving her highly professional team, and therefore a hindrance to their success. Unless one of them was deliberately hindering this investigation. The newspaper story could have been an attempt to destabilise her.

"Any joy?" Ken called over, as he laid the tables for dinner.

"Haven't looked yet, sorry. I was miles away." She turned the pages until she found the crossword. "Which one was it again?"

"17 down. *A sign post victory proves me right*. What you reckon?"

Beatrice read the clue but her mind drifted.

"Have you got an event tonight, Ken?"

"S'right. Skool Dinners. Bunch of geezers from one of the banks come down, eat sausage and mash with boiled cabbage, spotted dick for afters, drink a good hundredweight of Chablis and chuck bread rolls about. Messy, but we make a fortune."

"I feel for your poor waiting staff."

"You want to see 'em. We use the girls what work the *Oktoberfest*. Mess with one of them, they'll break your arm. I keep out of it, get down the Oscar Wilde for a pint till it's all over. You off already?"

"No rest for the wicked. How much do I owe you?"

"Call it fifteen. No luck with 17 down, then?"

She counted three coins. "'Fraid not. My brain is elsewhere today."

The American's blonde head rose from the magazine. "Vindication?"

Beatrice and Ken turned to her.

"A *sign post victory proves me right*. Vindication. Does it fit?"

Beatrice checked. "It does. Perfectly. Thank you."

The woman smiled and returned her attention to glossy

photographs.

Ken picked up the paper, filled in the letters in and gave a satisfied sigh. "God bless you both, ladies."

Beatrice said her goodbyes and made her way back to her apartment.

Two weeks to make some kind of breakthrough. You can't even grow cress that fast.

Chapter 15

St Germain du Bois 2012

Hearing Conceição speak French was such a turn-on. Her throaty pitch seemed designed for the musical cadences of the language and several sounds required her to purse her lips. Chris couldn't concentrate. The manager of the carp lakes seemed equally hypnotised and his desperation was obvious as he scrabbled to think of something helpful to say. But the facts were that Edwards paid his fees, bought some bait, and departed. The manager heard no more until the police arrived to inform him that a body had been found at Etang Gallet. With some eagerness, he volunteered to show them the spot. Conceição expressed their thanks and politely but firmly refused the man's offer.

As they returned to the car, Chris looked at her sideways. "Did I understand that right? You told him we'd seen the site."

She put the car into gear and drove off, with a small wave at the manager. "Yes. I didn't want him there while we look around. It will interfere with my thinking."

"You could have told him that."

"Sometimes a little white lie spares someone's feelings. Do you want to eat first, or shall we go to the lake now?"

"Let's do the lake. And hope we don't bump into the manager."

Parking on the road, they followed the photocopied map, walking up the track to where the police had discovered the Volvo.

Chris stopped. "Here. Good location. Can't be seen from the road or the lake and few people would pass this way."

"And even if you did pass, you would assume the person was sleeping. He could have been here a lot longer if his wife had not raised the alarm."

"The killer must have drugged him before fixing up the exhaust. How did he do that?"

Conceição flicked over a page. "The report says there was a full flask of tea in Edwards's bag. It hadn't been touched. How do you get a total stranger to ingest debilitating drugs?"

Chris inclined his head. "Assuming the guy was a total stranger to Edwards. As I said, I think this individual was known to the dead men."

They walked down to the swim and stared out at the lake. Olive-coloured water reflected the tree tops opposite and steady ripples oscillated across the surface. While Chris had no interest in fishing, he could see the appeal of sitting here, at peace.

Conceição thought aloud. "He came here to spend the day fishing. It was raining. Did he even get out of the car? He was still wearing his seatbelt."

"Perhaps he stopped for lunch and someone slipped him something then. Talking of lunch, we're not going to find much here. Want to try that restaurant on the square?"

St Germain du Bois was quiet, giving Chris the strange feeling that everyone was somewhere else. They parked on the market square and entered the restaurant. The sun was warm enough for them to sit on the terrace, and enjoy the view of the tree-lined main street. After ordering, Conceição asked to speak to the owner. The square remained empty, dominated by the shadow of the church, until a man walked past with a small dog, which stopped every ten paces to urinate against a tree. Its owner seemed glad of the frequent stops.

"Geraldine Lefèvre. You wanted a word?"

The woman's English was perfect and unaccented. She wore a white kitchen coat over jeans. Her silvery blonde hair was held back in a clip, and her expression suggested curiosity, revealing their interruption was a break from routine. The upside was they could speak to her in English, giving Chris a better chance of understanding. The downside? He wouldn't see Conceição do her pout *à la française*. He withdrew his ID.

"Yes please, Ms Lefèvre. Would you like a seat? We won't take long. My name is Chris Keese of Europol, and this is my colleague, Conceição Pereira da Silva of Interpol. We're just doing a routine follow-up of the death of Brian Edwards, who was found near here in 2010. Do you recall the event?"

"I certainly do. I knew Brian and Sheila vaguely, through the expat network. They'd been coming here for over a decade. To St Germain, I mean. And they generally ate here at least once or twice each holiday. When he did away with himself, I was shocked. Firstly, I had no idea he was the boss of that water-poisoning company. Secondly, how could he go and leave his wife and kids like that? A disgusting way to behave."

"During that particular holiday, did you see them at all?" asked Conceição.

"No. They kept their heads down. A wise decision after all the fuss in the papers. As far as I know, they avoided all their usual haunts. Natalie, who runs the hotel here, saw them in the pizzeria in Bletterans. Over there, no one would know who they were, you see. And I once I saw him at the café on the Louhans road. But he wasn't with his wife." She dropped her chin and gave them a meaningful look.

Chris picked up his cue. "Did you recognise the person he was with?"

"No. A tourist, I think. Young, blonde, pretty. I must say, Brian Edwards's true colours surprised us all. He was not the man he seemed."

"Thank you, Ms Lefèvre. You've been most helpful. Sorry to have dragged you away from work," Chris smiled.

"Oh, I was glad of the break. End of the session now, so all that's left is the washing-up. What did you order?"

"*Poulet de Bresse.* The regional speciality."

"Not just the region's, it's mine too. Hope you enjoy it. Good luck with your follow-up. All the best."

Despite finding nothing of interest in Burgundy, Chris had enjoyed his day. Even the journey provided some attractive scenery. He stretched out his legs and looked at his companion. Conceição drove along the A36 at exactly three kilometres over the speed limit. Her gaze focused on the road, while he admired her profile, knowing she was aware of it.

"What?" she demanded, eventually.

"Just wondering what you're doing tonight."

"You are unlikely to find out by studying my right ear. I arranged to have a drink with Sabine if we get back early enough."

"What's early enough? We won't be back in Zürich till about eight. Why don't you have girls' night tomorrow, then you and I can stop for dinner somewhere en route?"

She remained silent.

"It would be the sensible thing to do. You've been driving for two hours," he added.

"Somewhere en route? Where?"

"I'm sure we can find a charming little bistro somewhere near the border. What do you think?"

"Yeah, OK. I could do with a break. Although I'm not that hungry," she added.

He grinned and picked up his phone. "I'll find a nice romantic little salad bar, then."

"It doesn't need to be romantic. This is not a date." She took her eyes from the road to give him a stern look.

"Course not," he agreed, still grinning.

Not perfect. A shabby roadside Imbiss, for a cervelat and a beer. But he made her laugh, offered to drive, encouraged her to have another drink and slipped in some compliments. Everything was going according to plan as they returned to the car, discussing theories on contract killers and which countries made the best sausages.

He took the wheel and she chose the music. A little more light flirtation and laughter as they approached the city and Chris's confidence grew. He needed to make a plan. He wouldn't ask her to come back to his place, not tonight. But he would plant a seed. Make it look as if he was wrestling with himself, forcing himself to leave her alone. That always rang two bells with women. His passion for her and his noble nature. Just a polite, but longing kiss before saying goodnight. Pretty much guaranteed she'd be in his bed by the weekend.

So she surprised him outside her apartment, by inviting him in. He accepted, but went over his plans again while she fetched beers from the kitchen. OK, he definitely had to refuse sex. Otherwise the noble nature bit goes to shit. The difficulty being, how far to go? He'd play the 'we can't, but I want to, no, it's so unprofessional, you drive me crazy, I'd better leave,' card, with a long, lingering, more-where-that-came-from kiss at the door.

She came back, handed him a beer and flopped into the armchair opposite. Not beside him on the sofa. Was she making a point?

"So what's your story, Chris? Got a girl pining for you beside a canal somewhere? *Prost*!"

He laughed and raised the bottle. "*Prost*! No, no one's pining for me. I'm getting to the stage where I'd like a regular relationship, but in this job? You know what it's like."

Conceição acknowledged the problem with a tilt of her head. "Yeah. Difficult. But not impossible. I find it easier to date people in the same line of work. Fewer explanations."

That was a come-on. All evening, little candles lit up as they chatted, laughed and found common ground. But this was a colossal flare, lighting up the room.

Tread carefully and you could be under the sheets in less than five minutes. Noble nature has a time and a place.

He sipped some beer. "Sure. Perfect solution. If you can find someone in your line of work who makes you laugh, who's intelligent, who's beautiful, who makes you ..."

The shrill blast of the telephone made Chris clench his fist as Conceição reached across for the handset.

"Hello?" Her forehead wrinkled in concern. "Sabine, are you OK? What's wrong?"

Chris faked an intensely concerned expression. Intensely concerned wasn't too far from pretty pissed-off so it was no effort.

"Of course you can. Chris is here, but he's just leaving. Come over. You shouldn't be alone if you're feeling upset. No, Sabine, it's fine. We were just having a beer! Sabine, listen ..."

She shook her head at Chris and shrugged an apology.

He picked up his laptop case. "Don't worry. I'll go. See you tomorrow."

She nodded, distracted, but waggled her fingers to say good bye. He blew a silent kiss as he left the room. She smiled.

OK. That would have to do.

As he started the car, he glanced back at the window. He could see her silhouette. He waved but she was shaking her head.

Chapter 16

Zürich 2012

The worst thing about getting up at 06.30 and leaving the apartment at 07.00 was missing the *Today Programme* with John Humphrys. That one-hour time difference could really upset a person's routine. Beatrice ate her porridge sprinkled with raspberries and scowled at the BBC website. She could listen to the recorded version later, of course, but cold news was as appetising as cold porridge. She snorted and closed down the machine. Her temper had not improved since her shower. Another restless night, caused by the prospect of a fractious day ahead.

Interpol's blunt, unflattering assessment of their progress two days ago had put the whole team out of sorts. Yesterday, Sabine sulked. Xavier worked at double speed and consequently achieved about half his usual output. And Kälin disappeared completely. Not in his office, not answering his mobile, just gone. Chris and Conceição escaped the atmosphere, driving to Burgundy to visit the scene of Edwards' death. Two weeks, and already the General Secretariat were stamping their feet. Journalists popped up everywhere they went, demanding results on behalf of the public. On top of everything, the Swiss government suddenly chose to question the validity of having a specialised Federal Task Force to deal with international crime.

Beatrice had every expectation of being home by the end of May. It seemed the whole exercise had been a waste of time and resources.

She packed her computer, brushed her teeth and set off for the office in a foul mood.

The walk to Zeughausstrasse cheered her somewhat. Joggers along the river greeted her with a friendly *Grüezi*, she stopped to pat a St Bernard, and the daffodils and irises on the verges raised their heads to the sun. As she trudged up the stairs of the police building, Beatrice realised she was not gasping for breath for a change. Usually, she had to take a moment to regain her wind before entering the investigation room. A pleasant notion crossed her mind. Could she be getting fitter? Her smile dissolved as she heard angry voices behind the door. She grabbed the handle with a sinking feeling.

The guilty silence restored Beatrice's foul mood. Xavier, Conceição, Sabine and Chris stood in a confrontational circle. She dumped her bag on the nearest desk and resisted the temptation to fold her arms.

Sabine gestured to Chris and Conceição. "It seems that these two have other priorities than investigating this case. They spend the day in France and come back with nothing apart from a big smile. Now he thinks there's nothing to investigate! Am I wasting my time here?"

Chris gave an exasperated sigh. "Beatrice, I didn't say there was nothing to investigate. What I said was …"

"That my theory …"

"That your theory is not the only one! If you will stop shrieking for one minute, we can clear this up."

Sabine's face flushed raspberry-red. "I am not shrieking. I am trying to make myself heard. Why am I the only one who can see what's going on here? Xavier has spent days researching similar kinds of crime. I have explored hospital and pharmacy records for links. And you two, you two proceed with your theory that this is a professional hit man that we'll never catch. Ask yourself why this hit man leaves his DNA behind, if he's so professional. But you're clearly far too busy with each other to think this through."

Beatrice intervened. "Sabine, that is enough. Can you all please take a seat, and we can discuss this civilly. Now, I am aware that the news we received from Lyon and London was not good. But as professionals, that should not distract us from the job we are trying to do. I think it might be a good time to reassess our progress, or lack of, and consider altering our approach."

Xavier seemed uncomfortable, looking towards the door. "Beatrice, if we are thinking of changing our strategy, should we wait for Herr Kälin?"

"No Xavier, I don't see that as necessary. Herr Kälin, as he often reminds us, is a consultant to the team, not a part of it. I decide how we operate. Chris. You wanted to make a point."

"Yes, I did. The trip to France was pretty fruitless. It was two years ago, and most people have forgotten about it. The police records we already have, the locals recall seeing Edwards fishing, and that's about it. I'm not sure these visits to the scene of the crime are getting us anywhere. Especially as this character operates so efficiently. We discussed the possibility of this being a professional job, but that's the one theory we haven't followed up. We are all chasing this 'profile' Sabine created, but to tell the truth, I'm not sure that it's leading anywhere."

Beatrice held up her hand to forestall Sabine's outrage.

"Thank you for being honest. How would you like us to progress?"

"Do you mind if I jump in, Chris?" Conceição waited for his nod. "Beatrice, Chris and I have talked about this a lot." She ignored the snort from Sabine. "We think we should provide the General Secretariat with a report that states we believe different people or organisations employed a professional to get rid of these men. And then Interpol or Europol can make use of their databases to check suspected hired killers. It really does seem that we are chasing down cold leads and wasting a lot of time."

Beatrice bristled at the criticism, but nodded her understanding. Her mind raced through the conflict mediation training she had received and she played for time.

"I see. Well, that's one perspective. I think Sabine sees things differently."

The blonde head gave a sharp nod. "I see things very differently. This profile is not some fantasy I made up. It is based on serious research and tested methodology. Of course, we can write a report based on vague assumptions and go home. But I for one do not consider that to be a professional job. We have identified a series of markers which can help us locate this person. But as Beatrice said at the start, it involves a lot of boring, dull paperwork. However, it seems that only part of the team take responsibility for that. Others are enjoying themselves on their European Tour."

"Sabine." Beatrice had to act. "I take your point, but I must ask you not to make this personal. If you feel duties have been unfairly allocated, we can look at the situation. But what people choose to do in their private time is no concern of ours. Xavier, I'd like to hear from you."

Xavier hesitated and darted a glance at Chris. "In my opinion, to write a report saying we think it was probably a professional and leave it there would not be satisfactory. The traces of DNA, and nothing else, at each scene makes me think it could be deliberate, to confuse us. It is possible to fabricate DNA, and make us hunt someone who is not existing. Beatrice, this is the first international project I'm working on. I learn a lot. But I would be interested to stretch myself further. For me, visiting a scene of crime could be an education."

"Am I allowed an opinion?" Kälin spoke from the doorway, making everyone jump.

"Herr Kälin. Good morning. Please, come in. We'd be most interested to hear what you have to say. I'm not sure how much you heard while hiding outside. Would you like us to recap?"

Beatrice wrestled with her temper.

"Two things before I begin. The morning briefing happens at 08.00. It is now 07.53. If you expect your team to participate fully, I suggest you stick to the agreed time. I think I may have said that before. Secondly, this team is intended to be a covert, discreet operation. Having an internal argument with the door wide open is, in this regard, counter-productive. I heard quite enough while ascending the stairs to form an accurate picture of what you are doing. I agree with Frau Stubbs, personal feelings should be kept out of this, which prevents me from agreeing with Frau Pereira da Silva. I think we should exhaust all the leads we have before giving up and going home. It might be a good idea to change duties, and I suggest Frau Tikkenen accompanies Herr Keese to St Moritz."

Beatrice inhaled. "Thank you everyone. I appreciate your candid responses. And as Herr Kälin mentioned, it will shortly be time for morning briefing. I suggest you get yourselves a coffee etcetera before we begin. And he is absolutely right. Leaving the door open was a foolish mistake. Entirely mine. I apologise, everyone. Finally, I have decided to rearrange duties in order to maximise efficiency and learning capacity. Sabine and Xavier, you will take the next scene of crime investigation. Right, five minutes, everyone."

She didn't even look at Kälin. Why bother? She could mimic that expression of utter loathing by now.

Twenty minutes later, the depressing lack of progress was evident. Sabine had turned up no one in her search for pharmacological employees, despite an impressive search system in three countries. Chris and Conceição learned nothing of obvious value from Burgundy. The local villagers mentioned that Edwards had rarely eaten in local restaurants during that visit, only seen once in a pizzeria with his wife, and once in a café with an unidentified blonde. Beatrice confirmed that Interpol were prepared to give them another two weeks to produce some concrete results, or their status would undergo review. The atmosphere was despondent.

Xavier cleared his throat. "I may have something. It's not definite, but looks possible. Sabine suggested this person commits one of these offences per year. February 2007. March 2008. September 2010. April 2011. I did a search for unusual deaths across Europe in 2009, with a filter for high-profile businessmen. Several incidents showed up. One of them in particular could be worth investigating. It was not reported as a suicide, as the Czech police suspected a gang execution. The man was an arms dealer from the Ukraine, and killed near Brno, in the Czech Republic. Shot in the mouth. The site was completely clean, apart from some DNA, on a vodka glass. I cannot say if the sample is good, but I have asked to see the results of their tests."

A fizz of excitement surged through Beatrice. "In that case, it seems like your first scene-of-crime visit is on the agenda, Xavier. But first I want you to thoroughly brief Chris, who'll do the legwork while you're away. Chris, make sure you check for any connection with D'Arcy Roth. Sabine, I hope you'll forgive me. If we need to verify DNA, it will have to be Conceição who accompanies Xavier."

The girl received the news with such equanimity Beatrice wondered if the objections to task allocation were simply a ruse to get closer to the Dutchman. Judging by Conceição's expression, it seemed Chris had provoked some rivalry. Sometimes, it was such a relief to be beyond all that. Xavier's expression glowed like a chestnut-vendor's brazier, triggering a concern in Beatrice.

"Ja?"

Kälin's office was dark, his expression lit solely by the computer screen. His moustache, eyebrows and frown cast shadows, making him look impossibly grim. Despite her unease, the urge to laugh bubbled up inside Beatrice's throat.

"Apologies for the disturbance, Herr Kälin, but I have a

question which I'd rather ask discreetly."

"You can sit, Frau Stubbs."

"Thank you. My question concerns Herr Racine. I've chosen him for the Brno investigation because although he's young and lacks expertise, I believe in giving him the benefit of the doubt. He's shown real aptitude in his work so far and I feel he deserves a chance."

Kälin leant back and folded his arms. "You said you had a question. This sounds like a justification of your decision."

Beatrice refused to rise to the bait. "I can't help noticing that Xavier is a little clumsy, in terms of physical coordination. Obviously he'll need to be armed for this trip. Going on my existing knowledge, I'd take the risk and send him to Moravia, particularly as he was the one who discovered the Brno incident. But as one of his superior officers, you know him better. Would it be safer to send a more experienced officer now that firearms are concerned?"

Kälin smoothed two fingers over his moustache in a thoughtful gesture while watching the fingers of his other hand drum a pattern on the table.

Beatrice had just begun to suspect him of playing status games when he answered.

"Your question is intelligent. Racine has not yet learned to control his mouth, his enthusiasm or his gestures. There is only one area in which we can trust his abilities."

Kälin stood and pressed the button to lift the blinds. Light flooded the room, prompting an odd feeling of exposure in Beatrice. She quite liked talking to Kälin in the dark. Now his ice-blue eyes settled on her like a glacial lake.

"I'm not sure how deeply you researched this country before coming here, Frau Stubbs, but I suppose you know that all Swiss men do military service, including weaponry training. Those who excel are encouraged to rise in the ranks, to constantly improve their skills. When Herr Racine took his first firearms assessment with the Stapo, or Stadtspolizei, he scored higher than any previous trainee. Xavier Racine ranks as the top ... what would you say ... sharpshooter?"

Beatrice pondered. "I'm not sure. It's not terminology I'm familiar with. Crack shot? Sniper? Ace gunman?"

"Hmm. So I can tell you that he is one of the top ten sharpshooters of the Swiss Army and top five in the police force. Unbeaten in many cantons. I hope he will soon learn to apply such precision and care to the rest of his behaviour."

"Thank you, Herr Kälin. I'm very grateful to you. Not only do I feel my decision was valid, but you've put my mind at rest. I'm sorry for disturbing you."

Kälin watched her leave. "It's always better to ask when you aren't sure. Have a nice evening, Frau Stubbs."

The computer clock showed 18.15. Time to go. Tonight, the opera. Beatrice's spirits lifted as she closed down her machine. A casual chat with Xavier last week resulted in his telling her about his sister, the Box Office Manager at the Opera House, the number of unclaimed tickets left for most performances and the fact that *Die Zauberflöte*, or *The Magic Flute*, was scheduled that week. She planned to change, walk down to the lake and have a snack, before making her way over the river to the Opernhaus. She had practised her speech in German and all she needed to do was wait till the five minute call. Apparently, unclaimed tickets were then released. A free performance. And there was no better way of taking her mind off work, or herself, than a large dose of Mozart.

"Beatrice?"

"Hello, Chris. Shouldn't you have left by now?"

"Just about to. Sabine and I were just finishing off. I wondered if I could persuade you to come for a drink with me."

"Me? Well, I'd like to, Chris, but …"

"You're washing your hair?"

"No, no. I'd planned to … never mind. Mozart can wait."

"You sure? I don't want to mess up your arrangements."

"I know. But with Conceição out of town, someone must keep an eye on you."

He looked shocked.

"I'm joking, Chris. I've heard there's a rather good place called Oscar Wilde's. Shall we try that?"

"Sounds perfect."

She smiled. There's never any need to chase gossip. If you're not interested, gossip comes to you.

"Ein Gespritzer und ein Grosses." The waitress placed the drinks on small paper coasters and a bowl of nuts between them. *"Möchten Sie etwas essen?"*

Chris looked at Beatrice. "You hungry?"

"Not just now."

"*Nein danke. Es ist gut.*"

Beatrice lifted her drink. "What do you suppose this is?"

"A spritzer. That's what you asked for."

"With lemon? A slice of lemon in wine?" She fished it out with a cocktail stick.

Chris laughed. "I'll tell her to skip it when we order the next one. So, cheers!

He raised his pint glass and Beatrice remembered to meet Chris's eyes over the toast, before looking around the room. Deep purple banquettes, a long wooden bar, Art Nouveau murals on the wall and pale floor tiles matched more her idea of a gentleman's club than an Irish pub. There was even a glassed-in cigar area, with two serious besuited chaps sampling something from the humidor. Everything was muted, subtle and discreet, even the small stage area. Changing colours lit a single microphone. Beatrice liked it enormously. She helped herself to nuts.

"Without sounding patronising, I have to admire your facility with languages. I can just about order a coffee in French. How did you get to be so fluent in English?" she asked.

"Lived there. I trained at the NHTCTC in Wyboston."

"In Bedfordshire? National something Centre ... what's the rest?"

"High Tech Crime Training Centre. I learned a lot, mostly British slang and the strengths of real ale. Oh, and some computer forensics."

"And where did you pick up your German?"

"It's not so different to Dutch. I almost feel at home, apart from the culture. It must be harder for you, I think."

"The language or the culture?"

"The situation."

Chris lifted his glass and drank without taking his eyes from Beatrice's.

She acknowledged the kindness in his comment. "It's been quite a week, hasn't it?"

He gave her a smile. "We were ripe for that, in terms of a team. We'd done forming, and now we've got to get through storming. It gets easier from here though. Norming and performing come next."

"Hmm. You sound like someone I know. A concept for everything."

"I work for Europol. It's all very well in practice, but will it work in theory?"

Beatrice chuckled. "So what is the theory behind this case?"

"This is an administrative exercise, in my view. A non-case, but a signal of 'close co-operation between member states'. I believe they're getting us to go through the motions, turn up nothing at all, but ticking the box that says all irregularities must be eliminated."

"You're very cynical, Chris. I imagined you had more idealism."

"I work for a European governmental organisation. Idealism smothered by bureaucracy. Are you telling me you think there's really something to this?"

Beatrice checked herself. Her method was to exhaust all possibilities, follow every lead and never to act on that most ridiculous of fictional detective accessories, the hunch.

But she had a hunch.

"I actually think there is. And I have a strong feeling there is a connection through more than just money to that D'Arcy woman. Even if I'm wrong, I want to take this case, turn out its pockets, hold it by the ankles and shake it upside down. If there's nothing here, I want to know that for certain."

"No stone unturned?"

"Precisely. Now, if I may go off on a tandem, tell me what's going on in terms of relations between Interpol and Europol."

"Oh hell." He took a long draught of his beer. "I don't know exactly, but somehow, we get on. I like her, she's very attractive and it seems she likes me. I'm trying to be discreet, but it looks like Sabine caught on and doesn't like it. Does it bother you?"

"Not unless it is likely to bother the case. In my experience, these things can be a force for the good. The destructive element comes when it ends."

The animation left the Dutchman's face. "It hasn't even started yet."

"Sorry, *if* it ends. I'm not concerned, as I trust you both to be wholly professional."

"Thanks, B."

"I beg your pardon? What did you just call me?"

"B. What? You don't like it? I'd better prepare a team email, then. We all refer to you as B."

"What do you mean, you *all* call me B? Even Kälin?"

Chris grinned. "Not quite. He calls you *Frau* B."

Several groups of people entered the bar. The place grew lively, with an air of anticipation. When the stage lights brightened, and those of the bar dimmed, Beatrice realised why. At eight o'clock precisely, applause pattered around the room and a door opened beside the stage. Receiving her welcome as a cat receives the sun, the performer lifted her face to the light. A work of art. One could only guess at her real appearance under the layers of exquisite camouflage. Her turquoise dress sparkled and a blue velvet wrap was draped across her throat before cascading down her shoulders. A torch singer! Chris ordered more drinks and Beatrice beamed at him.

"This is marvellous, I have to say. Our seat is in the perfect spot, we have fresh drinks, without lemon, and a chanteuse is about to perform. I am glad you dragged me away from Mozart."

"You like these guys?" he asked, with amusement.

"What do you mean?"

"I would have thought you'd be more into *Il Divo* than drag queens."

Beatrice frowned at him, before turning her attention to the stage. That was a man? Was Chris pulling her leg? A glance around the bar confirmed that the majority of the audience were male couples, so he might be right.

"How can you tell it's a man?" she whispered.

"Scarf around the neck. Dead giveaway. They can't hide the Adam's apple, you see. So they cover it up."

The singer opened with '*My Funny Valentine*', and whatever the gender, that voice was rich, sweet and glorious, like a chocolate fondue.

Beatrice crossed Sihlbrücke in a distinctly positive mood. Chris had made her laugh with his indiscreet observations on the team, on their assignment and on the Oscar Wilde. She'd enjoyed herself and relaxed. Tomorrow, she would try the opera, and try to extract herself from the case in the evenings. All work and no play ... Beatrice smiled. It was almost eleven and time for two of her favourite chaps; Earl Grey and John Humphrys.

Chapter 17

Zürich 2012

Detective Karl Kälin left his office a little after seven. As his BMW pulled into the traffic, a black Ford Mondeo followed at a respectful distance. Kälin drove directly to Adliswil, always observing the speed limit, and parked outside the shopping centre. He took the lift to the supermarket, where he selected some broccoli, cauliflower and a packet of freshwater fish, which was on special offer. Afterwards, he visited the off-licence, buying a bottle of Swiss white and some sparkling water. All this was covertly recorded on a digital camera.

In Austrasse, Kälin reversed his car into one of the blue bays, placed the residents' parking permit on the dashboard and hauled his laptop case from the back seat. The black Ford Mondeo drove past and pulled in further up the street. Its lights went out.

Kälin locked his car, took his mail from the post-box and crunched up the gravel path. His apartment block was the last of the four in this development and therefore furthest from the road. Lights shone from various rooms on the first and second floors, but in the bottom apartment, all remained in darkness. He entered the building and several minutes later, lights flickered into life on the ground floor. The driver of the Mondeo didn't move.

A pair of teenagers sped down the street on rollerblades. Several cars went by, some descending to underground garages, some continuing towards Soodring. A cat shot across the road and under some bushes. It had something in its mouth.

Five minutes passed before the internal light glowed in the Mondeo. The driver's door opened and a figure slipped out, following in Kälin's footsteps, but making considerably less noise. At the entrance, the figure stopped, waited and bent to check the name plates beside the buzzers. The black-clad shape then padded around the corner of the building, turning back sharply when voices drifted down from one of the balconies above.

A set of concrete steps led to some terraced gardens, with shrubs, ornamental trees and a communal barbecue area. The figure checked for observers before finding a vantage point behind some shrubbery which allowed a view into the uncurtained rooms of the ground floor. Using the camera's zoom function, the figure located the detective. The apartment was open-plan, with a wide work surface separating the kitchen area from the lounge. Kälin was cooking, although most of his attention was diverted to the TV screen and *Tagesschau*, the daily evening news programme. The figure took several more shots, returned to the vehicle, and with a last glance at the apartment block, drove away with a smile. This job was going to be easy.

Chapter 18

Rome 2011

Seven missed calls. *Oh, Giuliana, please. This has to stop.* He slid onto the back seat of the car, and took out his handkerchief to mop his lip. The air-con and silence, usually so soothing, could not compete with the heat and noise in his head. What a total waste of a day.

"Via Veneto."

The driver nodded and pulled away.

He dialled the number, but did not press the call button. *Give me an hour, and I'll deal with it.* With a few swift thumb movements, he turned his phone to silent. The driver swung across two lanes, into Via Napoleone III, leaning on the horn. The Vittorio Emanuele monument blazed white across the piazza, a wedding cake crawling with brightly coloured parasites. One more thing he hated about *Roma*. Tourists. Another reason, apart from the obvious, why he could never live here. The Infernal City. Not that *Milano* didn't have plenty of badly dressed gawpers, it most certainly did. But like *Venezia* or *Firenze*, the sheer numbers here spoiled its appearance, like blighted fruit.

At least he'd changed hotels. Why his assistant had booked that horrible place at the top of the Scalinata, the most crowded tourist spot in the whole city, was beyond him. The last thing he needed was to be forced into finding a new room, using his own credit card and organising his own taxi. He intended to have harsh words with her when he got back. Then to make matters worse, his room in the second hotel was too close to the ventilators, so he'd insisted on being relocated. One's hotel room played a major role on trips like these, whilst trying to persuade lazy, useless bureaucrats to recognise the exception and grant the exemption.

God, he hated politics. Worst thing this country had ever done, joining the EU. And now look at the situation. Italy in the same leaking boat as Greece, Ireland and Portugal? Too late now to reverse the damage done by that buffoon while Prime Minister. Impossible. The country's situation made his position untenable. Sweat returned to his forehead. Downgrading *Ristorex* to a safety level C would cause a firestorm in the media, wrecking their reputation and crippling their sales forecasts. It was impossible to contemplate. Impossible. He replayed his passionate arguments. The government had a responsibility to recognise the company's reports, and acknowledge that the anti-depressant could not be proved to be teratogenic. Of course it could not be disproved either, but in their study of over one hundred women who had taken *Ristorex* while pregnant, not one delivered an imperfect child. It was irresponsible and controlling to deny this medication to depressed women. Without it, these unbalanced females might drink, smoke, take drugs and self harm. How dangerous would that be for a foetus? He snorted, expelling the dusty air of bureaucracy from his Milanese nose.

Eyes closed against the hordes on Repubblica, he visualised the next two hours. The hotel. Cool room, silence, shower and change. A beer, perhaps, while researching FC Roma in preparation for tonight's dinner. A knowledgeable comment on the team's performance would earn him far more status than any research statistics. The hotel. A safe haven. But Giuliana knew where he was. He envisaged his arrival.

Signor Boldoni? We have some messages for you. Thirty-two urgent faxes – all from your wife.

His eyes opened and his idyll soured. An hour. Just one hour of peace. Not the hotel. Not now.

"Eccoci arrivati ..."

Cesare waited for the driver to open his door, exited and gave him instructions.

"Grazie. Venga a prendermi alle otto in punto, per favore."

"Certamente, a più tardi."

Eight o'clock. He had three hours. One hundred and eighty minutes of freedom. He could steal an hour, not doing, not thinking, not dealing. Just being. He turned from the hotel's portico and strode down the street, ignoring the endless tourist bars, glancing up alleys for something small, cheap, Roman. *Café Don Pomeranus* had two tables outside and an awning striped in red, white and green. One table was free. At the other, two old men looped through an argument about coffee houses. *Sant Eustachio* versus *Frontoni dal 1921*. They both supported their views with passion and dismissed each other with aggression.

He ordered a *Peroni* and sat still. He watched the paint flake from the building opposite. The waiter poured his drink. He thanked him and observed bubbles crawl up the glass. A dark blue Vespa sped by. The rider wore no helmet. And back again, this time with a passenger. Long dark hair rippled behind her, as she grasped the driver's waist with one arm and punctuated her speech with the other. An ancient Fiat 125 filled with three large women and their shopping trundled past, barely missing his table. He watched. He breathed. It couldn't last.

His hand reached for his phone and he scrolled through the missed calls. Nine, now. He listened to Giuliana's increasing hysteria with a sense of mild numbness. It's an emergency, Cesare, the baby is crying, I can't stop him, something is wrong, Cesare, I've sent the nanny home, your mother is unavailable, I am taking him to hospital, Cesare, it was a fit of some sort, I am desperate, Cesare, this is unfair on me, I can't go on like this, where are you for the love of God, have you any idea of how exhausted I am, Cesare, the doctors told me not to get so stressed, there's nothing wrong, I want a second opinion, these people are a disgrace, Cesare, uncivilised, it wouldn't happen in *Roma*, people care there, this city is so cold and its people are hateful, Cesare, you don't care, I'm so alone, and our son, your son, Cesare, how can you be so cold, so remote, I wish I'd never moved north, Cesare, it's destroying my sunny nature, my lust for life, I can't bear it, Cesare, Cesare, Cesare.

He hung up and considered another beer. After all, he deserved it.

A voice interrupted his internal monologue. "Do you mind if I sit here?"

Tourist. No attempt at Italian. American, probably. Nasty bright clothes.

"Prego." He gestured for her to sit opposite him. His expression was cool. She smiled gratefully, sat and took off her shoes. How ill-mannered. Two angry red blisters on each foot. Are these people not used to walking? The waiter's sneer was visible as she massaged her foot and asked for a sparkling water and coffee in a poor accent.

Cesare pulled his sunglasses down from his forehead over his eyes to observe her while still appearing uninterested. His mobile phone vibrated in his pocket. He ignored it. Giuliana's voice now bored him.

The tourist had the minimum of accessories; no camera, no sunglasses, a small handbag, a map and bad clothes. Her hair was frizzy and she had caught too much sun. How stupid were these people? He should keep his mouth shut. Yet the habits of finding a way into a person prevailed.

"First day in Rome?" he asked, in English.

A flicker of mistrust. "Yeah, first day. I guess that's obvious, right?"

"You are American?"

"Canadian. Close."

"Close but yet so far."

She looked at him properly for the first time. "Right. It doesn't usually matter to Europeans. We're all the same to you guys."

"Fair point. But isn't it also true vice versa?"

"No, I don't think so. For us, Europe has many strong identities. OK, we may get confused between Norway and Denmark, but I know a lot about Italy. And Spain. And France. I'm touring, trying to learn more, you know what I mean?"

"*Bene*. How did you find the Eternal City?"

"No fair. I landed this morning, but my luggage went to Germany. I started my tour in borrowed clothes and none of my cosmetics. Believe me, for a woman, that's not good."

"Bad luck. So your first day in Italy was not a success?"

"It's not my first day in Italy. I spent a few days in Florence and Milan before coming here. That was so great."

"You like the north?"

She sat back and tilted her head to look at him. "You're a Roman, right?"

"Wrong. But that's all I'm going to say."

"OK, whatever. To be honest, I totally loved the north. Maybe I'm a little culture-shocked, I don't know, but I find Rome kinda hard work."

Cesare pushed his sunglasses up onto his head to allow her a view of his eyes. He gave her a smile. "I would say you have excellent taste."

"Phew! Looks like my gamble paid off." Her laugh softened her face and her blue eyes crinkled.

"Signora." The waiter shoved a bottle and a glass on the table, tucking the bill under the bottle.

"Excuse me? The coffee?"

The man blanked her and returned to the interior.

"Shoot." Her face burned with something more than an excess of sun.

He leaned towards her. "Can I help?"

"No, thanks. I wanted cold sparkling water and a coffee. But I got warm still water and a whole bunch of attitude. You know what, I think I'll skip it and get back to the hotel."

"Wait a moment."

He swung out of his chair, grabbed her water and strode into the café.

"The woman outside. She ordered cold water, *frizzante*. And a coffee. Is that too complicated an order? Or do you always treat tourists like this? No wonder Rome has the worst reputation in Italy. You are all arrogant, lazy and stupid as pigs." He threw ten Euros on the counter along with the warm water and stormed out.

"Come. Let's find a place with better service."

She slipped on her shoes and joined him, limping slightly.

"This is ridiculous. You need to bathe your feet. Where is your hotel?"

She gave him a grateful smile. "Right up the street. Regina Baglioni. Listen, thanks for the knight in shining armour stuff. Good to know there are some nice guys out there."

"I too stay at the Baglioni. I will walk with you and arrange a cold drink."

"Can you please ensure room service deliver a bottle of cold *San Pellegrino* and a cappuccino to this lady's room as soon as possible. Have her luggage taken up as soon as it arrives, please." He slipped the clerk five Euros, disguising it as a firm slap on the reception desk, before guiding her to the elevator.

"Which floor?"

"Five, please."

The doors closed and he pressed levels three and five.

She turned to him. "You are so kind, I'm totally overawed by this. Thank you so much."

"I am simply trying to reinforce your prejudice. North good, south bad. Your baggages should be here soon, and maybe tomorrow, you can see the clean face of Rome. Wearing comfortable shoes."

"Right. Oh, is this your floor already? Ok, well, thanks again. Hey, could I get you a drink at all, maybe later? Just to show my appreciation?"

"I have an engagement, unfortunately. But perhaps we could enjoy an aperitif before I go. I imagine you and your feet would prefer not to go too far this evening. How about the bar at seven?"

"Excellent. Or, even better, could I just swing by your room? That way I can keep my slippers on."

"Of course. I'm in room 302. See you later."

Not his place, really, but he would have to tell her. These women, alone, in strange cities, no grasp of the language. You cannot just invite yourself to a strange man's hotel room. Naturally she was safe with him; he was a man of honour, *Il Cavaliere* in more than just a title. But any *figlio di puttana* could play the gentleman and she would trust him. Far too risky. The phone rang. Maybe she just had the same thought.

"Pronto?"

"Cesare!"

Giuliana was sobbing with relief. His mother, the doctors, his son, their son, this city, these people and the knowledge that he was in her beloved Rome. It was too much for her, her heart was beating strangely, she needed him, she felt so bad, she couldn't cope with this, she needed him. Cesare!

Cesare put his head in his hands. His wife needed him. He had a dinner engagement and more meetings tomorrow. Giuliana sounded terrible. It was a self-induced panic attack. She couldn't work herself into such a state every time he was away from home for a few days. He had to work, had to keep the business healthy. A sedative would buy him time, but he would never permit his wife to take any medication while still breastfeeding. Cancelling tonight's dinner would lose him anything he had already gained from the *Guardia di Finanza*. Not forgetting that drink with the grateful tourist.

From nowhere, his mother's voice arose. 'Cesare, what are you thinking? Putting a stranger before your wife's pain? What kind of man are you? You should be ashamed!'

He made a decision.

"OK, Giuliana, I'm coming home. I'll be with you in a few hours. Please rest, my love. I will be there tonight."

As the car drove away from Malpensa, he regretted not informing the Canadian woman that he couldn't make it. But finding a flight, calling his contacts to cancel and packing had eaten away all his time. And without knowing her name, he had no way of leaving her a message. Still, he hated to be impolite and really should have warned her about trusting strangers.

Chapter 19

Zürich 2012

Sabine's contact arrived at the *Rote Fabrik* on her bike. Chris assessed her in seconds. A beach bum without a beach. And not much of a bum to speak of, either. A camouflage vest and denim shorts covered a limited amount of her wiry, deeply tanned body, accompanied by ancient Converse trainers, vaguely Celtic tattoos and dangling things from her wrists, neck and plaited rat's tail in her hair. He wondered why these independent alternative types all bought into exactly the same uniform. *Look how different I am.* She joined them at the wooden table.

"Ursula, this is Chris, my colleague. Chris, Ursula may have helpful information."

After greeting Sabine with a handshake and a smile, Ursula turned to him with a hostile look. She cocked her head in an affected enquiry at Sabine.

Sabine seemed unruffled. "Chris is part of my team, Ursi. Did you find anything for us?"

"Yes and no. I'd like a beer."

Sabine went inside to order and Ursi fiddled with her mobile, paying Chris no attention. Each blunt finger was stained yellow and burn marks crossed her inner arms like the rungs of a ladder. He'd seen marks like that before, on a tandoori-oven cook at an Indian restaurant. Ursi either had an addiction he'd not heard of, or more likely, she worked in a pizzeria. Absorbing the many shades of colourful and alternative passing by on the lake path, he realised he may as well have a blue flashing light on his forehead. Everyone looked at him and saw *Polizei*. He looked past them at the lake, watching the early evening light play across the opposite shore.

Sabine returned with three bottles of *Vollmond*. Ursi drank a good third without waiting for a toast.

Chris knocked his bottle against Sabine's, met eyes and drank.

"So, let's hear the good news first," said Sabine, wiping her lips with the back of her hand.

"Good news is I fixed a meeting. Bad news is, I don't know if they'll talk. Look Sabine, I'm pretty sure that if *he*'s there, they won't say anything at all." She flashed a contemptuous look at Chris, her dark eyes reminding him of a rodent as she swigged at the bottle.

He smiled and prepared to reply but Sabine got in first.

"I'm going nowhere without him. We come as a pair. Otherwise, forget it." She took a sip of beer and shrugged, as if unconcerned by Ursula's opinion.

An awkward silence settled, but Chris's instinct held him back. He'd leave it to Sabine. Let the ferret deal with the rat.

Ursula dug into her tatty fringed bag, pulled out a book and retrieved a piece of paper from between the pages. "Up to you. I've done my bit. Here's the address, mention me and don't be late. I said you'd get there by eight."

Springing up, she drained the beer and pointed at Sabine.

"Call me." She turned her back on Chris and headed for her bike.

Navigating Stauffacher as dusk leached the colour from the city took all Chris's concentration, so he barely registered Sabine's call, informing Xavier of their location and intention. Driving onto Ankerstrasse, he found to his frustration he couldn't turn left. Sabine spotted a space.

"Park it here, we'll walk."

He locked the car, conscious of wary stares from doorways, windows and the benches on Helvetiaplatz, and positioned himself on the inside of the pavement. A gentleman would usually do the opposite, but Chris had the feeling that on Langstrasse, the traffic was less dangerous than the street. The building they were looking for had a series of pink-lit windows and a sign: '*Nightclub*', depicting a naked woman in heels reclining on a crescent moon. Without hesitating, Sabine pushed open the door.

Just inside, a heavy velvet curtain screened the room from prurient eyes. Chris pulled it back, allowing Sabine through first. The room was tiny, with a bar, a stage, which was closer to an Olympic medal-winner's podium, and a few poorly lit tables. No more than ten people populated the room and every one of them gawped at the new arrivals. Chris had to admire Sabine's relaxed manner as she bid the punters good evening and settled herself at an empty table. Chris sat beside her, rather than opposite, giving him a chance to survey the room.

His eyes got no further than the barmaid. The woman hypnotised him; long black curls, black sooty eyes and skin that seemed to soak up light. Laughing with one of the customers, she showed a wide, gap-toothed smile, reminding him of Beatrice Dalle. Everything about her suggested sex; scary sex, sex without boundaries, sex limited only by imagination, and he'd bet she had plenty of ideas. Nothing about her clothes was overtly revealing, but low-slung jeans hinted at a tight belly and her scoop-necked T-shirt clung to her contours as she moved. As if she sensed his stare, she looked right at him. He ordered two Cokes, relieved the dim lighting spared his blushes. Her eyes lingered for a few seconds, weighing him up, before she gave an understanding nod.

Most people sat alone, apparently waiting for something. A small, balding man perched at the end of the bar, chain-smoking, where more burgundy velvet screened another door. As Chris watched, he ducked through, spoke to someone, came back and summoned a man at a table near the door. The john downed his drink and slipped through the curtains with a nod to the doorkeeper.

"Looks like our contact is yet to arrive. Still, it's only just eight," said Sabine.

"Yeah. I'd be surprised if he was one of this lot. Aren't all left-wing anarchists a bit younger than this crowd?"

"Of course he's not one of them. These men are all sad middle-aged perverts taking advantage of the economic circumstances of exploited women."

"Sabine, keep it down. If we get asked to leave before our guy arrives ..."

A tobacco-roughened voice interrupted. "She's right. The women *are* exploited and these losers *are* middle-aged perverts." Betty Blue stood at their table with three Cokes. She placed one in front of Sabine, gave one to Chris with a half-lidded look and sat down opposite. "This one's for me. It has vodka in it and officers shouldn't drink on duty." Her accent sounded Spanish. She grinned at them with that incredible mouth. Chris wanted to grab her, throw her over his shoulder and run through the velvet curtains.

Slipping a small leather pouch from her back pocket, she commenced rolling a joint. "I hear you want to talk to someone in the socialist action movement. Maybe I can help. No names, no inside information, but I'll answer a couple of questions."

Sabine seemed similarly struck by this goddess. "OK. You're not what we expected but ... thank you for meeting us. I understand you don't want to give us your name, but I'm Sabine and this is Chris."

The balding man sloped off his stool and moved behind the bar to serve a customer. He looked over at their table and whined.

"Yolanda?"

Without turning, she lifted her hand, middle finger to him and returned to crumbling resin onto tobacco strands. The guy sighed and filled a glass with lager.

"And you can call me Yolanda. So, what do you want?"

Chris spoke. "We're investigating a series of deaths. Several men, whom you might call corporate fat cats, died in suspicious circumstances. Looked like suicide, but we have evidence the same person was with them when they died." He was pleased at the professional tone of his voice, as he suspected he might be drooling.

Sabine took over. "I'm a psychological profiler, Yolanda, and my research leads me to think this person is performing what he believes to be social justice. A diamond dealer from South Africa, an American vulture fund boss, a media magnate with fingers everywhere, a British CEO of a polluting water company ... you can see what Chris means about *fat cats*."

"Yes." Yolanda lit the joint and the sweet distinctive scent crept up Chris's nose. "So you think this is direct action from a left-wing activist? An anarchist on a crusade? And you want me to tell you his name and where he lives?" Her laughing eyes reflected the pink lights in the opaque windows.

Chris smiled back. "That would be great, thanks."

Sabine shot him a look. Fair enough, he was flirting with a potential informant. But who wouldn't?

At least Sabine kept focused. "We were really looking for more of an insight into how these things work. As far as I understand, most direct action groups target material things such as buildings. But I've yet to find a group which advocates physical harm to individuals."

Yolanda blew smoke into the air above them. "Ursi was right about you, Sabine. You *are* smart. And what you say is true. We don't believe in violence against people. We believe property is theft. We believe information should be public. We believe in righting capitalist wrongs and redistribution of wealth. Needs not profits. But we don't do murder."

Chris's ardour cooled. Sex, yes. Slogans? Such a turn-off.

Keeping his smile in place, he asked, "Property is theft? So where do you live?"

She took a long draught of her vodka and Coke, her eyes not leaving his. "In a disused railway terminal. Me and seven other squatters. You should come round sometime; I think you'd like it."

Chris broke eye contact, knowing he was being played with. And enjoying it.

Sabine had her teeth in and was unlikely to let go. "So if your group, and those similar, don't believe in violence to the individual, might there be someone who feels you don't go far enough? Can you think of someone who was frustrated by such policies and wanted to go further? Maybe someone who left your group because you weren't as radical as he hoped?"

Yolanda's smile faded as she listened to Sabine. "Yes, such people exist. But the one thing that doesn't make sense here is the range. People I know tend to have one cause. Anti-war. Animal rights. The diamond racket. Corruption in the pharmaceutical trade. Shit, there's even an action group against FIFA. But not all together. Yes, a lot of people feel very aggressive towards bankers and their obscene activities and I think that's probably the closest we've come to a desire for physical retaliation. What you need to understand is we're attacking the system. We want governments to take control of the banks and use the profits for social projects. We want to massively increase taxes on the rich. We want to fundamentally change the system to serve the people and the planet, not exploit them and plunder its resources. And much as it might serve some short-term satisfaction to punch a banker in the face or drag a key along an ugly great SUV, it will not achieve change. Thought and action must work together as part of the struggle."

Chris blinked, mesmerised by that supple, articulate mouth, those flashing, passionate eyes and the fact that some of what she said made sense to him. Sabine, on the other hand, retained her laser precision and sharp teeth.

"So you think it unlikely that a renegade activist would take it upon themselves to serially kill high-profile capitalists as a symbolic anti-establishment action?"

Yolanda re-lit her joint and nodded. "If the dead guys were all part of some kind of chain, like fur farmers, importers, fashion designers, owners of fur shops, that would make some sense. It's just these different random men ... to me, it feels personal."

Sabine sighed. "I agree. Thanks for your time Yolanda. I appreciate your talking to us. How much do we owe you for the Cokes?"

"Any donation you'd like to make to the cause is always gratefully received." The laughing eyes were back.

Chris withdrew a fifty and slid it across the table. She placed a hand over his, stroked it down and withdrew the money. Her hand felt cool and soft. Chris felt precisely the opposite.

Sabine stood up and thanked her again while he mumbled a goodbye, ignoring the invitation in her expression. Thrusting his way out through the red curtains, Chris appreciated the chill evening air restoring some of his perspective.

"I have to say, Sabine, you do play the left-wing sympathiser very well. Very convincing."

She zipped her jacket and looked up at him. "That's because it's not an act. As for her, useful, do you think?" she asked.

"Yes. I think she was. It sounded pretty rational to me."

Sabine's eyes narrowed. "I agree. Intelligent analysis. I'm going to add this to my profile tomorrow. But right now, I want to go home and have a bath. Listen, I can take a tram home, if that's more convenient?"

Chris looked at her, puzzled. "Why would you do that? I'll drive you."

Her sharp little face softened into a sly smile as she glanced sideways towards the pink windows. "I thought you might want to go back in, now you're off duty."

He grinned. "Was it that obvious?"

"Frankly, any minute I expected you to start humping her leg."

Chapter 20

Zürich 2012

"Kälin?"

"Hello, Herr Kälin, Frau Stubbs here. Would you be able to join us upstairs? It seems the trip to Brno has turned something up."

"Now?"

"Yes. Now."

He hung up.

His behaviour did not affect Beatrice in the slightest. An almost-forgotten buzz hummed through her system; this was a step forward. Her innate caution warned her not to get too enthusiastic, yet the news was a boost to the team's confidence. She began drafting an email to Lyon in her head, while observing Xavier's animated conversation with Chris.

Kälin arrived, his traditional scowl lightened by curiosity. Beatrice clapped her hands for silence.

"OK, Conceição and Xavier have some news. Over to you."

Conceição began. "The DNA found at the scene is a match. A thirteen-point match, which means the chances of it coming from two different individuals is effectively nil. The same person was with Belanov before he died. But as to who that person is? Xavier?"

"Thank you. The Czech police had some background on

Belanov. Officially a used-car dealer, he actually traded in small to medium-calibre weapons; handguns, rifles, and so on. However, the police strongly suspected his involvement with the East European grey market arms trade. They know he supplied rocket launchers, mortars and cannons to Georgia, for example. So I got the name of Belanov's associate in Brno, Ivan Sykora, and met him at his office. He would tell me nothing about Belanov's business, but he explained a little about the methods. According to Sykora, Belanov rented a cabin in the Brno region every year, for the duration of the arms fair. He took clients and colleagues there 'to enjoy themselves without inhibition', as he put it. Belanov usually did a good trade at the event and was generous with his hospitality. Sykora knew of no problem or dispute which may have caused his death. He attended the fair on the day Belanov was killed and spoke to him several times. He noticed Belanov leaving mid-afternoon. He remembered because he was with a woman he didn't recognise. All he can recall about her is that she was good-looking and had red hair."

Kälin's eyes fixed on Xavier. "Anything else?"

"No fresh evidence. The police analysed the vodka bottle. Just vodka. They also checked the glasses. Clean. And I mean clean. Freshly washed and polished, but with saliva on one. Our DNA. We checked the cabin, of course, it is very remote. Belanov's Porsche was spotless."

"Why did they assume it was a gangland killing and not see it as suicide?" asked Sabine.

"Good question." Conceição flicked through her notes. "It looked like suicide at first. The only factor which made them suspicious was the initial report of the forensic team. The body was found by the cleaning company the following morning, so there was plenty of blood, but the police did pick up one strange detail. Most of the skull and brain matter was spread across the floor behind him. But there was a significant amount of it down his upper arms. As if his hands had been above his head. If he'd pulled the trigger himself, his arms would have been out of the way. They think he was tied up, shot and later his body arranged to look like he'd done it himself."

"How do you see this as fitting into what we already think?" Beatrice asked.

Conceição answered without hesitation. "It fits in several ways. Another morally suspect line of work…"

"Although not as high profile as the other men," added Xavier. "Which helped us."

"Yes, because there is one vital point we uncovered which we haven't even mentioned yet." Anticipation brightened Conceição's eyes.

"Please tell us, Frau Pereira, I cannot stand the suspense," Kälin drawled.

Conceição gestured to Xavier. "Go ahead. You found it."

"Well, actually, Chris was the one who made the connection. I just did the digging."

Kälin sighed. "This politeness is charming, but not particularly time-efficient. Will someone explain what has been found?"

Xavier responded quickly, despite his high colour. "Belanov had several expensive hobbies. One of which was playing polo. He wasn't very good, from what I heard, so sponsored teams in order to be able to play. For the 2008 season, he sponsored the team of Antonella D'Arcy."

No one spoke.

Beatrice cleared her throat. "All the same elements again. A suspicious death of a morally suspect businessman, the apparent welcome from the victim, the same DNA, and now D'Arcy again. She is the strongest link here and I want to talk to her again." She met Kälin's eyes. He remained expressionless.

"Not forgetting Sabine's identification of each method of killing as 'just'. How else would you kill a gun-runner?" Conceição shook her head, apparently amused by the cause of death.

Chris nodded. "And the super clean glasses, with his saliva on one, support Sabine's and Xavier's theory. He drugs them, kills them, cleans up and the DNA is a red herring."

"A what?" Sabine's frown was as severe as Kälin's.

"*Eine Finte.* A false trail," Chris replied.

The team stayed silent, absorbing the implications, when Kälin spoke.

"So, as Herr Racine enquired some time ago, our fundamental assumption – that we are hunting a man – could be completely wrong. Where does that leave your psychological profile, Ms Tikkenen? Or can we simply change the pronouns?"

Beatrice opened her mouth to dilute the acidity in Kälin's voice, but stopped short.

"Good Lord."

Chris watched her intently. "What is it, Beatrice?"

"Xavier could be right. It could be a woman. Think about it." She looked from face to face. "Belanov left with a woman, according to Xavier's source. And the uniform, in Utrecht. A staff member's uniform went missing, a female receptionist. Didn't you say that Edwards was seen with an unidentified female, in a restaurant or something? And Thompson, halfway down a dangerous ski run, was carrying condoms. Hence the access. Men would open the door much more easily to an attractive woman. And the chemical element. She can't do the physical stuff, so has to drug them first. It makes perfect sense to me."

"That has something." Kälin focused out of the window. "And if it's a woman, leaving male DNA behind in saliva is quite a clever strategy."

Xavier shook his head. "But it wasn't just saliva. She left a hair in Burgundy."

"So where does she get it from?" asked Conceição.

Sabine perked up. "I mentioned that many serial killers live with someone older, or who depends on them. If our killer has an elderly or disabled male relative at home, there would be an inexhaustible supply."

Beatrice shook some unpleasant images from her mind. "So, we may have been barking down the wrong hole. We need to retrace our steps. Chris, the case files. Go through them all and see if we missed anything because our focus was too narrow. Sabine, as regards the medical connection ..."

She groaned. "I need to do it all again. I only looked for men."

Xavier spoke. "I'll help you. I am very quick with database searches. Unless Beatrice has another job for me?"

"I do, Xavier, I'm afraid. I need you to check D'Arcy's alibis again and also to do a flight search from Zürich to Utrecht and Brno on and around the dates in question. See if there are any names that were in both places at the right times. Both genders.

"Conceição, find out if there is some kind of care-at-home support agency here. Possibly there is a register of carers who have live-in dependants. Cross check with Sabine constantly, to see if we can use her profile to narrow the net. I am going to inform Lyon about our progress and then Herr Kälin and I are going to visit Antonella D'Arcy. And this time, on our terms."

Kälin raised his eyebrows and to Beatrice's disbelief, gave her a genuine smile. She was appalled at herself. Good God, she hadn't blushed like that in twenty years.

Chapter 21

Zürich 2012

Beatrice was underdressed and it was all Kälin's fault.

The plan was to arrive unannounced at the D'Arcy Roth offices once again, so Kälin made a reconnaissance call to ensure the woman herself would be present. On discovering she had taken a long weekend to prepare herself for the first polo match of the season, he suggested the embarrassment factor would be heightened by their turning up to interview her in front of clients, colleagues and competitors at Polo Park Zürich. Beatrice could see the logic, but felt some trepidation. She had never attended a polo match before. Kälin advised her to dress '*as if for an English wedding. Or Ascot*'. She was horrified. English weddings and Ascot meant one thing.

Hats.

She called Matthew.

"Don't have to take it literally. And anyway, hats are awfully last generation. What you need now is a fascinator." Matthew spoke with conviction.

"Sounds like something you dangle in front of a child."

"It wouldn't last long. No, this is more feathers and frippery, normally stuck on one side of your head. Tanya wore one for Luke's christening, if you remember. Trouble is, in all the photos it looks like someone's doing bunny ears behind her." He laughed at the recollection.

"Well, I have no time to buy a fascinator, or even bunny ears for that matter. I have to leave early tomorrow morning; it's halfway to Germany, so I need to cobble something together tonight."

"Co-ordinate, then. A dress of one colour, with matching bag, earrings and lipstick."

"How did it come to pass that I need fashion advice from a Classics lecturer?"

"A Classics lecturer with two fashion-forward daughters. Which reminds me, Marianne wants you to bring her back a cuckoo clock."

"She can whistle. Do you have any idea how much they cost? I'm thinking about that grey two-piece, with my good handbag and some black pearl earrings."

"So you'll be wearing grey, grey and greyish. That's one way to stand out in a crowd."

"I don't want to stand out, Matthew. I want to be serious, intimidating and cast a threatening shadow over her day."

"Perhaps you should go as Darth Vader."

"Perhaps you should be less facetious. The sooner I find out how she's involved in all this, the sooner I can come home. And I want to come home. I miss you. I even miss bloody Hamilton."

"Not in the same way, I hope. I miss you, actually. Odd how a spring weekend can look so drear when there's no one to appreciate my fish stew."

"Let's see how this week goes, and if all looks good, I may fly over next weekend."

"May the force be with you. And I want to see the *gris et gris* ensemble for myself. Get Happy Bear to take a picture."

Polo Park Zürich lay just outside Winterthur. Verdant forests of pine created the backdrop for the crisp green field ringed by white. Like a cricket pitch, Beatrice thought, wondering if she and Matthew would be able to attend some village matches this summer. It seemed rather important that they should. Kälin spoke to an official, who waved them through. The lad was awfully young. Of course, it was traditional to exclaim at the youth of police officers and dentists as one aged, but this boy really could be no older than twelve. Her imagination danced away as she envisaged the youth of Mile End left in charge of traffic.

As she and Kälin approached the field, the deceptive familiarity of faded green and shabby white disappeared. The brilliant white of the pavilion was almost painful and the grass looked as if it had been combed. Close to the field stood a series of tables, covered with stiff, white tablecloths. Some high for those who wished to stand, and some lower with chairs which did not look at all comfy. Umbrellas created pools of shade, in which the glamorous gathered; chattering, laughing and tinkling. Everyone wore pastel; duck-egg blue, beige, powder pink, taupe, pale yellow, cream, lilac and ecru. It could have been the set of *Steel Magnolias*, but for the men.

"What now? Shall we wander about, flashing ID and asking where she is?"

Kälin shook his head. "We'll find someone with a badge, and ask him. Or her. And let's get a drink. It's warm. For now, we just wait."

Beatrice's eyes followed him as he threaded his way through the sea of Easter egg colours inside the pavilion. Spectacular flower arrangements stood between the tables, and the place settings themselves were a work of art. Pity they weren't invited to dinner. Children darted around the legs of tables and adults; elsewhere several small dogs sized one another up. The sparkle from champagne, sunglasses and jewellery did not distract Beatrice from noting how many heads turned her way. Matthew, infuriatingly, was right. The grey suit made her look like a thundercloud over a spring meadow. She pulled a face to match. Kälin handed her a glass.

"She's playing in the first match, for the Royal Blues. We won't have the possibility of talking to her for a while. However, we will have a chance to watch her play. Should we sit?"

Beatrice led the way to a table near the picket fence, marvelling at the snowy starched cloths, the effortless small talk and delicate colour coordination of the crowd. The scent of wealth and perfume of power was overpowering. She sipped at her drink.

"Herr Kälin, this is champagne."

"Correct, Frau Stubbs. Let us toast your skills of observation."

"We are on duty, you know. I prefer to keep a clear head when trying to needle someone. For an interview, I mean. I hardly think alcohol is appropriate."

"The police line is, '*Ein Glas ist OK*', so I plan to stick to that. And it is a quality brand, don't you think?"

Beatrice took another sip. It was rather good.

"And it is polite in Swiss society, as in most civilised countries in the world, to toast one another before drinking. Cheers, Frau Stubbs."

"Cheers, Herr Kälin. Thank you for the tip. Here's one for you. In Britain, we tend not to advise other people on how to behave."

"True. You give no advice and then despise foreigners for not knowing the rules. It is a mystery to me why the British have no word for *Schadenfreude*."

Beatrice stared at him, unsettled by the turn the conversation had taken. He looked like his old adversarial self, but the amusement in his voice and the light in his eyes reminded her of the photo she had seen. The one in which he looked like fun. She surveyed the polo field and sipped her champagne.

The tannoy, after a lengthy welcoming speech in three languages, announced the first chukka. Ten horses came onto the field and the excitement became tangible. Beatrice, having one of her more observant days, registered the players wearing royal blue were all on the same team. One of whom was Antonella D'Arcy. Impossible to tell which player at this distance. The other team wore white, and the two black-clad individuals were evidently referees.

Tension built, the horses snorting and skipping with excitement, the audience arranging themselves into optimum viewing positions, and the players faking confident laughter. When the action began, Beatrice was entranced. Hooves drummed into the hard earth, players charged one another like jousting knights and all the while, mallets swung with horrifying force. The speed, the confusion, the danger from these large sweaty beasts, violent mallets and whizzing ball absorbed her completely, although she had no clue what was happening.

The crowd gasped and sighed and applauded, at what Beatrice knew not. But even she recognised when a goal was scored. D'Arcy's team celebrated, and without warning, after barely ten minutes, it was over. She turned to Kälin.

"Talk about fast and furious. Is that it?"

"For the first chukka, yes. The Royal Blues lead. They have a short break, change horses and play another. There will be four in total."

"How do you know so much about polo?"

"Like a good police officer, I do my research."

Beatrice chose not to respond. She too had done her research, into the dress code. And look where that had got her. During the changeover, she took the opportunity to observe the crowd. Standing at one of the higher tables behind them was a slight figure Beatrice recognised.

"Isn't that D'Arcy's secretary, the shy girl? The table at one o'clock. She's wearing peach."

Kälin let his gaze roam over the crowd, past the girl in question, and on to the pavilion. His attention returned to Beatrice. "Daughter *and* secretary. It looks like the same person, yes."

"Does the poor creature have to attend all D'Arcy's sporting events and cheer her on?"

Kälin watched the field, but Beatrice found the girl more interesting. She sat alone, hunched over her handbag as if she were trying to remain unseen. An older woman with a sour face to match her lemon ensemble approached the table and offered pleasantries. Beatrice could see the girl's awkward discomfort at answering questions and evident relief when the yellow lady left. As she continued to watch, two men greeted the girl in passing and she dropped her head.

"Typical of such a bully. Drags that poor child here, leaves her alone and embarrassed while she prances about on her pony, then insists on hearing fawning praise all the way back to Zürich."

"Frau Stubbs. You are making assumptions."

"Perhaps. But look at her, she can't even meet people's eyes, she so shy."

Kälin glanced up at the girl. "Low status body language, I've seen it before. Either that or she may have noticed you staring."

The Royal Blues won the match, and crowd reaction showed it was either well deserved or a popular result. The applause swelled again as the players emerged in small groups from their paddock. Beatrice watched Kälin's sharp eyes follow the pastel tide flowing around the blue shirts. He chose his moment with deliberation, nodded to Beatrice and stood.

D'Arcy laughed with her acolytes and shook her head modestly, every bit the gracious winner. As Kälin moved into her sightline, her face stiffened. She took in Beatrice, excused herself with great charm and moved towards them. Her smile was restrained, lacking any kind of warmth. Clocking the heads turning to watch D'Arcy's progress, Beatrice was suddenly glad she had worn grey. She could be mistaken for nothing other than a police officer. Exactly what she'd hoped. She must remember to tell Matthew.

"Good morning, Frau Stubbs, Herr Kälin. Did you enjoy the match?"

"I'm sorry to say we are not here for the entertainment, Ms D'Arcy," Beatrice replied. "We need to ask you some more questions. We tried to reach you at your office."

"And this must be done now?" Her eyebrows lifted.

"It has to be now, but not necessarily here. We can return to the police station in Zürich if you prefer?" Kälin offered.

D'Arcy's jaw was taut and she turned her blue eyes to Beatrice.

"Follow me. If you insist on disrupting my day, I insist on some degree of privacy."

She turned back the way she had come and into the players' enclosure, with a brisk word to the attendant. Weaving a path through the horse-boxes, she led them into a large tent. Clothes rails lined the walls and a sizeable table surrounded by camping chairs took up the middle. D'Arcy perched on the edge of one of the chairs.

"I'd appreciate it if we could make this as quick as possible."

Beatrice seated herself and took her notebook from her bag.

"What can you tell us about Symon Belanov?"

The beautiful face didn't flicker. She appeared to think for a moment.

"Belanov. Very poor player. Almost dangerous, I would say. But he paid his way onto teams, one of which was ours. 2008. Not a good year for us. That was the end of our association. I recall hearing he'd been involved with some sort of arms dealing and fell foul of a rival gang. If you lie with dogs, you get fleas."

"A maxim that could be D'Arcy Roth's motto. What else did you know about Belanov?"

"You know very little about me or my company if that is your impression, Ms Stubbs. As for Symon Belanov? Independently wealthy, but always looking for the next opportunity. He dealt in small weapons, although the shop window was cars. A social climber, rather ill-mannered. Reasonably attractive and made the most of it, so naturally popular with women."

"Not you, by the sounds of it," Beatrice commented.

"No. Not with me. I'm hardly his type but he still made a pass. Probably more of a reflex than anything else. But he took offence at my refusal and made life extremely uncomfortable that season. I was relieved to see the back of him."

Kälin pointed his pen at D'Arcy. "Why aren't you his type?"

"The man had rather clichéd preferences. His ideal woman would have large breasts and ginger hair, usually accompanied by a loud laugh and the manners of a peasant."

Beatrice noted real spite in D'Arcy's tone and wondered at the truth behind the rejection story.

"After that season, did you have any further contact?"

"Not much. We met once more in Argentina, for a tournament, but his team were knocked out in the first round. He deserved it."

"Don't you find it puzzling, Ms D'Arcy, that the only connection between these high-profile men is you, or your company?"

"No. As I explained before, I make contact with a lot of people, the vast majority of whom are still alive."

Kälin spoke. "The dead men. Do you know of anyone else who knew them all? Any mutual friends?"

She leaned her head back and looked at the roof of the tent, silent for several moments. Beatrice had to admire how the polo kit suited her. The dark blue matched her eyes, the white jodhpurs clung to her fit, shapely legs, and her hair, escaping in damp curls from her ponytail, gave her a touch of vulnerability.

"I believe some people are acquainted with two, even three, of the men you mentioned. I'm not aware of anyone who knew them all. Yet many such individuals must exist and some solid detective work will undoubtedly bring them to light. Perhaps when you find them, you might stop hounding me."

Kälin ignored her jibe. "I'd like you to provide us with an alibi for the third of May 2009. Here is my card; you can call me anytime on Monday."

Beatrice stood and put away her notes. "You are quite likely to see more of us, Ms D'Arcy. A fact I dislike just as much as you. Best of luck with the tournament today. We'll be off now."

D'Arcy didn't move. "I'm sure you can find your own way out. Goodbye, officers."

Kälin led the way back into the sunshine. Maybe it was watching sport, or sparring with that woman, but Beatrice had worked up quite an appetite.

"Herr Kälin, I know it's Saturday and you have already given up a large chunk of your free time. But I wonder whether I can persuade you to have lunch with me? We could throw a few ideas around; see if we can make some progress. What do you think?"

Kälin looked suspicious. "Only if I can choose the restaurant."

Chapter 22

Zürich 2012

Kälin seemed on friendly terms with the staff of *Restaurant Rössli* and offered to choose for Beatrice. He ordered the same dish and when their meals arrived, Beatrice was glad she'd placed her trust in him. At least where food was concerned. A pat of herby butter melted into rivulets down a startlingly large steak, surrounded by golden chips. Substantial, greasy and just what she fancied. And it smelt divine.

"*En guete*."

"*En guete*. This looks delicious." Beatrice tucked in and chewed on a rich and juicy chunk of meat.

"If you don't like it, we can change ...?"

Beatrice shook her head. "No, not at all. I was just thinking about today." She tailed off, trying to grasp that elusive thought which kept returning, bouncing and vanishing again. She ate her food and, although deep in thought, relished every mouthful.

Kälin eyed her. "You wanted to discuss ideas?"

"Mmm. It's about that woman. I can't quite pin my finger on it, but there's something peculiar about Antonella D'Arcy."

"You don't like her."

She took a sip of red wine. "No, I don't. And the strange thing is, it bothers her. Now why on earth would that be?"

"You judged her." Kälin added salt to his chips.

"Yes, I did rather, didn't I? But why ever should she care?"

"I don't know. But your comment on her lack of conscience, at her villa, touched her. And again today, what you said about her company ..."

"Yes, I definitely seem to rub her up the wrong way. Not that she harbours a soft spot for you either. I must say, your idea to catch her off guard at the polo match was inspired."

"As was your threat that she will see us again." He stopped and Beatrice realised they had just exchanged compliments.

They ate in silence for several minutes.

"Would you mind ordering me another glass of red, Herr Kälin? I find it goes down very well with this steak."

He raised his eyebrows, but did not comment and communicated her request to the waitress.

Beatrice continued. "You know, Sabine used the word 'chameleon' to describe our killer. It's rather appropriate for D'Arcy, too."

"True. She is skilled at adapting to her environment, blending into her surroundings."

"Precisely." The waitress brought the wine. "*Danke*. And what happens to a chameleon when it has camouflaged itself blue and another environment intrudes, say, orange."

"Blue and orange? In which country is this chameleon?"

Beatrice gave him an unamused look. "What I mean is that the woman seems at odds with herself. She wanted to meet us at her home, so we would see a particular side of her. The mother, a charming woman with a weakness for macaroons. Today, she was the hard-nosed ball-breaker, out to win. It is a role, just like any other. I don't think we've met the real D'Arcy yet."

Kälin replaced his cutlery. "This is why you dislike her? Because she has two faces?"

"Partly. But I think there's something suspicious about her performance. Two of her comments stick in my mind."

"The dogs and fleas remark?"

Beatrice was surprised at his insight. "Yes. How can she judge

Belanov's business operations while she profits from all manner of dirty dealings? And the second was her attitude to the dead men. She asked if they might have developed a conscience. The implication being that their actions were sufficiently reprehensible to justify their sudden deaths."

"But where does this take us? D'Arcy didn't kill them; her alibis are solid."

"I don't think for a second that she did. But she most certainly runs with the horse and the hounds."

"And this expression means what exactly?"

"She gets the best of both worlds. I think she plays the corporate cynic, but her heart is not in it. I think she genuinely despised these men and feels no sorrow at their passing. If anything, there's a sense of righteousness. Whether she was involved or not, I don't know. At least not yet."

Kälin angled his head in a half-shrug, half-nod. "What are your thoughts on our press leak? Do you think it was just D'Arcy's opportunism after my interview?"

"No, I don't. Unless you gave her substantially more information during your second encounter, she didn't know about the DNA. Which could still mean she leaked the information, revealing she knows far more about these deaths than any old innocent witness."

"I gave her some extra information about the strength of our team but nothing about the reason we linked the killings. So, you're right, she may have shown her hand. But we still should be aware the leak may have come from within."

She met his eyes with a challenge. Deflecting attention from oneself by suspecting others was an old trick. "Yes, that thought had occurred to me."

He stared right back, giving nothing away. "It might be worth squeezing the journalist, to get him to reveal his sources."

"We can but try. Let's get a bit of background and identify his weak spots." She patted her mouth with her napkin. "Herr Kälin, your recommendation was excellent. I thoroughly enjoyed that meal."

"Good. Would you like coffee, or shall I get the bill?"

"I've taken up enough of your time. Let's pay up and head for home." Beatrice finished her wine.

Kälin hailed the waitress. "I wasn't sure you'd like this kind of farmer's food."

"Farmer's food is my favourite sort. Solid and unpretentious. Not the sort of fare they would serve in those crisp white tents at the polo park."

Kälin let out a short laugh. Beatrice cocked her head in enquiry.

"It would definitely be inappropriate at the polo park, Frau Stubbs. We've just eaten *Pferdefleisch*. Horse steak."

Chapter 23

Liechtenstein 2011

His secretary waited, as he flipped through the stack of message slips and made frequent notes. He'd noticed an air about her recently. Mouth permanently upside-down, constant worried frown and her shoulders slumped in defeat. Not the kind of attitude which added value. Ryman needed positivity, dynamism and energy. And, it had to be said, youth. Sibylle's competence was unquestionable, but she was over forty and it showed. Ryman filed the issue as something to consider over the weekend and to act upon next week. Maybe bring in an assistant, so Sibylle could train her the way he liked, then 'promote' Sibylle to a position where her skills would be better used. Out of his sight.

"Right. These have gotta be done today, the rest can wait till Monday. Is there anything else, because I'd like to hit the road pretty soon."

"No, not from my side. Your suit is ready, hanging in your closet. And I booked *Restaurant Adler* for your lunch meeting."

"Sorry? What lunch meeting?"

"That journalist, Jack. You asked me to slot her in for lunch today, as you have already cancelled on her twice."

"Hell, I don't have time to talk to a journo today. Cancel. Tell her to put some questions in an email and if I get time, I'll answer them."

"No problem. I'll cancel the reservation at the same time." She gave a sad shrug and left the room. His mind was made up. Sibylle had to go. She should know him better than that. The last thing he'd want to do before heading off for the weekend would be a chat to a hack. Let's face it, Sibylle wasn't happy here and he sure as hell wasn't happy with her. He removed his files from the drawer and laid them in his briefcase. His desk was as clear as his conscience. After a quick glance around the huge office with its view of the Kunstmuseum and the distant castle, he picked up his jacket and left the room.

Voices reached him as he locked the door, speaking that weird German he disliked. Sibylle seemed to be giving someone a hard time, judging by the tone of her voice. He rounded the corner, his expression deliberately mean and impatient. He would not be delayed. A svelte blonde in a gray suit was arguing with Sibylle, whose face registered exasperation.

"Problem, Sibylle?"

"Yes, Jack. This is the journalist who had an appointment today. She wants to reschedule your interview. I'm trying to explain to her it's not convenient."

The girl swivelled round and blushed. Cute. A natural blonde with a tiny nose and blow-job lips. His eyes flicked downward as he held out his hand. Slight figure, not all that much up top, but a killer pair of pins.

"Hi, I'm Jack Ryman. Listen, sorry for the inconvenience. You caught me at a busy time."

"Melanie Roche. Pleased to meet you, Mr Ryman. I understand that today is difficult. It's just your secretary mentioned you were leaving for Zürich this afternoon. That's where I'm based. I was wondering if there would be a window while you're there?"

"Not this weekend, Ms Roche. I'm playing in a polo match on Saturday and meeting friends on Sunday. I'm kinda all work or all play, know what I mean?"

"I see. Never mind. Perhaps I could return to Vaduz next week?"

"Nope. I'm leaving Zürich Sunday and flying to New York. I can't say when I'll be back in this office. It's only one base of many."

Sibylle folded her arms. "So, you see, Frau Roche, as I already explained, we'll call you."

A surge of irritation at Sibylle's smug manner caused him to clench his teeth. "One second. Which paper is this for?"

"I'm freelance, Mr Ryman. But this article has been commissioned by *Time* magazine. They want to give the banking world a chance to voice their side. A response from the 1% to the other 99? Here's my press pass."

He glanced at it, his mind elsewhere. "I can give you a half hour. Let's grab a sandwich. But I want to be out of here by one thirty. That do you?"

Her smile lifted her face from pretty to beautiful. The girl was a fox. "That would be great, Mr Ryman! Thank you so much."

He gestured to the lift. "Talk to you Monday, Sibylle. Have yourself a fine weekend."

Because next week, you're gonna get one hell of a shock.

"We'll take my car, as I need to dump these bags. Where are you parked?" he asked, as the doors opened into the basement parking lot.

"I came by train today, so I don't have a vehicle."

"By train? You serious? Yeah, well, I guess that's a whole lot easier here. So how are you getting back to Zürich?"

"Same way. It's not bad. I have my laptop so I can work, you know."

"You got any other business in Liechtenstein, Ms Roche?"

"No, none. I only came here to interview you."

"What say I give you a ride back to Zürich? You get to ask your questions and I get some company on the journey? That suit?"

"Really? Mr Ryman, that is so kind of you. So much more than I could have expected. I really appreciate it."

"Not a problem."

Placing his case on the back seat and hanging his jacket on the hook, Ryman made some rapid calculations based on optimistic forecasts. Taking the freeway would give him just over an hour. The scenic route could double the time they spent together, giving him chance to get past the interview and into the personal. Good thing he'd kept plans fluid. He opened the passenger door of the Audi S5 and she tucked herself in butt first, swinging her legs after her. Classy, very finishing school. She gave a quick, nervous smile up at him as he closed the door. She was intimidated. He liked that. Lucky girl. She was gonna get a whole lot more than she expected.

"I kinda like to avoid the freeway, Melanie. I figured we'd go up the other side of the lake. Takes a little longer, but gives you more time for questions."

"Whatever you like, Mr Ryman. I'm just grateful for this opportunity to talk to you."

He flashed her a benevolent smile as they emerged from the underground parking lot into the rain.

"Hell, the view's gonna be lousy if it's raining." The climate irritated him. Europe always had such shitty weather.

"It might be sunny again by the time we get there. *April, April, macht was er will.* Do you speak German, Mr Ryman?"

"Nope. Not really necessary." He waited for the inevitable. Just one snippy comment, lady, and you can walk. He stopped at lights in Schaan, his knee jumping impatiently.

"Oh. Well, it's just a saying. Basically, April does whatever it wants. I suppose the language of banking is English, so there's no need to learn anything else. You're lucky."

"Damn right. I'm an American. You're a German Swiss, right?"

"I was born in Fribourg, to a French mother and a Swiss German father. So I'm half-and-half. Where were you born?"

"You know what? You can Google all that bullshit. Let's cut to the chase here. *Time* magazine want you to get the bankers' side of the story? Well, you got a banker right here, so make the most of it. I'll tell you the truth. Because, more than most people, I can."

They crossed the border into Switzerland and he accelerated, feeling better. Open road, a weekend of fun ahead, and on Monday, he'd be back home. The journo took a notepad from her huge handbag. Why the hell did women need such epic bags? And carrying them around on one shoulder all day; in the long-term, that's gotta hurt.

"OK, Mr Ryman. Let's begin. The newspapers blame ..."

"Call me Jack. And the newspapers don't have a goddam clue who's to blame. Here's the thing. Everybody is a party to what goes on. No one is blameless. The banks have to take some responsibility, but not as much as the mortgage brokers, who set up the home buyers with real estate they couldn't afford. Add that to the central banks, reducing interest rates to stimulate liquidity. Don't forget the credit rating agencies, who gave triple-A ratings to the collaterized debt obligations, making them very attractive to those who didn't understand them. Governments? Forget it. Their aim is to keep the big boys sweet and the people passive. So everybody's got dirty hands. Sticking it to the banks is ill-informed, but typical."

She took several seconds to scribble down his words, as he turned onto St Gallerstrasse. "You see these parties as equally guilty? Although the central banks' choice to lower rates was intended to kick-start the economy, no?"

Ryman gave a tsk of exasperation. "They had to. After the dotcom collapse and 9/11, the market needed to keep cash flowing. But with lower rates, investors are forced to take bigger risks to get decent return on investment. The CDOs looked like a damn good bet. Mortgages and house prices were rising, and everyone believed they would continue to do so. You know, between 2001 and 2005, US subprime mortgages increased by 300%."

"But that kind of growth can't be sustainable."

"We're all wise after the event, right? Demand for housing was high. The economy was doing fine, people were paying their instalments, the debt obligations had guaranteed collateral. What's not to like?"

"So what went wrong?"

Ryman was enjoying this. She had him on home ground, where he was at his best.

"The real estate bubble burst. It had to happen sometime. Prices dropped, mortgages were reset, buyers couldn't pay, lenders foreclosed. Supply starts to outstrip demand. And now the collateral underpinning your debt risk is just part of that excess of supply."

Approaching Gams, their upward route remained in shadow and mist, while the sun threw an enticing light on the mountains ahead as they climbed. He drove faster.

She looked up from her notepad. "So the CDOs weren't, after all, a 'damn good bet'. Yet the investment banks were pushing them well into 2006, after the property crisis had already hit. My research tells me that around the world, CDOs issued leapt from 120 billion dollars worth in 2005 to 475 billion in 2006."

"You walk into MacDonald's and order a Big Mac with fries. You're hungry as hell and that's gonna hit the spot. You been thinking about it for the last 50 miles and now you're at the counter. Your mouth is watering; your nose is full of the smell of prime beef. Gimme a Big Mac with large fries. The kid behind the till says, No Ma'am, I can't serve you one of those. I have it on good authority that in a few years time, you'll have high cholesterol and hardened arteries. So for your own good, I'm gonna have to refuse."

"So if demand for toxic products is there, someone has to sell them. Is that what you're saying?"

"You know anything at all about economics, Melanie?"

"Can we turn to another area which has upset people? You had one of the highest severance packages of last year. People ask how this is possible, when your company went bankrupt, losing millions of dollars of shareholders' money."

"A contract is a contract. I negotiated hard before I joined Mendoza, and made sure that whatever happened, I would be remunerated for my work."

"Well done. And yet, you were the strongest advocate of performance-related pay for your top executives."

"Like I said, I fought for what I got."

"Do you think the performance-related elements contributed to these executives taking bigger and bigger risks, in order to guarantee their bonuses?"

"I guess you'd have to ask them, Melanie."

She took a couple seconds. Out of her depth and drowning. She scribbled away but you could see she knew; she'd grabbed a fully grown tiger by the tail and had nowhere to go.

Still one more try. He had to hand it to her, she didn't give in easy.

"Can I ask you about RAM's policy of buying poverty-stricken countries' debts and prosecuting them through legal loopholes? Many of our readers ask how you can demand repayment from a country which has no functioning hospitals."

"Kid, if you buy anything on credit, time's gonna come you have to pay it back. Hell, even a child can understand that. It's a matter of principle. Borrow from me, I'll want it back."

"But they didn't borrow from you. You bought their debts from someone else. How are these countries supposed to recover from civil war, drought, pandemics and so on when everything they generate goes to paying your and your investors?"

"Hey, so the system's unfair. I didn't make the system, I'm just the repo-man. Just doing my job and getting back what's owed."

"Fair point. Um, Jack, do you think we could stop quickly at a garage? I need to use the bathroom."

Her face was a little pale. Maybe the speed upset her, not just the car but the conversation. "Sure. There'll be something in this next village. You okay?"

"I'm a little dizzy. Trying to write shorthand, keep up with you and watch the road is a bit too much for me."

He shot her a wink as he pulled into the gas station. She hurried towards the rest rooms. He thought back over their conversation. Was she trying to trap him? The minute she got back in the car, he was going to ask her about her angle. If she planned to stitch him up, he would oblige, and give her totally uncensored material. A few decent sound bites would show he was unrepentant, and whining is for losers. She was back.

"Jack, I'm just going to get a bottle of water, can I get one for you?"

"I'll take a Coke. Thanks, Melanie."

Watching her walk to the shop, he knew she was watching him watching her, reflected in the glass doors. Good. Women love it when they're being admired. Fastest way to make any woman fall at your feet? Let her see you watching. Pretend to hide it. Every Jane Doe wants to be wanted. Look away that second too late. Tell Jane's best friend you're crazy about Jane, but ssh, okay? Let her think she's caught you, when she's the one who's trapped. The female ego can be used to your advantage, just like everything else. His eyes flicked to the clock. She was taking her time. How long does it take to get a water and a Coke? He looked back to the shop and saw her emerging from the restrooms once more, carrying a plastic bag.

"Sorry. Looks like I inherited my mother's Gallic stomach. I can eat anything, including snails, but movement makes me sick."

"Yeah, these roads are a little crazy. I guess the freeway woulda suited you better, right? What say we put the roof down?"

The sun had emerged with conviction, drying the roads and illuminating the landscape.

She shook her head. "As I said, April's unreliable. Maybe we're safer with the roof on."

He accelerated onto the main road with a flamboyant screech. It felt fantastic. Shit, he didn't want to talk about work anymore.

"My turn to ask some questions, Melanie." The tone of his

voice told her who was boss. His car, his company, his time, his choices. She pulled the Coke from the bag, unscrewed it and handed it to him. He took a long swig.

She drank several gulps of her water and licked her lips. "We're taking turns? So what do you want to know?"

"What's your angle? Are you really telling the other side of the story? Or are you gonna do a hatchet job?"

"That depends on what you say, Jack. We're interested in what drives the bankers, what part they played in this mess and what lessons have been learned."

Ryman didn't know this route all that well, but the sun, the car, this babe beside him and the awesome scenery encouraged him to put his foot down. The car roared along the road to Wildhaus. Life didn't get much better. Whirling up a Swiss mountain in a fine automobile, with a beautiful foreign girl at his side, a weekend of fun ahead of him and a first-class flight to New York, where they were all waiting to welcome him home. How in hell could he feel guilty?

"Jack?"

"To tell you the God's honest truth, Melanie, I don't know. As for the role we played, I'm pretty sure I answered that. We were a part of the problem, but it's not like we had an alternative. So as for lessons learned, ask around. Are humans ever gonna stop wanting more than they deserve? How can you blame people for making the most of an opportunity. You know what? If you had the chance, you'd do the same. But I'll be honest about what drives me; moments like this. I feel better than ... hey, what's up? You look terrible."

The girl's skin looked pale to start with, but now she was green. Her notebook fell into her lap and her hand lay limp, pen wedged between her fine fingers.

"Sorry, I'm so sorry. I think I need to get out. Could you pull over?" She pointed to a small lane into the forest. Sweat broke out on her forehead. She looked sick as a poisoned rat. He pulled over, driving a little way into the trees, so she'd have somewhere to hide. He was such a goddamed gent. She opened the door and lurched toward the forest, but he made no move to follow. First off, she wouldn't want a man like him to watch her puke. Second of all, he was tired. His whole body weighed him down like it was made of wet sand. He had to shape up. He fumbled for the Coke bottle and struggled to get the top off. Caffeine. He needed to sharpen his mind. She'd be back soon and most of the journey was ahead of them. Not to mention the evening. He hoped she'd stop puking by then. Wouldn't it be great if he could just throw a switch and they'd be there? In his Zürich hotel, on his king size bed, with soft pillows, white linen, and nothing to worry about. He lifted his head and looked into the brush. Nowhere, goddammit. This was the last time he gave anyone a ride.

The skirt suit rolled up in the bottom of her bag, her bag folded into her rucksack, the figure emerged in hiking hues of grey, brown and green. Her hair was stuffed under a woollen hat, and she wore hygienist's gloves. His head rested against the door, mouth open, snoring deeply. She sat still for a full five minutes, checking for any signs of movement through the trees. Satisfied, she hauled him sideways and took his place, driving the car off the track, through the forest and as far into the foliage as she could go. She altered both seats to a full recline and pulled a clear plastic bag from the pocket of her rucksack. She broke two small capsules into it and pulled it over his head, tying it tightly around his fleshy neck. She watched and waited, listening to the movements of the plastic.

In, out. In, out.

In.

Out.

She waited until the sounds ceased completely before clearing up after herself. The sun broke through the tree canopy and an idea occurred to her. It took her a few seconds to find the right switch, but she finally pressed the roof retraction button and watched the mechanics open them up like a sardine can. She got out, slammed the door and walked around to the other side.

"How's that for a hatchet job, Jack?"

Chapter 24

Zürich 2012

First chance he got, Chris intended to shake Xavier by the hand. The man was inspired, though he didn't realise it. His suggestion of a picnic on the lake was prompted by his kind nature, a sense of being the host. It would never cross Xavier's mind it meant they'd get to see Sabine and Conceição in bikinis.

But Chris spotted the whiff of opportunity instantly and had to play down his enthusiasm in case he gave himself away. Sabine was all for it, persuading a curiously reluctant Conceição. She caved finally and even got excited as they planned the route. The only drawback being that Chris couldn't ask her for a date on Friday night as well as spending all Saturday in her company. That would look over-eager. Instead, he would see if the picnic might be extended into the evening, possibly as a foursome, but at some stage ditching the other two. Play it by ear and who knows how Sunday might look.

Anticipation filled the air on Saturday morning. As Chris took the tram along the lake to the jetty, everyone seemed to be going somewhere. Twenty-seven degrees forecast for the day. Plenty hot enough to swim or sunbathe. The sun flashed off the water, reflected from car windscreens and lit hopeful faces as they set off for their weekends. Chris's grin was a match for any one of them.

"Chris! Over here!"

Conceição waved from the boat. She was wearing a wraparound sundress in bright blues and purples and wearing a headscarf. She looked stunning. Xavier, in shorts and a baseball cap, messed around with the ropes holding the boat to its moorings. He spotted Chris and motioned for him to get aboard. Chris obeyed, throwing his backpack in before clambering onto the deck. Not a luxurious vessel, but in good condition, comfortable and with a sun deck. Sabine smiled up at him from the leather banquette, shading her eyes, despite her oversized sunglasses. She wore white cut-off trousers, a white halterneck top which showed off her pale shoulders, white deck shoes and her platinum hair up in a silver clip. Chris felt he should be the one shielding his eyes.

"Am I late, or are you early?" he asked.

"Bit of both, I think. Conceição and I brought the picnic." She tapped a cool box with her foot.

Xavier threw the ropes up to Conceição and leapt on board with surprising grace. He shook Chris's hand. "We have good weather so the lake will be busy. We'll go further down, direction Rapperswil, to escape the crowds. Is everyone ready?"

Chris chose to stand next to Xavier, watching him steer a course southwards, using the shore as a guide. The speed and spray created a buzz of enjoyment in Chris and he looked round to see the girls lifting smiles into the wind.

"Is it expensive to rent a boat, Xav?" he shouted above the noise.

Xavier shook his head, maintaining his constant scan of the water. "The expensive part is taking the Captain's licence. It costs a lot of time and money and even then many people fail the test."

"You can't take a boat out without a licence?"

Xavier grinned. "Welcome to Switzerland."

Sabine sighed, shoving around the potato skins on her plate. "That was a perfect meal. You know, this has been a lovely afternoon. I hope B enjoyed herself as much at the polo match yesterday. I wouldn't want to spend a day in the company of Kälin."

Xavier helped himself to more salad. "Herr Kälin is ... special. To understand him, well, it takes a while. Anyway, I'd be very surprised if they found out anything more from D'Arcy. She's tough. I don't think she'll give much away."

"No, she'll be very cagey," Conceição agreed. "I think waiting for D'Arcy to slip up is a waste of time. In fact, I wonder if we should suggest pursuing a more dynamic approach."

Conceição poured more wine for the three of them. Xavier stuck to Ice Tea.

"What I mean is research. I think we could predict where D'Arcy is likely to strike next. Or arrange for someone else to strike. With some intelligent analysis of high-profile corporate scandals, we could pinpoint who she's likely to hit and why. Then cross-reference that data with her personal or professional contacts. I think we'd probably end up with a shortlist of around five or six men, all of whom could be tailed and the killer trapped."

Sabine pursed her lips. "It's a good idea, but Interpol would never agree to the extra expense. We couldn't tail six men for however many months ..."

Conceição shook her head. "We wouldn't have to. If we alerted the personal security these men employ, and they *all* have bodyguards, they would have the profile, know what to look for. If they suspect something, they call a professional squad and catch her or him in the act."

"It could work as a parallel approach to what we do now," agreed Xavier. "We could share these thoughts with B when she gets back."

"Yes. Why not use some time this week to prepare a presentation? B and Kälin are visiting Vaduz and St Moritz, so we have a few days. Good idea, Conceição!" Sabine's face shone pink. With her colouring, she should really keep out of the sun. Xavier too. So that left him and Conceição.

Sabine turned to him. "Chris, what do you think?"

"I need to rest and digest. I'm going to lie in the sun and think this idea over. Anyone else feel like sunbathing?"

Predictably, Xavier and Sabine shook their heads.

"I'll come with you." Conceição stood up. "I want to explain exactly what I mean."

Xavier, once again, set up the perfect circumstances, suggesting a drink to round off the day. Sabine seemed reluctant, glancing at her watch. Chris willed her to refuse, especially because Conceição agreed easily. But she gave another of her disappointed sighs and said yes.

Wandering up the Niederdorf, Chris just followed Xavier. The choice of bars, restaurants, cafés and beer gardens was overwhelming. Xavier, whose nose was sunburnt, guided them up a side street to Bar Corazon and recommended the *Weissbier*. Conceição and Chris took up the challenge, but Sabine ordered a mineral water, claiming dehydration.

"This is a great area," enthused Conceição. "I've never come this far off the main streets. Good tip, thanks, Xavier."

"You're welcome. Yes, it's always lively at the weekends. And there are several art cinemas around here, where you can see films which are not so commercial."

Conceição looked up. "I noticed. *Gainsbourg* is playing this weekend. I'd love to see that film."

Chris seized his moment. "Me too. I've heard such great things about it. How about checking it out later?" He remembered his manners. "What do you say, Sabine, Xav?"

To his delight, Xavier pulled an apologetic face. "I'm sorry, Chris, I can't. I have an appointment this evening."

Sabine's nose wrinkled. "No. I've had enough for today. I prefer to go back to my apartment."

Chris shrugged. "Looks like it's just you and me, Conceição."

She hesitated and glanced at Sabine. "Could we see it another evening? Sabine and I already arranged to have dinner and watch a video tonight."

"No problem. Hey, here comes the beer. *Prost*, everyone, and thanks to Xavier for a great day out."

They raised their glasses and Chris drank deeply. Choosing to spend both weekend evenings in the company of that sour-faced little ferret instead of him? It didn't give him much confidence in Conceição's taste. As he met each pair of eyes for the toast, he saw Sabine's smug expression reflecting off every surface.

Chapter 25

Zürich 2012

She should have called James. Just because there had been no real signs, and she was preoccupied with the case, she hadn't. She'd cancelled their session, choosing to send him a jaunty text message instead. She regretted it now. She lay under the duvet, staring at the ceiling. Foolhardy and irresponsible. The only way to cope with the dogs is to consciously, constantly manage them. And she'd done extremely well. Weekends were a danger zone, so Beatrice prepared herself with care. As other people's anticipation built on Friday afternoons, Beatrice's dread of forty-eight hours of nothing grew in inverse proportion.

She'd taken to arranging a cultural event on Fridays; the opera, a concert in one of the churches, a play by the English-speaking theatre group, giving her something else to think about. Saturdays she did some shopping, had lunch at Ken's and spent the afternoon writing a report on the week's activities for Lyon. Saturday night was her television programme evening, for which she would cook something special. And on Sundays, she explored. A long hike up Uetliberg, a trip to Schaffhausen's waterfalls, a wander around the animal park; anything that tired her out before returning to her apartment and making her Sunday phone calls home. But this week, she had slipped up, due to the polo match yesterday. And found herself with a long empty Sunday ahead of her, when the dogs were pacing.

This time tomorrow, she would be preparing for work, with a routine to follow. All she had to do was weather the next twenty-four hours. Whether she liked it or not.

Whether the weather be mild or whether the weather be not,
Whether the weather be cold or whether the weather be hot,
We'll weather the weather whatever the weather,
Whether we like it or not.

Tears leaked into her hair as she recalled her mother reciting the verse. It would not do. She sat up. Find something to engage your mind. Force yourself. Shower, breakfast, read the news. But even as she threw back the duvet and headed for the bathroom, she felt defeated and tearful, in the knowledge that whatever images were dominant on the news website would drag her down, with their litany of cruelty, hunger, disease and abuse. So leave the news alone. She would not spend a day weeping over the death of a maltreated child, or the struggle to survive in a war-ravaged African state. When she had one of these days, even feel-good stories gave rise to agonies. Sweet that a little kitten had been rescued from a chimney breast, but what about all those poor wretched animals kept in cages and beaten so their meat is tender when eaten?

She'd taken her pills without fail so it did seem odd to find herself dragged into such depths without warning. Yesterday, she'd felt quite energised and chirpy, only to wake with this black shroud. Beatrice realised she was standing in front of the sink, staring at the bath mat. It would not do. With a shake, she got into the shower.

At quarter to ten, she put a bottle of water and mini-pack of After Eights into her handbag with her guidebook and walked with determination to the Hauptbahnhof. She would decide where to go when she got there. *Think positive.* One of the wonderful things about Switzerland was you could go anywhere by train. All those magical sounding names; Prague, Dijon, Lugano, Geneva, Bellinzona ... but not one of them held the attraction of Brampford Speke. International adventures at her fingertips when all she wanted to do was potter around Tesco's with Matthew. She shook herself. This was going to be a bad one. Staring up at the departures board in the huge hall of the main station, her vision was blurred with tears. It just wouldn't do. Perhaps she should just go back to bed. *Make your mind up, for heaven's sake.*

A blonde woman in a Grace Kelly dress and white neckerchief stood beside her, looking up at the board. She glanced at Beatrice and gave a polite smile. It took a considerable effort for Beatrice to do the same. Then the woman did a double take.

"Oh, hello again. I recognise you from Big Ben. The tea shop? You're the crossword expert, right?"

Beatrice gawped at the woman for a moment before her memory recovered itself. Glossy blonde hair, a perfectly made-up face and astonishingly white teeth; the Tatler woman.

"Yes, well. I can hardly be called an expert. I seem to recall you were the one who assisted Ken."

"That was a one-off. I'm normally useless with those things. So when I figured it out, I just couldn't keep it to myself. I'm Madeleine Lassiter."

"Beatrice Stubbs." She shook the proffered hand, observing that Madeleine was married and wore false nails. "Nice to meet you."

"Same here. So, where are you headed today, Beatrice?"

A panicky sense of incompetence swelled in Beatrice's throat. She looked back at the board and grabbed a name at random. "Interlaken. I've heard it's beautiful. And you?"

"Oh, I'm not actually travelling. But some Sundays, when my husband has to work, I just like to come down here and enjoy the bustle. There's not a whole lot else to do with all the stores closed and I get bored of my own company."

The woman's truthful reply touched Beatrice. "I know what you mean. I usually organise trips for myself at the weekends. Keeps me occupied."

"I hear you. Say, you're a little early, aren't you?"

Beatrice checked the departure time and saw she had picked a train due to depart in forty minutes. Small talk with a stranger would be an excellent distraction.

"Yes, I have a pathological horror of being late. But I was planning to have a cup of coffee first. I wonder if you'd like to join me?"

"Sure, I'd like that. How about that place?" Madeleine indicated some incongruously rustic benches in the main hall. "We could sit outside and people-watch. And that way I can smoke, too."

She pulled open her bag and dug out some cigarettes, offering the pack to Beatrice.

"I don't, thank you."

"Good for you. I'd given up until I got here. Seven years as a non-smoker. But you're never really free of the weed."

"No, I suppose not. I never tried, so I think I'll keep it that way."

At least Madeleine was considerate, fanning the smoke away, as they settled at a table outside *Brasserie Federal*. Beatrice noted the Chopard watch, studded with diamonds. Up close, the immaculate grooming was no less impressive, although she did look unhealthily thin. Beatrice suspected diet pills. Madeleine seemed to be assessing her in a similar way, but was unlikely to come to the same conclusion.

Beatrice did her duty. "I'm guessing from your accent that you're not Swiss."

"Nope. I'm from Michigan. But you come from Great Britain, right?"

The waiter appeared.

"Hi there. We'd like two coffees, please. Cafe latte okay for you, Beatrice?"

Although Beatrice generally disliked the common assumption everyone should speak English, Madeleine's manner towards the young man was friendly and pleasant. He gave her a smile as he took their order and returned back through the glass doors.

Beatrice looked up at the gigantic blue angel hanging from the roof of the Haupthalle. "Yes, I'm British. A Londoner. Lived there all my life."

"London's so cool. A great city. So why are you in Zürich?"

"Same as most expatriates in Switzerland. I'm here to work."

"Right. Banking?"

Beatrice deflected the question. "More advisory. What about you?"

"I represent the other expat trend. The spouses and significant others. My husband works in finance, so we're here on a two-year contract before heading back to New York." Her introduction was rehearsed, probably through repetition, yet a wistful note could be heard in her sigh.

"I see. And does he often have to work at the weekend?"

"He does at the moment. So I'm left to shop, or read, or explore the galleries on my own. It works out pretty well. When Michael is free, he always wants to do something active. Ski, hike, cycle, you name it. The cultural stuff doesn't interest him, whereas I love it."

"So do I. Much more stimulating than hurtling down a mountain. I'm the antithesis of active, I'm afraid."

Madeleine's smile bloomed and faded, like a distant firework. "I like both. But whether it's snowboarding or a jazz concert, I prefer to have someone to share it with. You know what? During my first couple weeks here, I got so lonely that if I heard someone speaking English, I'd deliberately bump into them so I could start a conversation. That's why I hang out at places like Big Ben. Just for someone to talk to."

The woman's honest need for companionship shamed Beatrice. There was such a thing as trying to be too independent. The coffees arrived, with the bill rolled up in a shot glass.

Beatrice picked it up, making a decision. "I'll get this, Madeleine. You can buy next time. Now listen, I think I'll give Interlaken a miss today. Have you been to the Kunsthaus at all? They're open on Sundays and have the most fabulous collection."

Madeleine's smile lasted much longer that time.

The dogs were quiet. Temporarily.

Chapter 26

Zürich 2012

The package in locker 939 at Baden Station contained no surprises. Just a Pay-As-You-Go mobile. The figure, aware of curious glances from the teenagers loitering on the concourse, moved outside to the sunshine. Noisier, certainly, but far better cover. Taxi drivers looked up enquiringly, so the figure walked away in search of some privacy, phone in hand.

Eight minutes later, it rang.

"This week. Do it as soon as you can."

"Tuesday's a good day. Fewer tourists. Latest, Wednesday. I want to be back in Zürich for Thursday evening. "

"Excellent. So you're ready with the other one?"

"Almost. It's not going to be difficult. Just a question of timing. And timing is one of my strong points."

"I can't argue with that. I'd like this finished by the weekend. Then I'll take the heat while both of you get away for a holiday."

"No problem. Get away where?"

"Wherever you want to go. Maldives, Seychelles, Acapulco? Take a break until you feel ready to go back to work."

"Back to work? So you've changed your mind about it being the last one?"

The voice contained a smile. *"No, no. It's definitely the last one. I was talking about your* real *work. Complete by Saturday, take her on holiday somewhere and you can go back to tending the Third*

World when you feel the time is right. I'll arrange everything. Now, do you foresee any problems?"

"Not in Ticino. It's all scoped and everything's in position. You're going to love my artistic flair with this one. Inspired, even if I say so myself. Rosaria will approve." The figure laughed. "As for here, at such short notice, I think I can organise something prosaic but effective. Unless you want something more fitting."

"I'd rather it wasn't prosaic. In fact, if you don't mind, I've chosen the method I find most appropriate. And the ideal location, too. It's achingly apt. One might even say this is poetic justice. The details are on their way via our friend. Just make sure the evidence is planted somewhere other than the scene."

"Why?"

"Because I want to be sure they find it. Shouldn't be complicated, so I'm sure you'll find an opportunity. I'm leaving tomorrow but I'll be back on Saturday morning. If anything remains unfinished, it puts me in an awkward position."

"I know. I'll contact you as soon as the job's complete."

"If anything goes wrong, I can always delay my flight. Just let me know."

"Relax. Nothing will go wrong."

After the call was over, the figure put the phone in the padded envelope, posted it and headed back to the car, all the while softly singing their song.

" ... *And I can take or leave it if I please.*"

Chapter 27

Liechtenstein, St Moritz 2012

"Sibylle Keller, Jack Ryman's PA. It is a pleasure to meet you. We can speak in here. Can I get you some refreshments?"

Beatrice and Kälin both accepted a coffee, and Frau Keller disappeared into a side room. The immense office had glass walls, offering a view right up to the castle. Liechtenstein fascinated Beatrice. What appeared to be a simple turn off the motorway was the gateway to a tiny principality, with its own monarchy, number plates and tax laws.

The woman returned and joined them at the conference table, placing a tray with two tiny cups, two small glasses of water, and a bowlful of chocolates in front of them.

She smiled. "So how can I help you?"

Kälin ripped open his colourful paper tube of sugar and poured it into his cup. Without thinking, Beatrice handed over hers. He took it with a nod and repeated the procedure.

"Thank you for talking to us, Frau Keller. We are attempting to clarify the details surrounding the death of Jack Ryman. I know you have spoken to the local police on more than one occasion, but we would like to try your patience once again."

The woman gave a genuine smile. Pepper and salt hair formed a curly frame around her face; the onset of laughter lines around her hazel eyes. Her navy suit was smart yet subtle, and she projected an air of effortless efficiency. A young Joan Plowright came to mind. Beatrice had a feeling they might get along.

"I would like to help in any way I can. My opinion, like that of everyone else who knew him, is simple. Jack did not take his own life."

"Thank you. In the police report, you state when he left the office, he was accompanied by a journalist. They planned to have lunch together," Beatrice prompted.

"Correct. Melanie Roche had made three appointments and on both previous occasions, Jack cancelled at the last minute. But that day, he gave her half an hour."

"That's not long for lunch," observed Kälin.

"No. That was typical of Jack. Everything done in a hurry. In fact, he asked me to cancel Ms Roche again that day. But he met her as he came out of his office and decided to give her a brief interview."

"Why did he change his mind?" asked Beatrice, unwrapping a chocolate.

Frau Keller glanced from her to Kälin, apparently searching for the right words.

"Was Ms Roche attractive, Frau Keller?" Kälin helped her.

"Yes. Young, blonde and very pretty. Just Jack's type. I wasn't surprised when he changed his mind. Although I know they didn't have lunch at *Restaurant Adler*, where I made the reservation, because the owner called me to complain. I don't know where they went."

Beatrice made a note. "Do you remember anything else about this woman, Frau Keller?"

Judging by her stillness and her frown, she was concentrating hard on recalling every detail. A detective's favourite kind of witness.

"Very pretty, early thirties, I would guess. Pale complexion, light-blue eyes. Minimal make-up. She wore a dove-grey skirt suit, which could have been Jaeger. Rather than a blouse underneath, she wore a scoop-necked T-shirt, which was powder blue. She had a silver chain around her neck, with no pendant. I seem to have crystal earrings in mind, Swarovski, but that could be because she told me she was from Zürich. Her press pass looked authentic, and she said she'd been commissioned by *Time* magazine. Her Swiss German was more Luzern than Zürich, and she wore low heels. Black, if I remember well."

Beatrice raised her eyebrows. "If only everyone remembered in such detail, our job would be so much easier. Thank you, Frau Keller. So Jack Ryman left with Ms Roche at 12.45?"

"Closer to one."

Kälin replaced his cup. "Can you think of anyone else who might have wanted to harm him?"

Frau Keller's face creased with amusement. "I'm sorry, Herr Kälin, but it might be easier for me to give you a list of the people who didn't despise Jack Ryman. Not one person who worked for the man had any respect for the way he did business. I don't approve of people acting as judge, jury and executioner, which is why I want to help find the person who killed him. But if I can be completely honest with you, the world is a better place now he's gone."

Beatrice nodded. "And one last thing: Ryman's car: automatic or manual?"

"Automatic, Frau Stubbs. Can I get you more coffee?"

The safety bar locked into place, the machinery hummed and the ground dropped away from them. Tugged into the air, Beatrice's stomach took a second to catch up. A rush of childish excitement filled her and it was all she could do not to shout 'Wheee!' in a high-pitched voice. Given the circumstances, however, that would have been quite inappropriate. Kälin sat grimly beside her, while Herr Müller and Herr Franchi of the Kantonspolizei occupied the chair behind. The two officers probably spent much of their time scampering up and down mountains and Kälin must have grown up on skis. Her frivolity would stand out like a sore thing, so she chose to stay quiet as if visiting a crime scene via a chair lift was a totally commonplace occurence. Keeping a check on her exhilaration, she looked down at the receding car park, the people becoming as featureless as Lowry's matchstick men. She gazed around at the vibrant shades of late spring, relishing the rush of air round her ears, watching the everyday details diminish. Tops of trees skimmed past, almost close enough to touch. She lifted her head to watch the absurdly slight cable winching them to the top, before focusing on their destination. Even as summer approached, the peak remained white and crisply delineated against the blue sky. A sigh of admiration at such pure, powerful beauty escaped her and she turned to Kälin to share the moment. He faced forward, his expression pale and set.

"Herr Kälin?"

"I'm fine, Frau Stubbs. Just a small problem with heights."

Beatrice hid her amusement at finding a chink in Karl Kälin's defences and patted his arm.

"Nearly there now."

After they dismounted from the lift, she watched him taking conscious deep breaths. Herr Franchi leapt onto the platform and indicated two snowmobiles parked beside the station. He handed Beatrice a helmet. Relieved that she had plumped for the trouser suit that morning, she straddled the machine and clutched the officer's jacket. He accelerated and sped off toward the piste. Her attempts to stop grinning were unsuccessful, so she relaxed and beamed her way down the mountain. Why had she never done this before? It was terrific fun. Snow flew up as they skimmed the surface, her cold nose inhaled Alpine air and the speed at which her driver attacked the slopes made Beatrice want to throw back her head and whoop. This is not a holiday, she reminded herself.

The Kantonspolizei Graubünden had been enormously helpful. Their records were well organised, enabling the detectives to respond to all their questions efficiently. Dougie Thompson.

Booked two weeks in St Moritz, only lived till the end of the first. He skied daily, taking difficult, off-piste runs, while his wife spent her days in the wellness centre. The two children attended *Skischule*, group lessons in the morning, individual tuition in the afternoon. Thompson left on Sunday afternoon to tackle terrain near Morteratsch, one of the less accessible off-piste routes. His wife raised the alarm at 12.10 on Monday.

"According to your report, she received an SMS from her husband on Sunday afternoon?" asked Kälin.

Herr Müller checked his notes. "Exactly. A message was sent from his phone on Sunday at 16.55, saying the weather was bad. It said he planned to stay at a lodge on the mountain overnight and try the run the following day. So his wife did not become concerned until Monday lunchtime."

"Excuse my ignorance, Herr Müller; I'm not familiar with this region. He was reported missing at midday on Monday. His body was located on Tuesday morning. So why did it take so long to find him?" enquired Beatrice.

"That's a good question, Frau Stubbs. Normally, a lost skier would be found much faster."

Officer Franchi chimed in. "However, bad weather from Sunday to Monday meant that search teams could not achieve much. Rescuers located him on Tuesday morning, and he was not registered at any lodge on Sunday night."

"Time of death was established as 36 to 48 hours earlier," added Müller.

Franchi carried on. "It was clear his death was no accident. The Stapo found his clothes and his drinking flask beside him."

"Suicide." said Müller. "We see this frequently. It is not an unpleasant way to die. Alcohol makes you sleep; your body temperature drops and your vital organs cannot survive hypothermia. These alcohol-related winter deaths look like accidents, but the truth is that many are deliberate."

Franchi's expression revealed some irritation with his gloomy partner. "His wife was convinced there was something wrong.

She insisted that Stadtpolizei called us and that we contacted Interpol."

Beatrice sympathised with the police, but had it not been for the family's insistence that something wasn't right, they would not have checked the body for DNA.

"Did you run a toxicology report, Herr Franchi?"

"Yes, this was performed on Wednesday afternoon. After we found the saliva on his flask. And the condoms in his pocket."

The roar of the snowmobile dropped and after far too short a ride in Beatrice's opinion, the officer pulled over towards the trees. He cut the engine and turned to assist Beatrice. Aware she looked suspiciously as if she was enjoying herself, she forced some sobriety into her expression as she turned to greet Kälin and Müller.

"Here is the site. The body was found like this." Officer Müller arranged himself in the snow to give them the picture, for a second, before pushing himself to his feet. "Easy to imagine that he drank the alcohol, undressed and went to sleep."

Franchi chipped in. "But he sent a message on his mobile to his wife, knowing no one would be concerned until after the storm."

Beatrice thought aloud. "So if this was not suicide, or an accident, someone else wrote that message."

Kälin frowned. "I find that hard to believe. Possibly Thompson was forced to write it himself. How could this person plausibly write a message from husband to wife? Even with a certain amount of familiarity, can a stranger reproduce the tone, the terms of affection used between a couple, without in-depth knowledge of their relationship?"

Beatrice wondered for an instant what terms of affection Kälin would use for his significant other, if he had one.

Franchi nodded. "That's an interesting point, Herr Kälin. Because the wife had no doubt it was from him. He referred to her as *Hon*. Our unit assumed Hon was the short form of

Honorable. But it seems that is a foreshortened version of Honey, an endearment like *Schätzli* in Swiss German, or *Darling* in English."

"What I don't understand, Herr Müller, is how someone could know that he would be here, at this precise time?" Beatrice asked.

Müller and Franchi exchanged a look. Franchi spoke. "Nor do we, to be honest, Frau Stubbs. The only lead we have is the children's ski instructor. Thompson told his wife that he was going to do a run recommended by one of the staff at the *Skischule.* After questioning the boy, it seems Thompson spent a lot of time talking to this particular woman, and had asked her to go with him on more than one occasion. It seems that on Sunday afternoon, she agreed. The son only knew her as Anni, but he mentioned that she understood Portuguese. Julia Thompson comes from Brazil and both children speak Portuguese as easily as English."

Müller agreed. "And when we uncovered this link, we checked with the *Skischule* on Thursday. Ana-Maria Lima, a Brazilian, had left their employment on the previous Friday. She only worked there a month. Seasonal workers, it happens a lot here. We weren't able to trace her."

"And why do you think he was he carrying condoms?" asked Beatrice.

The three men looked at the ground.

Beatrice clapped her gloves together. "I see. So if someone set a honey-trap and lay in wait to kill him, how would that person escape?"

Franchi's slight smile indicated admiration. "Down the run. You can't go back up. And this one is a real challenge, so whoever it was must have been an expert. Not only that, but the conditions on Sunday evening and Monday were horrible. I am skiing since two years old, and have done this run on many occasions. But I would never attempt it in bad weather."

Beatrice shivered as a breeze lifted her hair. Müller noticed.

"Should we go down? Or is there anything else you would like to see?"

"How are we getting down?" asked Kälin, with some concern.

Frost decorated the ends of Müller's moustache. "As I said, Herr Kälin, you can't go back. The lifts are not insured for return journeys. We'll take the snowmobiles across to the cable car."

Kälin blanched and Beatrice replaced her helmet. "Herr Franchi, I do envy you working in such a spectacular location."

"Thank you, Frau Stubbs, but like everything else, after a while, you get used to it."

He started up the machine and Beatrice looked back. No matter how many mountains she climbed, she doubted she'd ever get used to it. And, she smiled to herself, neither would Kälin.

As the BMW rolled along Route 3 towards Chur, Beatrice sifted through the facts. A Portuguese speaker and an expert skier. Must also speak English to access Ryman and Edwards. Maybe van der Veld, too. Knowledge of pharmaceuticals and time to embed herself into the situation ahead of the event. Not to mention the detailed background information on each of these men. The woman had just too many advantages.

Kälin's growl drew her back to the present. "Frau Stubbs? Does anything strike you?"

Beatrice spoke without hesitation. "She's not alone. She has an accomplice who possibly performs the heavy stuff. Maybe she acts as a lure; she is most likely very attractive. Or one is the researcher and one the actor. The amount of information she has allows for intricate preparation. She knows so much, not just what these men did, but she is aware of their weaknesses. Remember what D'Arcy said about Belanov? A penchant for women with ginger hair. According to Xavier, he left the Brno arms fair with a redhead the day he died. One person to house all these skills? It's too much for me."

"I agree. I support your theory the killer has been carefully briefed. She has enough time to gather a sample of DNA to leave at each scene. And a varied source of it. Saliva, hair. The preparation must be immense, so this is a full-time job. There must be some kind of back-up."

Beatrice looked across at his profile. "You can understand why Chris and Conceição lean towards a professional hit."

"They overlook the other link. D'Arcy Roth. The person who caused these deaths had a great deal of information on all these men, both personal and ..."

The theme from *The Godfather* rose tinnily from Kälin's jacket. He pulled over to the kerb before answering the call. His gruff tones indicated it was work related, so Beatrice studied his severe expression as he listened.

"*Scheisse*!" He closed the phone, glanced in the mirror and wrenched the car around, facing the direction they had come. He accelerated, shaking his head.

"This is getting ridiculous. That was Xavier Racine. The Ticinese police have found the body of Giuseppe Esposito on the Valle Verzasca dam."

"Esposito? He was the lawyer who defended that airline ..."

"Hermair. Yes. He killed himself today. The police think his suicide looks suspicious. They found some skin underneath his fingernails. Not his."

Beatrice tucked her hands under her armpits, feeling unsettled and cold.

"You think this is another one of hers? How did it happen?"

"The man was infamous for defending a negligent airline. It seems he went bungee-jumping from the top of the dam, but rather than the rope being around his feet, it was around his neck."

Beatrice tensed. "How high is this dam?"

"Two hundred and twenty metres. This is not going to be easy, Frau Stubbs. A bungee rope contains elastic, to ensure the impact is not too great. Esposito, or our vengeful friend, used normal rope. As a result, his head came off."

Beatrice pressed her palms to her eyes and swallowed.

Chapter 28

Lago di Vogorno 2012

First sun hit the slopes above as he descended. The thrust and push of muscle thrilled less now, and weariness encouraged him to use his poles more as support than motivation. Yet a feeling of achievement transcended his fatigue. Seventeen days had transformed him. Taut buttocks, powerful thighs, cyclist's calves; he had a body to admire. His breathing was calm and he felt a relaxation, the kind only physical exertion could deliver. He would sleep tonight, deep and dreamless. Lean body, clean mind. Lean. He loved that word. Fat dropping away, baggage left behind, and a cleaner, leaner Sepp emerged. Who could have known that divorce was a man's best friend?

The sun rose higher, turning the sky a fishmonger's palette of red, silver and gold, and he watched an aircraft begin its descent to Locarno. He picked up his pace; experience had taught him when the sun hit the valley, it got hot and uncomfortable. Onto the straight now and he could move as fast as he liked. Freedom made him lean. While married, he was flabby, weighted down, hindered by responsibility and care for others. Divorcing Rosaria propelled him out into the world and he flew. Focused and free, he soared. He was a winner. The victor. Not only was his name recognised in Europe, but now the wider world had heard of Giuseppe Esposito. And his critics could go fuck themselves; he played the hard game and he won.

He caught his first sight of the dam as he emerged from the trees. In this light, if he didn't look directly, he could imagine the thousands of tonnes of concrete as water, tumbling, rushing and roaring to the bottom. But he did look directly. His eyes were drawn to it, just as they always were. The scale of this edifice would always impress him. A shocking smooth expanse of white between the beard of the cliffs, a dramatic V to draw the eye down, the elegant man-made arch which stood in the way of nature. Not the time to stop and marvel at the engineering, he'd be back tomorrow. Yet he interrupted his rhythm to pull off his fleece and sip some water. It was getting warm.

Pushing the car door shut, Beatrice caught Kälin's impatient look. It wasn't closed. She tried again. This time, the mechanics shut audibly and he walked away. She followed, her mood darkening as she spotted the thin crowd of ghouls standing behind the police tape. The late afternoon sun shone into her eyes, so that the individual moving down the slope towards them was a mere silhouette in uniform.

"Herr Kälin! *Es freut mich sehr Sie zu sehen.*" The men shook hands.

"*Grüezi,* Herr Valletta. Nice to see you too. This is Frau Stubbs, from Scotland Yard, London."

Herr Valletta turned sideways and she saw a genial pair of dark eyes light up. "Scotland Yard? It is me a pleasure, Frau Stubbs. Come please."

They threaded a path through police vehicles, TV crews and of particular interest to Beatrice, a catering van, before emerging next to the dam itself. She took a breath, amazed by the immense amount of concrete spanning the valley, and another as she looked down. The dam shot downwards, like the point of a colossal arrow, to a rocky riverbed below. As the light diminished, Beatrice looked up and watched the sun sinking slowly toward the mountain. She realised the urgency of making the most of the light. So did Kälin.

"The body?"

"In the morgue. We can go there later. But the site is more interesting. The bungee operators arrived just before nine today and noticed something wrong. We got a team down there by eleven hours. Freshly dead. The torso was found 420 metres from the head. Much damage. The coroner suggested to escalate this case. We searched the platform and found his poles. After testing, the team discovered this DNA. So we called you. Do you want to see the site?"

Despite her unease, Beatrice nodded. The officer marched with confident familiarity down the path to the dam. Beatrice had an urge to hold Kälin's hand. For his sake, naturally, not hers.

Sepp thanked his mental discipline for getting him out of bed while it was still dark, so that he could arrive at Vogorno at this time in the morning. The sun lit the forest behind him, transforming it into a kaleidoscope of shivering jade, teal, emerald, lime, bottle and leaf. Across the valley, a blank dark-green mass promised shade and coolness, enticing him across, luring him in. He replaced his water bottle in the pocket of his rucksack, picked up his poles and headed down towards the dam. At the rate he was moving, he would escape the strengthening rays around halfway across, a moment of natural beauty.

One could feel part of the planet here, sensing the history of earth, the dynamics of geography, the joy of rock formations, water reflecting sky. Yet the human influence stood out. Mastery of nature and its forces was one of the most striking things about the valley. The dam – its magnificence, its power, its strength against millions of tons of water – was a testament to the will of man. And he was part of it. Alone on this enormous edifice, staring into the abyss below, he felt a pride and nobility in his homeland, his people, himself. Emotion rose in him as he stared down the valley. There were people in this world who shot for the stars, who could achieve greatness. How many people had told Dr Lombardi that his beautiful concrete arch, holding back the whole of Lago di Vogorno, was an impossible dream? Yet, here it was. Lombardi ignored the disbelievers, and built something both fundamentally practical and aesthetically magnificent.

Rosaria would always be a chicken, scratching at the ground, head down, pecking at scraps. She'd always dragged him down. He might remarry, it was imaginable, but this time he would choose a genuine partner. Someone who complemented his lifestyle and was as free with her admiration as his ex had been with her criticism. He wanted a woman who had vision, who could see his potential and help him reach the stars. At the centre point of the dam, he left the light, stepping into the shadow of the mountain.

Kälin crossed the dam on Beatrice's right, looking out at the lake, allowing her the dramatic view of the valley below. Had she not known about his vertigo, she would have presumed it a chivalrous gesture. Ahead there was some sort of structure, with a platform protruding over the edge. Something about it made Beatrice hesitate. Dusk bled colour from the scene.

"The bungee-jumping station is the centre point of the dam. It is very popular; everyone wants to be James Bond. This is where Esposito jumped, or was pushed. Come, I show you." Herr Valletta offered his hand to guide Beatrice beneath the various supports and up onto the platform.

Kälin shook his head. "I wait here. I will be of no use up there."

Valletta shrugged. "You see, Frau Stubbs, the jumpers put on a harness, climb up here, and throw themselves off the edge. It is thrilling, but totally safe. The operation is run by professionals with the highest safety standards. The elastic rope drops you 220 metres, you bounce a few times, and they winch you back up. Now, Signor Esposito had no harness, simply a noose around his neck. The rope was only 80 metres long, and attached to the grid above us. For a suicide, it was not a quiet way to go."

Four small steps took Beatrice closer to the edge. She gripped the barrier and leant forward. To leap off here would be a horrifying prospect, attached to elastic or not. The floor of valley below looked many miles away and full of unreceptive materials. Bungee-jumping would not be on her list of things to do once retired. She gave a shiver and turned back to Valletta. The sight was no more appealing. He held a noose in gloved hands.

"The rope, tied with great security to the main structure, which was around his neck. We have not moved it."

"There's not much blood, considering ..." Beatrice could not quite say the words.

Valletta shook his head. "No, you're right. But the impact was so great that his head came off quite cleanly, leaving the body to continue to the ground. There is much blood on the dam below, if you want to see."

"Perhaps not tonight. The rope has been tested?"

"The rope, the bungee station, everything. There's nothing here but Esposito's prints. But not many. None on the metal to which this rope was attached, for example. And the rope is standard marine use, you can buy it anywhere."

Beatrice edged back to the small steps, away from the edge. Kälin was looking the other way. "Herr Valletta, if someone did this to him, how could they manage it?"

"The laboratory can help us there. They discovered traces of a sedative around his mouth, similar to chloroform, but nothing in his blood or urine. It is possible that someone disabled him, then dragged him up here, put the rope around his neck, and ..."

"How many kilos did he weigh?" interrupted Kälin as they descended.

"Eighty-two."

"Not possible. To lift eighty kilos up these steps? No, someone could not do that alone." Kälin dismissed the idea.

Valletta thought about it. "If he was strong enough, he could.

I have seen labourers lift two sacks of cement, each weighing fifty kilos."

The sun dipped below the mountain, leaving them in rapidly cooling shadow. Beatrice took Kälin's point on board. "As you say, Herr Valletta, if he were strong enough. Perhaps we should head to the morgue? This skin under his fingernails ..."

"Yes, this is how we found the DNA. He had damages to his hands, of course, but our coroner is a careful man. On Esposito's right hand, someone else's skin was under two of his nails. He also had a rosary tied to his wrist."

The lake glinted and flashed in the early sunshine, trying to attract Sepp's attention, to pull his gaze from the other side, the valley below. Yet, the natural beauty of the lake could not compare to the elegant intervention of man. He had performed this hike eleven times already, each time getting off one stop earlier from Contra to improve his fitness, and each time, he was no less awed by the Verzasca dam.

As his eyes adjusted to the shade, he saw a figure on the platform of the bungee jump. That was early; they were never normally around at this time. It could be a special event; they might be doing a film, or a photo shoot. Although he couldn't see a crew. He kept up his pace, eyes fixed on the figure at the edge. It seemed to be praying. Sepp looked behind him, and ahead, straining his eyes to see if there was anyone else around. The dark shape took on more detail as he strode closer and he saw it was a woman. No harness, no elastic, and she seemed to be holding something to her face. A rosary. His body temperature dropped and his stride faltered.

She was kissing a rosary. He stopped, resting his poles silently against the rope barrier which marked the jumpers' area. Her words were inaudible, but the tone of impassioned prayer was recognisable and he understood. Standing in such a place, wearing black, and at this hour, there could be only one reason. He slipped off his rucksack and reached for his mobile phone.

Keeping his eye on her, he dialled the emergency number of *la polizia*. At that moment, an idea dawned, and he locked his handset. If a reputation could be reclaimed, if individual heroism and courage could dilute cynical business decisions and public scandal, here was a golden opportunity. This was a challenge and a potential gift. Sepp took his chance.

Walking boots and metal steps up to the platform did not make it easy to be stealthy, but he reached halfway up the steps before he could hear her words.

"*Salve, Regina, madre di misericordia, vita, dolcezza e speranza nostra, salve. A te ricorriamo, esuli figli di Eva; a te sospiriamo, gementi e piangenti in questa valle di lacrime.*"

His instinct advised him to go no further. In trying to save her, the ultimate stupidity would be in frightening her and making her fall. She continued and he joined in.

"*O clemente, o pia, o dolce Vergine Maria.*"

She stopped, but did not turn. "Get back! Get away from me."

"I won't move. I'm here, on these steps. Do you want to check?"

She stiffened, but flung a rapid look backwards, before facing forward once more. "Please go from here. I need solitude."

Younger than he thought. Wild eyes, thin trembling body.

"Of course. I will be happy to give you what you want. But I see you are a Catholic, signora, like me, and I have the most terrible feeling that you want to commit a cardinal sin. My faith allows me no choice but to try to prevent you from throwing yourself into Eternal Hell."

"I am NOT a Catholic! I no longer believe. And my choice is already made. You cannot stop me. Please, I beg you, just go."

"*Va bene.* Fine, I'll go. A non-Catholic who does the rosary. Before I go, will you just tell me your name?"

Her back did not move, apart from the occasional shiver. "Why?"

"So when you've gone, I can find out all about you and shake my head, and say 'Oh Luisa/Ana/Grazia, it didn't have to end that way. It will happen, I guarantee it."

"My name is Mara. But it does have to end this way. This is my will. And no one can change this. I deserve eternal damnation."

"Funny, my ex-wife says the same thing about me. But I'm not standing over a 200-metre drop; I'm planning to hike to Brione. What's the difference?"

"You haven't killed someone."

His mind whirled through possibilities. She wasn't a teenager; she couldn't be talking about abortion. A rival in love? A faithless husband? And now she planned to end it all off the dam. Just keep her talking.

"Not exactly, no." His tone was casual. "But many people see me indirectly guilty of many deaths. Yet I still plan to eat lunch in a grotto today."

"Indirectly or directly, one must take the consequences." She stared out at the vast space. Sepp's instincts provoked him to speak, to keep her with him. But she began again.

"I am, or I should say I was, a nurse. Geriatrics. I care for ageing women, and some men, every day. But my own mother ... my own mother died in a pile of her own waste, because I was too occupied with my own life. I cannot forgive and do not deserve absolution, no matter what penitence. Now you know and if you have any mercy, you will leave me." Her voice gave no sense of emotion, as if already dead.

He'd reached the top step by now and crouched on the platform. "I've listened to your story, heard your confession. I offer you a deal. You listen to mine and I will leave this place. I will give you your privacy if you allow me my honesty."

She was silent. Her body swayed as the light and heat grew. He added one point more. He was a lawyer, after all.

"And your last act will have been one of compassion, a Samaritan, giving time to a stranger."

She turned, her eyes streaming. "I will listen." She moved slowly towards him, black leather gloves tucking her rosary into the folds of her widow's weeds. She was attractive, if a little haggard. The news conference would look even better. So fragile, next to her muscular, modest rescuer. She came closer, eyeing him with tearful concern. Her pupils were dilated with fear. He opened his palms, his arms and his face to show his trust. The Hollywood moment; she's back from the brink. She smiled and rushed into his embrace, forcing a cloth over his mouth and knocking him to the ground. He lay back, winded and disorientated, before attempting to throw her off. Her hand remained clamped over his nose and mouth, her knees on his upper arms. He writhed with enormous force, intending to buck her off. His body responded with an ineffectual twitch. His mind threw a punch, but still she sat, a Gothic demon crouching over him. His body was not responding. As if it was separated from his head.

Chapter 29

Zürich 2012

Sometimes, sometimes. Words, a phrase, or an expression just stuck. In the small hours, Beatrice would wake in the knowledge that if only she could go back to sleep, tomorrow would be perfectly fine. Yet a phrase kept popping into her head. Round and round. Sometimes it was music – Leonard Cohen made frequent appearances – but it could just as easily be a sentence in German, or a half-remembered exchange from the day.

"I don't need to ask you for the keys to all my joys, I don't need people like a baby needs a toy."

"Das weiss ich auch nicht!"

"Maybe we could pre-act as opposed to post?"'

If this were a dramatisation of her life, one of these phrases would be relevant and her recognition of its hidden meaning would solve her problems. But it wasn't, they weren't and it wouldn't. They were merely thought-mosquitoes, buzzing around her brain, sapping her energy. She looked at the clock; twenty past four. So, what was left of the night was mapped out. Restless shifting position for an hour, maybe two, before falling into a profound sleep sometime before six. Then hauling herself to the surface mere minutes later at the shrill insistence of the alarm.

Silence, blackness and a comfortable sense of peace. Perfect kipping conditions. Arriving back from Ticino past one, Beatrice had hit the pillow like a stone. Banshees would have wasted their breath. Yet now, in the pre-dawn anticipation of the day, she had a refrain from a song in her head. And a myriad of concerns.

"Man may escape from rope and gun
Nay, some have outlived the doctor's pill
Who takes a woman must be undone
That basilisk is sure to kill."

What was the matter with her? What did she want? Her mind roamed over her world. Matthew in Exeter. Her job in London and the respect of her colleagues in Zürich. Control over the dogs, everywhere. A resolution to this case. Peace. And as a consequence, sleep.

Fat chance.

"Man may escape from ..."

Oh do shut up.

"Morning B. Are you all right? You look awful."

"Thank you for the welcome, Chris. I am full of life, and tact. Yourself?"

"Not bad. We've had some thoughts while you were on your Helvetian tour. I think you might like what we've got to say."

Beatrice's tired eyes widened. "You found something?"

Chris lifted his shoulders and wagged his head in irritating ambiguity. Quelling an impulse to grab his tie and pull, Beatrice turned to get a coffee. Xavier burst through the door, as bright-eyed and gleeful as a squirrel remembering where he'd put his nuts.

"Xavier. Good morning. How are you?"

"Thank you, fine. Are you well, Beatrice? You are looking, what is the expression?"

Chris opened his mouth to reply, but Beatrice cut him off. "Perfectly well, thank you. A few more hours rest would have been helpful, but we have a case to solve and the pressure has just increased fivefold."

"Yes, exactly. Conceição and Sabine are finishing some slides. They come directly."

"No hurry, Xavier. It's ten to eight. And Kälin never bothers to show his ... Good morning, Herr Kälin. You are unusually early."

Kälin carried a cup of peppermint tea, the scent accompanying his freshly showered smell. He looked clean as a cucumber. "Good morning Frau Stubbs, Herr Keese, Herr Racine. Are you feeling well, Frau Stubbs? I am afraid yesterday's scene was too much for you."

Bloody cheek! Who was it that stood on that platform and looked down into the void? Who held still as the mortuary staff pulled back that blanket? And who had no difficulty polishing off a sausage and mustard roll afterwards?

"I am stronger than I look, Herr Kälin. Hello, Sabine, Conceição. I hear you have some thoughts."

At least harmony seemed to reign in the love triangle. Sabine greeted everyone with a smile, as her colleague set up the laptop. Beatrice, disconcerted by the change in dynamic, watched and waited as Conceição took charge.

"Good morning everyone. As you know, Giuseppe Esposito's death seems to have been orchestrated by the same person. We find ourselves with a problem. Lyon is screaming for results, our approach so far has produced none. Beatrice, we talked about this while you and Herr Kälin were away yesterday and we think there might be another way to tackle this. I hope you don't mind but we have done some work on a proactive approach."

Beatrice said nothing, but lifted up her head in enquiry. The team's choice to follow a different tactic had better not be at the expense of the detailed duties she'd allotted before leaving. Her smile was tight.

Chris took over. "Beatrice, Herr Kälin, we think the procedure we have followed so far has merit, of course. But we all agreed that it is not producing results. If we know enough about the killer's MO, then we could overtake her or him and jump one step ahead. We researched the press during the six to twelve months before the deaths of the victims so far. Each one had the most negative press of the year, with the exception of Belanov. We think we can look at this from the opposite angle. Rather than chasing this person, we believe we can predict with reasonable accuracy where he or she might strike next. Sabine?"

The presentation was slick and well prepared. Beatrice's jaw clenched. All this had taken some time. Her team had indeed ignored her orders and followed their own course. What the hell did they think they were playing at? She flicked her eyes toward Kälin, whose eyebrows had knitted.

"Thanks, Chris." Sabine flashed him a smile as she stood up to speak. "Beatrice, Herr Kälin, listen. We don't want to take over, just simply to propose another way of looking at this. Presuming D'Arcy is involved in the orchestration of these killings, we can look at how she picked her targets. In each year, the dead man had the most negative newspaper inches in the business press. She, or 'the killer', selected the most unpopular man of the year. Only Belanov was different, and we know from your investigations that he was personal for D'Arcy. Going on these assumptions, we have identified three men who could be the potential victims for 2013, or even 2014."

She clicked the remote and three faces emerged on the screen.

"Based on a search of bad press on business figures linked to D'Arcy, we have reduced our net to these three men. If we act now, we can place someone close to each man, and lay a trap. For example, the first ..."

Beatrice had heard enough. "Sabine? I'm sorry to interrupt. You have all clearly done an impressive amount of work on this. However, as you rightly point out, all of this is based on an assumption. Or, if my guess is correct, a presumption. Am I right in thinking that you collectively chose to abandon the tasks I allocated in favour of developing an alternative approach to the case?"

The enthusiastic warmth in the team's faces disappeared as if doused with cold water. Xavier, unusually pale, stood up. "Our intention was not to try to change the investigation, Beatrice. We simply wanted to provide a parallel track. So we can attack on two sides, you see."

Tired, irritable and frustrated, Beatrice was in no mood to conciliate. "I am very happy to hear that. So *my* assumption is that you achieved all I asked; Sabine has rechecked all medical records, Xavier has a detailed breakdown of D'Arcy's activities and flight records on the relevant dates, Conceição is fully conversant with the Swiss home-care system and Chris has identified any gender markers previously missed in the police reports. Is that correct?"

Chris shook his head. "No, it isn't. We devoted a lot of time to preparing this angle. I think you could at least listen to our ideas. This could save us all a lot of bullshit."

Beatrice placed her coffee on the desk, stood up and switched off the screen, before turning to face the team.

"A reminder, if you will. This is a team, a group of people working together for a common goal. I have been given the role of team leader and thus it is my judgement which guides our strategy. I have no objection to being presented with alternative ideas or techniques, unless my team drop my instructions to follow such an alternative without permission. And much as your glamorous idea of lying in wait for the next attack and catching our killer in the act may appeal, it is the stuff of television dramas, not reality. Bullshit, as you term it, the daily slog of checking under every stone, is the foundation of solid police work. And performed with diligence, will eventually yield results. I would like the information I asked for on my desk by the end of the day. Chris, you can present this concept to me at one pm, presuming you have completed all the tasks detailed. Have a good day, everyone."

She picked up her coffee and headed for her office. The team dispersed in silence, resentment and negativity charging the air like a thunderstorm. It was foolhardy to expect support from Kälin, but Beatrice wondered if he found the team's actions as offensive as she did. After all, this had all come to pass while she and Kälin were away from the office.

She wrote a quick email.

Subject: Daily briefing

Herr Kälin

When I hear these proposals from Herr Keese, would you like to be present?

Frau Stubbs

He replied instantly.

Subject: re Daily briefing

Frau Stubbs

No. I could have heard them this morning.

Herr Kälin

Beatrice decided she would go out for lunch for a change. Nordsee did excellent fish and chips.

"Shut the door, Chris. Do you want to set up your laptop?"

"In a minute. First, I want to apologise. You're right, we did get carried away with our idea and made an error of judgement in neglecting our duties. But I want to stress that we can do both. I think a combination of the two strategies is most likely to yield results. And I'm sorry I was blunt this morning. Tact, as you know, is not one of my strong points."

Beatrice smiled. "Apology accepted. I know I came down hard on you all, but to be presented with such a vote of no confidence after yesterday felt like a slap in the teeth. I am prepared to listen to your ideas and to give them the credit they deserve, as long as we maintain our daily duties conscientiously."

"Fair enough. Shall I set up now and take you through what we think? Or should we wait for Kälin?"

"He won't be joining us. Can I ask if you have uncovered anything from the file reviews at all?"

"Nothing concrete, although certain elements do support

our theory. Sabine may have got something. She skipped lunch to travel to Luzern. I'm not sure what she found, but she was pretty excited. OK, I'm ready. What about you?"

"Fire away." Beatrice sat back with her bottle of water and trained her attention on the screen.

"The theory behind this you know. We can make a pretty intelligent estimate as to how D'Arcy, or whoever, selects the victims. And as Sabine explained, there seem to be three candidates for the next hit."

"Yet if Esposito was the latest in line, won't we be waiting another year for our next one? I'm not raining on your fireworks, Chris, but how can you be sure that between now and then some corrupt government official, or avaricious trader will not come to prominence and unseat your trio?"

"We can't. But the killer leaves a cooling-off period, we believe. It was over a year in Belanov's case. It may be that the victim is marked up to twelve months before he's taken out. If another possible target arises, we just have to add him to the list. If they have any connection with D'Arcy Roth, if they attract negative media attention, or if they piss off Antonella herself, these are the guys we need to watch."

"It's a smart strategy. My concern is mostly to do with timescale. How do you propose that we ..."

A knock at the door caused both of them to frown. Xavier's head popped round, his face animated.

"Sorry for the interruption, Beatrice. I thought I should tell you, I am going to join Sabine in Luzern. She has found something, I think. May I?"

Beatrice nodded and gestured to a chair, but Xavier was too fidgety to sit. He closed the door and shifted from foot to foot. "Kantonsspital Luzern has a record of an anaesthetist who was ... how do you call it, when you stop someone from working in medicine?"

"Struck off. This person was struck off?"

"Exactly. Helene Richter was struck off after a case in 1993.

Found guilty of assisted suicide. She administered a fatal dose of pain-killing drugs to a patient with terminal leukaemia. His name was Jean-Baptiste D'Arcy. Antonella's stepfather."

The pace of the afternoon's activity kept Beatrice entirely occupied and filled with adrenalin. At 16.00, the team gathered for an update. In Luzern, Xavier and Sabine found a current address for Helene Richter and asked for permission to question her and search the apartment. Kälin spoke to D'Arcy's secretary and discovered that she would be returning from Buenos Aires early Saturday morning. Beatrice requested the search warrant and authorisation for D'Arcy's arrest. Conceição would accompany Kälin to the offices of D'Arcy Roth the following morning to test every male staff member's DNA, while Beatrice and Sabine did the same at D'Arcy's home. With considerable satisfaction, Beatrice updated Lyon, spoke to a GEOF representative of the Argentine Federal Police and forced everyone to go home at five. Not only did she want them fresh for the following day, but she also had an appointment. One she was dreading.

Chapter 30

Zürich 2012

"Come on, Beatrice, you won't regret it," Madeleine promised, when coercing her into this.

Beatrice already regretted it deeply and she hadn't even arrived yet.

Dragging her heels up Gessnerallee, her attention was drawn back to the Sihl, where a group of teenagers sat on a blanket, laughing and dangling their feet into the coolness of the river. The sun glinted off the water, the greenery of the bank provided a peaceful backdrop to the colourful party and an Appenzeller dog bounded in and out of the water after a stick. A Seurat come to life. A sudden swell of joy coursed through her, driven by optimism and vindication that her determined methodology had finally produced results. They had a suspect. This case could be closed by the weekend. She lifted her chin and picked up speed. After all, how painful could a haircut be?

"Hey Beatrice! Am I happy to see you! I thought you were gonna bail on me."

Dressed in a suit even Beatrice recognised as Chanel, Madeleine's glamour was such that a beautician seemed redundant. Her make-up seemed air-brushed, her jewellery co-ordinated exactly with the pinks in the suit and the silk scarf at her throat reminded Beatrice of Lauren Hutton.

"Hello, Madeleine. I did think about it. I already wish I hadn't agreed to this."

"Too late to back out now. This is Susana, who's doing our treatments today."

"Treatments? I thought I was just getting a trim."

Susana, a generously proportioned woman with a permanent smile, exchanged a look with Madeleine, before extending her hand.

"Pleased to meet you, Beatrice. Today, I'm going to cut and colour your hair while my colleague threads Madeleine's brows. Then our manicurist will take care of your nails while I deal with Madeleine's roots. Now, I'm going to put you side by side so you can chat. What can I get you to drink?"

"Beatrice, don't pull that face." Madeleine laughed. "It doesn't hurt, it won't take long and you'll feel a new woman when we're done. And this is my treat. You bought the tickets to the gallery on Sunday."

Beatrice succumbed to the pressure and allowed herself to be led to a leather chair in front of a mirror. She accepted a cup of tea and looked across at her companion.

"It's you I feel sorry for. Threading your brows sounds agonising."

Madeleine dropped her voice. "It's not so bad. Nowhere near as painful as sugaring your pits."

Beatrice shuddered.

The stylists went about their work in silence, gently adjusting heads and faces as necessary.

"So, how was your day?" asked Madeleine.

"Well, all things considered, not too bad. But I'm afraid the trip to Hiltl tonight must be postponed. I have to turn in early. I've got a big day tomorrow and I had a rotten night's sleep last night."

"Oh, that's a shame. Nothing wrong, I hope?"

"No, not particularly. Work problems, my own mind and some interference from John Gray. How are you?"

"Oh, I'm fine. Well, kinda. Michael just told me he has to attend a conference in Brussels this weekend, so I guess I'm a little bummed. But I was so looking forward to this girls' night, I almost forgave him."

"That makes me feel worse about pulling out of our restaurant arrangement."

"Forget about it. We can do that anytime. I just wanted to go somewhere after the salon so we could show off your new look."

Beatrice lifted her eyes to the mirror and immediately returned them to the magazine in her lap. She didn't want to know. And if the results were preposterous, there was always a hat.

Madeleine, her head stretched back as some girl performed God knows what atrocities on her eyebrows, asked a difficult question.

"So what's the deal at work? Anything I can help with? I may be only a *Hausfrau* right now, but there was a time when I ran my own company."

"It's kind of you to offer, but it's just the usual frenzy when a project comes to an end."

"Your project's ending? No way! Does that mean I'm gonna lose my new best friend?"

Beatrice smiled. "Not yet. But one way or another, I expect to be home by next weekend."

"Shoot. Bad news for me but great for you, I guess."

Susana finished snipping and a discussion began as to the most suitable colour. Beatrice's own opinion, that brown and grey worked perfectly well with her wardrobe, seemed the least influential. Madeleine thought honey and caramel lowlights; the eyebrow expert said dark chocolate with a hint of macchiato at the temples; while Susana put forward a forceful case for champagne and cinnamon as not requiring frequent touch-ups.

Beatrice lost interest and began to feel peckish.

The manicurist arrived and added her view in German, '*wie ein Dachs*', before settling down with a sweet smile to massage rich lotion into Beatrice's hands. Beatrice smiled back before recalling that *Dachshund* translated as 'badger hound'. She gave the skinny little teenager a frosty frown.

Madeleine interrupted her thoughts. "OK, so if you're taking a rain check tonight, how about tomorrow?"

Beatrice hesitated. Plans were likely to be disrupted if an arrest could be made. "That depends. We may be working late and over the weekend. Things have rather come to a head, you see."

"Wow, it sounds so exciting. Or isn't it?"

"At the moment, I'm not sure. But it certainly involves a lot of hard work. What did you have in mind for tomorrow?" The hair dye, whatever colour it was, began to sting Beatrice's scalp.

"Well, it's nothing important. But I've been getting about a bit, checking Zürich out. And I got a hold of a couple tickets to see a yodel choir, in Hotel Widder. It's one of the guilds of the city and it's so totally Swiss. Could be fun?"

"Yodelling? How absolutely marvellous! I would love to come with you, but as I say, it's crunch time at work. Could I call you tomorrow to confirm?"

"Sure. Don't sweat it if you can't make it. I know you're busy. Wish I was."

"It may come to nothing. These things often raise hopes then fall flat."

Madeleine paused. "OK, I'll wish you luck. And if you can come along, what say we check out the Fraumünster on the way? They have some stained glass windows by Chagall and Giacometti which I hear are quite something."

"Really? I am a devoted fan of Chagall, as you probably remember. Don't know all that much about Giacometti but I'm very keen on stained glass. I had a bash myself once. The tutor told me my work was 'energetic' and I felt about five years old.

You've really been bitten with the tourist bug, haven't you?"

Madeleine looked into the mirror at Beatrice's reflection. "I figured I may as well. What else have I got to do? Hey, how do my eyebrows look?"

Three hours later, no longer feeling sore, irritable or bullied, Beatrice was still gazing at the mirror in the bathroom. She couldn't stop. For the first time in her life, she was proud of her hair. She'd looked at her reflection in the microwave, in the TV and every shop window on the way home from the salon. Every half hour, she wandered into the bathroom to stare at the sleek, polished individual who waggled shiny fingernails back at her. She should take a photo because it would never last.

The phone rang.

"Beatrice, it's Madeleine again. I hope I'm not disturbing."

"Not at all. I was just ... actually, I was still admiring my hair. It's lovely. I can't get over it. Thank you so much."

Madeleine's satisfaction could be heard in her smile. "Isn't it? Thank Susana. She did a brilliant job and you look amazing. Listen, I was just calling to let you know the concert tomorrow starts at eight, but we can drop in anytime we like. Kinda takes the pressure off, huh?"

"Oh, eight should be manageable. I'll call you in the afternoon and hopefully we can do both the windows and the yodellers."

"Great! Let's talk then. You get some rest, OK?"

"I shall do my level best. And thanks again. Goodnight."

"Goodnight Beatrice. Best of luck tomorrow. Sweet dreams."

Fluffing up the pillow, Beatrice found she was smiling. She might be long in the hoof but was still capable of making new friends. Yodelling and stained-glass Chagall with Madeleine, the ideal antidote to work. Her eyes closed and her mind replayed the image of Madeleine's perfect make-up, beautiful jewellery and sensual scarf at her throat. Her mind wandered. Perhaps a classy scarf would bring her own image up to date. A natty knot at the side? No. Rather than displaying Grace Kelly elegance, Beatrice would look more like a drag queen.

Her eyes opened again. Throwing back the duvet, she padded into the living area and found her mobile phone.

"Conceição, I'm sorry to disturb you so late."

"It's fine, Beatrice. It's only ten past nine. Is something wrong?"

"Just a quick question. If someone has a sex change; you know, hormones, operations, the works ... it wouldn't change the structure of their DNA, would it?"

"No. There are some factors which may cause minuscule alterations in a few DNA cells, but nothing alters the building blocks. If you're born a woman, no matter how many external changes you make, female DNA runs through you for life."

"Like a stick of rock. Thank you, Conceição. That's given me food for thought. See you in the morning. Good night."

"Good night, Beatrice. Sleep well."

The chances of that were negligible.

Chapter 31

Zürich 2012

Trotting up the stairs to their workroom at five past seven, Beatrice was joined by Xavier, carrying a bakery bag.

"Good morning, Beatrice." He stopped short when he saw her hair.

"Your coiffure! You look so different. But it suits you. I brought croissants."

"Thank you, Xavier. They smell wonderful."

"My mother says that a good breakfast is the best way to begin the day. Did you sleep any better?"

"Not really. There's an awful lot to think about."

"You should try to do something else before bed. Watch TV, go out to a restaurant, take your mind off the case. When I need to clear my mind, I play football."

"Tonight, I plan to do just that."

"Football?" His eyebrows leapt upwards.

"Xavier, look at me. Can you seriously see me running around after a ball?"

He struggled to find an appropriate response so Beatrice saved him the trouble. "No, not football. However, I certainly intend to clear my mind. I wanted to ask you, is Fraumünster the one with the two towers?"

"No, that's Grossmünster. Fraumünster is on Münsterhof,

this side of the Limmat. Just before you go over the bridge. Please, let me."

Xavier opened the door for her. All the team, with the exception of Kälin, were present, bristling with anticipation like foxhounds on Boxing Day. Everyone did a double take.

"Beatrice! You had a haircut!"

"B, you look fantastic. I love the colour."

"Takes ten years off you, B! You look no older than f..."

"Shut up, Chris. Good morning, everyone. Xavier has brought us all breakfast."

Before Beatrice had even deposited her handbag, Chris was at her side.

"The search warrant is here. I think it would make sense if Xavier and I went to Luzern, to question Richter and search her apartment. Firstly, sending two men makes sense if she's potentially dangerous. Secondly, I can be useful if there's an opportunity for digital forensics. And Xavier's Swiss German will be essential for interviewing her or anyone else."

"All sound arguments, Chris. But before we plan our day, can I hear the latest and get a coffee?"

Xavier lifted his paper bag. "And a croissant."

"I just think it is important to get started because if we ..."

"Chris. It's seven am. We'll all be more effective if we know exactly what everyone is doing and why. Can you wait half an hour, do you think? We'll start as soon as Kälin gets here."

"And here is Herr Kälin, so now we can start." Xavier's bouncy eagerness reminded Beatrice of a Red Setter puppy.

She poured a coffee and turned to the team. "Under the circumstances, I think we could start. Chris tells me the search warrant for Richter's apartment is here. What else is new? Good morning, Herr Kälin."

Kälin opened a file and withdrew a slip of paper. "Good morning everyone, I received permission ..."

Kälin's eyes flicked over Beatrice and he appeared to lose his thread. He raised the paper as if to remind himself.

"... permission to test employees of D'Arcy Roth, and of Antonella D'Arcy. Arrest warrant for D'Arcy granted."

Beatrice sipped her coffee. "Sounds good. Does the permission state we can request DNA samples only from men, Herr Kälin?"

He looked at her, frowned and checked the permit. "Yes, of course it says men. Where else would you find male DNA?"

"It occurred to me last night that our quarry may have had a sex change. Outward appearances indicate a woman, but the DNA remains that of a man. I checked this with our expert."

Conceição gave a confirmatory nod.

"So I want to test everyone who works for D'Arcy. I know it's unlikely and I am adding a lot of extra work for the lab, but I want to look into every possibility."

"Beatrice, you have to be joking!" Conceição shook her head. "That would be a huge waste of time and money. And it means the lab will take twice as long to process anything relevant. I really can't agree to this."

Chris arched his eyebrows. "You really want to tell Lyon that we've invested so many resources in testing women for male DNA? Rather you then me."

Beatrice raised her chin. "It was not a request for permission, in fact. It was an instruction. I will submit another official form and explain why. We have to test everyone and turn every stone. I accept the consequences.

"Chris and Xavier can go to Luzern to search for this Richter woman, Herr Kälin and Conceição can begin testing at the D'Arcy Roth office, while Sabine comes with me to D'Arcy's villa. I'd like to talk to her staff, anyway, and look around the property."

"Be careful, Frau Stubbs. We don't have a warrant to search her home, and I would prefer it if you take some uniformed officers in case of difficulties," Kälin warned.

His words contained no criticism of her decision, thus acting as a balm.

"That's a fair point. I'll do that. Does anyone want to raise anything else before we head off? Yes, Sabine?"

"Conceição and I were talking about Helene Richter. From what the hospital told me, she was a rising star. To deliberately perform euthanasia on a patient would send her career crashing. And she must have known that. So why would she administer an overdose to Antonella D'Arcy's stepfather? We think D'Arcy paid her to do it. After the doctor was dismissed, she managed to retain her somehow and they worked together to 'arrange' these suicides."

Chris frowned. "If so, that was a long time in the planning phase. Richter was struck off in 1993. Van der Veld, the first death that we know of, was in 2007. And why did D'Arcy want her stepfather dead?"

"That's what we must find out," answered Beatrice. "Sabine and I will dig up as much as we can on D'Arcy's background and look into what happened to Richter after 1993. I want everyone to be thorough, check every story and make no assumptions. Take nothing at face value. We are extremely close, so we are going to get this right. Obviously, any major breakthroughs, I want to hear about it. Otherwise, I would like an update at lunchtime. In person or by telephone, let's speak at midday. Have a productive day, everyone."

Richter was not at home. The *Hauswart*, or caretaker of Richter's apartment building, took her job seriously. Refusing to believe the warrant, she insisted on calling the Kantonspolizei to confirm. Chris raised his eyes to heaven, but followed Xavier's example and gave her an understanding smile. As she closed her apartment door to telephone Zürich, Xavier reassured him.

"We'll get a lot more help out of her if we show her respect for doing her job. These people know a huge amount about the other tenants. I can guarantee she knows all their movements, right down to who had a shower this morning."

"Yeah, you're right. I just wish everything didn't take so long, you know." He leaned back against the wall and tried to remember his Tai Chi.

The door opened and Frau Pfenniger looked from one to the other. She frowned at Xavier and asked for their IDs again. Suppressing a sigh, Chris handed his over once more and the woman nodded. She led the way upstairs and after each reply to Xavier's enquiries, threw back questions of her own. Xavier's responses were brief, polite and guarded. Her accent and use of Swiss German made it hard for Chris to follow, but it was obvious she was trying to find out the reason behind their visit. After she unlocked the door, Xavier thanked her and with great diplomacy, persuaded her to leave them to it.

The slight figure disappeared down the stairwell, casting one last look back and returning their wave. Chris grinned at Xavier.

"Well done on getting rid of her. You refused her offer of tea, right?"

"Yes, I did. Otherwise, she would be up and down with all kinds of excuses. And we have work to do. But she did give me some useful information.

"She told me that Richter is a doctor and works away most of the time, as a volunteer developing countries. Apparently, she was last here on Monday. Very quiet, been a tenant since 2005. Doesn't smoke, very few visitors, but likes Chinese food and classical music. I told you, they know everything."

Entering the flat, Chris was immediately impressed by the space and light. Floor-length windows allowed sunlight to warm the large living area and the kitchenette, back against the far wall, had a wall of glass bricks. Drawn to the windows, Chris pulled back the white gauze curtains and studied the view. The street dropped away below to a river rushing past on its way to the lake. No one's apartment overlooked the building, so she could sit out here and enjoy the sun in privacy. He turned back to Xavier, who had donned gloves and already begun searching the desk.

Richter obviously went for the Zen approach to interior design. An L-shaped corduroy sofa faced the windows, the glass coffee table before it bearing nothing more than a remote control, and a vase with three artistic silver branches. The kitchen to Chris's left was all pale wood with dark marble worktops. So clean it looked like a kitchen in a showroom. Pausing to pull on his gloves, he opened the fridge. A half-drunk bottle of rosé, a butter packet and a variety of jars: pesto sauce, quince jelly, sauce bourguignonne and horseradish. The cupboards were equally Spartan: plastic containers with pasta, muesli, and packets of noodle soup. Removing everything methodically, Chris checked the cupboards, the dishwasher, the freezer compartment and the cutlery drawer. Nothing of any interest.

Xavier sat at the table, looking through papers, the picture of concentration. Chris decided to explore the two doors at the opposite end of the room. The bedroom, with large bed, fitted wardrobes and dressing-table was decorated in deep blue and white, giving a restful, expensive feel. Judging by the number of labels he recognised, she owned some quality clothes. A Donna Karan wool dress, two jackets by Dior, a long cardigan by Nicole Fahri, Gucci boots ... the wardrobe of a volunteer doctor? Next door was the bathroom, revealing a cabinet full of expensive products, thick towels and a power shower. Chris pulled several strands of blonde hair from the brush, and slipped them into a plastic bag. It wasn't much. He hoped Xavier was having more luck.

If Beatrice had never met D'Arcy, she would have felt some sympathy for her. Her history, baldly stated in black and white, was rather sad. No matter how spectacular her trajectory, the loss of both parents and a stepfather at a young age must have been terrible blows. Sabine lifted her head at Beatrice's sigh.

"Something wrong, B?"

"No, just feeling a bit sorry for the woman. Her father died of a stroke when she was nine years old. Then she lost her mother at seventeen. That's very tough."

"Hmm. I find it hard to feel sorry for someone who can take other people's lives."

"Sabine, we have no proof that D'Arcy has taken anyone's life yet."

"We will. You know that before she became partner at Hoffmann Roth, they had a reputation for honour? They would refuse any business not aligned with their principles of fairness, humanity and justice."

"How did it move from those ethics to its cut-throat reputation of today?"

Sabine read aloud. "From the annual report of 1999/2000. I'm sure you can translate this bullshit: 'Strategically, the company has embraced broader views, driven by our new Senior Partner, Antonella D'Arcy. As part of our ongoing mission to add value for shareholders and stakeholders alike, we will strive to explore new areas of business opportunity.' In other words, Hoffmann's moral code is thrown out of the window and we just want to make cash. Lots of it. And we don't care where it comes from."

Beatrice couldn't help but laugh at the fiercely cynical expression on Sabine's face.

"I would hate to get on your wrong side. It should have been you who accompanied me to that first interview. Bad cop and worse cop. Did you find anything in your material about relationships? From everything I have read, she has been linked with several men, but I can find no one special in her life. No indication of who fathered her daughter, for example."

"You won't find a father. The child was adopted from South America."

"Adopted? I didn't know that. But it fits, I suppose. I couldn't imagine D'Arcy pregnant. Do you have a date of birth there?"

Sabine shuffled through the papers from the local government office. "No birth certificate, apparently lost. But D'Arcy adopted her from a Brazilian hospital on 12 October 1994. And ... I don't believe it! The adoption certificate was signed by Dr H.

Richter."

Beatrice stared. "So. Struck off in Switzerland, Richter went to Brazil. Which is why she speaks Portuguese. In the right place at the right time to organise an adoption for Antonella D'Arcy. How convenient. Or perhaps D'Arcy sent her?"

"We should try to talk to the girl this afternoon, see if she lets anything slip."

"Good idea. Right, call that Brazilian hospital and find out what you can on Richter. Then it's catch-up time and lunch. My stomach is grumbling. I tell you, I could eat a scabby cat. Oh Lord, don't look like that, Sabine, it's only an expression."

Kälin had cream sauce in his moustache. As Conceição updated them on the lack of progress at D'Arcy Roth, Sabine made short work of *Fischknusperli* with salad, Beatrice enjoyed the police canteen *Schnitzel* with noodles and Conceição managed the occasional forkful of the fitness menu; or raw strips of vegetable. Throughout the conversation, Kälin stabbed at the slices of meat in his plate of *Zürcher Geschnetzeltes* as if he were spearing each awkward, obstreperous D'Arcy Roth employee who had caused them such problems.

Conceição explained. "And that means we're not as far forward as we'd hoped. But the first two batches are already in the lab, so they can get started. We should be done by mid afternoon. Unless we have any further 'I know my rights' big-mouths this afternoon." She shrugged as if it were inevitable.

Sabine patted her mouth with a napkin. "B and I have been going through all the documentation available on D'Arcy, her family, and her company. The only thing of interest so far is the fact that Dina is not D'Arcy's biological daughter. She adopted her in Brazil about eighteen years ago. And Helene Richter signed the adoption certificate."

Kälin glanced at Sabine in surprise. "Here, or in Brazil?"

"São Paulo, 1994. I called the hospital, they have no records of a Dr Richter employed there in the early 90s."

Conceição turned to Beatrice. "And news from Luzern?"

"Still waiting. I did tell Chris to call at twelve, and it's now twenty five past. But I know he will phone in as soon as it's convenient."

Sabine sighed. "If I only wait two minutes, this desire for a dessert will pass. I must be strong."

"No matter how long I wait, my mind will never forget that they have vermicelli, chocolate mousse and éclairs," Conceição added, mischief in her smile.

"You, Conceição Pereira da Silva, are a bad influence on me." Sabine picked up her tray and headed to the buffet once more, followed by Conceição.

"Any dessert for you, Herr Kälin?"

Fortunately, Kälin chose to wipe his mouth before replying, as Beatrice was perilously close to getting the giggles.

"Thank you, no. I think we both see this link to Richter as our way in." It was not a question.

Beatrice placed her knife and fork together. "Certainly. We can threaten charges of illegal child-trafficking and all sorts. All or any of this information about her could be useful."

He leaned his forearms on the table. "So tell me more about Ms D'Arcy."

Beatrice did so. He listened without interrupting. After she finished, he asked a question.

"Does anything here seem significant to you?"

"Apart from Richter, not especially. I was struck by how the steely female we see today experienced some dreadful losses in her youth. Yes, her upbringing was privileged in the monetary sense, but in terms of loved ones, everything was taken from her. Perhaps this is one reason why she needs to control her environment."

Kälin thought it over as he gazed at his empty plate. "Possibly. Can you see a way of using this information?"

"Not yet. We just need to keep doing the groundwork, covering all angles and see what happens when we arrest her tomorrow morning. Do you have flight details?"

He nodded. "Yes. I'll pick you up at six thirty. We'll take some back-up and be ready for when she touches down. You should warn the team that we'll probably be working all weekend. I hope you had no plans?"

"No. Well, I did for this evening, but nothing that can't be cancelled, if needs be."

"This evening shouldn't be a problem. We will all need some rest and relaxation."

"That's what I thought. And it's an opportunity to sample some Swiss culture."

Kälin frowned. "Please don't tell me you're going to have a fondue. Not in May."

A low buzz of electricity hummed through Beatrice. Tricky to tell the difference, but she was beginning to distinguish Kälin attacks from Kälin banter.

"No, I'm going to see some religious art and then I've been invited to a yodelling concert. And why, in the name of Emmental, can't I have a fondue in May?"

Before he could answer, her mobile rang.

"Chris! We were wondering where you'd got to. Is everything alright?"

"It's fine. But the caretaker person was hanging around just now, so I couldn't call. Richter's not here and we found nothing much in her apartment. But apparently each flat has a share of the cellar space. Xavier's gone down there with Frau Fish-Face to take a look."

"And you don't know where the Richter woman is?"

"Nope, but she's been here recently, after an absence of six weeks. We have her home computer, so as soon as we start unpacking that, we'll get more idea."

"Chris, listen to me. I want you to bring the computer back to Zürich. Any use of computer data has to be done with the utmost care."

"I know that, B, I am your digital forensics expert. Why do

you ..."

"Yes, and I am the case officer in terms of law. I am responsible for making sure all data has been handled correctly. We also need an independent party to vouch for all our processes. Bring it back and let's tick all our crosses. If there's anything there, Chris, we have to be able to prove we haven't fiddled with it. And let's not forget, if you do the analysis here rather than there, you get to spend the weekend in Zürich with us, your loved ones."

She heard his indignation deflate into a laugh. "OK. You're right. I'll pack up now and we'll head back. The machine will remain untouched until we can decide the best process and legal compliance. B, are you eating?"

"Yes. *Schnitzel* in the police canteen. It's excellent."

"I don't believe it. You're eating *Schnitzel* and Xavier and I can't even have a cup of tea. My stomach is ... what? Hang on a minute."

Chris's voice was muffled and Beatrice could hear the urgent tones of Xavier in the background, but could make out no words.

"B, I've gotta go. Seems Xav has found something in the cellar. We'll check it out and get back to you. Save me some *Schnitzel*." He rang off.

"Wigs." Xavier threw the various hairpieces onto the table with a flourish.

"And suits, bags, padded bras, accessories, jewellery and outdoor gear," added Chris.

"This gives us precisely nothing. What else do people keep in their winter wardrobes? This discovery is hardly the body in the basement." Kälin's tone was scathing.

Chris lashed back. "You're wrong. I will go back through these case files and show you that this stuff is not just a dressing-up wardrobe of your girl-next-door. What we found, what Xav found, were the disguises this female used."

"Good luck." Kälin left the room, a chill wind behind him.

Time for Beatrice to step in. "Chris, Xavier, I'm sure you're right. But can we prove it? None of it is anything more than circumstantial unless any trace of her DNA turns up at these scenes. Which, given the time lapses, is unlikely. It's much more feasible we can prove this woman had regular contact with D'Arcy. Then we might have a case. Our only hope is to get something from her home computer. Even there, I fear we may hit a dead end. If she has anything to hide, she will have taken it with her.

"Look, don't waste your time on case files. Get onto that machine and find out what skeletons are under the floorboards. Xavier will support you, and the rest of us can go through the files once more. We may as well face the fact we'll be working all weekend."

Chris shrugged. "I can live with that. Xav and I will go through the PC, and if there's anything to find, we'll drag it out. And you take the files and check details against this bag of tricks?"

"Relax, Chris. We got it. Now, we were wondering if you two might be hungry?" Conceição's voice drew a smile from both men.

Sabine held up two brown paper bags. "So we brought you a picnic each from the canteen. A sandwich, an apple and a yoghurt. Healthy and light enough to keep your brains alert."

Chris drew his eyes to slits. "A yoghurt? Are you serious? We've been working since 7am with nothing but coffee to keep us going. Haven't we, Xav?"

"Yes, that's true. Apart from the burgers and fries we ate on the way back."

Chris dropped his head onto the desk and as Kälin was absent, Beatrice allowed herself to join in the laughter with a sense of abandonment.

A security guard opened the gates as the police car approached, watching with a look of extreme suspicion as they rolled up the drive to D'Arcy's villa. Sabine's slow scan revealed her awe at the extent of the grounds, the view of the lake and the beautifully tended gardens. Unlike Beatrice's last visit, the front door remained closed as they exited the car. Beatrice spoke to the uniformed officers, reiterating her request they stay put unless needed and ascended the semi-circular steps with Sabine, who rang the bell. Several moments later, a heavy-set woman appeared at the side of the house, with her hands on her hips. She wore a cleaner's blue-checked smock and her hair was drawn back in a loose knot. Her face was unwelcoming.

"Good afternoon, Frau ...?" opened Beatrice. She received a blank stare.

Sabine tried in German. "*Können Sie Deutsch?*"

Transferring her suspicious glare to Sabine, the woman responded. "*Frau D'Arcy ist im moment nicht hier. Sie kommt morgen früh zurück.* She comes tomorrow."

Sabine smiled. "Yes, we know. But we would like to talk to you, and any other staff members available." She gestured in the direction of the gardener.

"This is not possible. *Ich darf keine Gespräche führen ohne Frau D'Arcy.*"

Sabine nodded her understanding and relayed her words to Beatrice. "She can't talk to us without her employer."

"Fair enough. But let her know that we have authorisation to test all D'Arcy's male employees for DNA. They may not want to talk to us, but they must give us a swab. You needn't tell her that we'll be back for hers tomorrow. I think we could use the officers now."

Sabine explained the reason for their visit to the housekeeper, while Beatrice asked the officers for their help in gathering all the household staff to the hall for the testing procedure. Five minutes later, the embarrassed officers returned with the grand total of the gardener and the security guard, both sulky and recalcitrant.

Indicating they should sit on the chaise longue, a gloved Sabine prepared her kit. The uniformed police retreated to stand by the front door and the housekeeper to the kitchen, while the gardener and security guard sat stiffly, listening to Sabine address them in German. Beatrice watched the preparations, feeling a little extraneous. The sense of the empty house resonated with all of them, including the awkward officers by the entrance. An air of being watched, being judged filled the hallway, making them all into performers, demonstrably doing their duty. D'Arcy's absence was the strongest presence in the room.

Sunlight from the cupola illuminated the space, highlighting the greenery of the indoor foliage and the inlaid colours of the floor mosaic. Golds, creams, purples and plums and more green. A hand, a vessel, some folds of cloth? With a glance at Sabine, who was evidently in control of the situation, Beatrice wandered up the stairs for a better look. Her curiosity piqued, this was her chance to see what the image was all about. All eyes observed her departure, but she had no intention of going far. On reaching the landing, she looked down. Directly beneath her sat the two unhappy staff members of D'Arcy's household. In front of them, Sabine sat beside an occasional table, reaching towards the gardener with a cotton swab. The officers stood against the main door, allowing Beatrice a clear view of the mosaic tiles.

Three women poured large golden jars of water into a central vessel, also made of gold, or brass. They wore draped garments of plum, rose and faded green, their limbs pale, their faces resigned. The water shone silvery as it flowed from the jars into the cauldron, and out again. At the base of the vessel was the mouth of a gargoyle, with two holes either side, allowing the water to flow away. The palette of colour was astounding, sitting perfectly in the generous hallway, light catching the auburn hair, the curve of the gilded jars, the blush of a bare breast. Whatever Beatrice might suspect of Antonella D'Arcy, the woman had fine taste.

"Beatrice? I'm finished here. Is there anything else you want?"

Hurrying down the stairs, Beatrice faced two reproachful

faces; three if you counted Sabine's.

"No thanks, Sabine. If you have everyone's details, I think we can let these people get back to work."

She tried to offer grateful smiles to the staff, but none returned the gesture. The guard closed the door behind them with a face so lugubrious Beatrice was tempted to laugh. As they loaded the car, Sabine seemed uncharacteristically quiet. They fastened their belts and the driver checked they were heading back to base. No one spoke as they drove back into the centre.

"I hope that wasn't too unpleasant an experience?" Beatrice enquired.

"Not at all. Only two people, all passive and silent. I'll bet Conceição is having a much harder time. You can see these people are used to observing orders."

"Yes. I have the feeling that D'Arcy rules that place like a dictator. One crack of the rod, everyone jumps. They're probably afraid to go to the toilet without permission."

"You know not one of them is Swiss? The housekeeper is Croatian, the gardener comes from Greece and the security guard, who's also her driver, is Lebanese. Which reminds me, she took two other members of staff with her. Her bodyguard and her daughter, or secretary. We should test them tomorrow morning."

"We will. What a life that woman leads. Private jet, staff of five, fabulous villa. Seems dirty money is rather profitable."

"Hmm. What were you looking at up there?"

"The floor. It's a mosaic, a beautiful piece."

"Modern art?" Sabine asked, as she watched shoppers along Löwenstrasse.

"Classical. Women with water jugs. Put me in mind of Rossetti."

Sabine gave her an indulgent smile. "Not a name I know, Beatrice. My kind of artist is more Warhol or Lichtenstein. Have you been to the Kunsthaus yet?"

"Yes, very enjoyable it was too. I loved those dark Nordic

Expressionists. And the Chagall room was a joy. In fact, tonight I'm off to see some more."

"Yes, I like Chagall, too, although I prefer Matisse. Less ambiguous. Cleaner."

At a loss as to how to respond to that, Beatrice checked her watch.

"So, it's four thirty. Let's go and see how the boys got on with the toys."

Chapter 32

Zürich 2012

"You sure you wouldn't like an apple, Herr Kälin? We have plenty of our healthy picnic left."

Kälin smiled. "I will have dinner later, thank you Herr Keese. *En guete.* Enjoy your meal. I am only here to ..."

"Ensure there are no mistakes?"

"No, not really. True, I have some authority reasons for being here. But my main purpose in observing is to learn. At my age, Herr Keese, I need to keep learning."

The detective's sudden humility and politeness took Chris aback and he instantly dropped the macho stuff. The problem with Kälin was you never knew when to hold up your hands, or come out fighting. That feeling of handling explosive material reminded Chris of his ex-girlfriend.

The basement area was smaller than their workroom and proximity unavoidable. Kälin, if he wanted to stay, would be up close. There was no room for hostility.

"OK, Herr Kälin. I'm happy to share what I know. So far, we've imaged the hard drive. Everything on Richter's machine, and I mean everything, is now on these little dynamos." He patted the laptops in front of him.

"So, after you copy the hard drive, what next?" Kälin asked.

Xavier, illuminated by the semi-circle of blue screens around them, corrected his superior. "It's not a copy, it's an image. While we make an image, we write-protect it. So no one can alter data during the process. That ensures our image is an exact replica of the original."

Chris shot Xavier an impressed look. "He picks up pretty fast. Right, so the original hard drive goes under lock and key. That's one of the reasons you're here. Chain of custody. And we continue our work on these. But we'll need to hash again sometime tomorrow."

Xavier nodded, frowning and watching the movements on the screens. Kälin stood in silence and asked no questions. Chris took another mouthful of water, waiting. It didn't take long.

"Once I take charge of the original machine, what will you do with the image?" Kälin's curiosity was as wild as Xavier's, but the old sod held back, as if uninterested. Chris swallowed and began his explanation, trying not to sound too excited.

"When we're sure the source data has not been corrupted and made sure it is safe for later reference, we start exploring. I want to know everything that's on here; obvious, hidden, deleted, encrypted, protected, and temporary files. I want to know what all the gaps are, why there's unallocated space and where there's slack. Finally, I want to produce a map of this machine. When we can see, as a geographer can, the valleys, tunnels and caves, we know where to dig for the hidden treasure. The only thing I cannot know is how long this will take. Sometimes, you get lucky and your first strike turns up gold. But those times are rare. We'll probably be here all night and we may have to call for more refreshments."

Xavier beamed. Kälin's eyebrows joined.

Chris reached for the mouse and continued. "Armed with our map, we'll split up. I intend to go for the areas which ... Beatrice! Hello ladies!"

Conceição and Sabine followed Beatrice into the room, bright with curiosity.

"How are you getting on?" Beatrice enquired.

Chris leant back with a smile. "Well so far, we've satisfied the compliance requirements. Now we can get to work."

"I see. I just wanted to tell you that it's approaching five o'clock and we have already done ten hours today. How much longer do you intend to keep going? And is there any way we can help?"

Chris let his eyes fall in stages from Beatrice to the floor. No one spoke, afraid to disturb his concentration.

"When does D'Arcy get in?" he asked.

Kälin answered. "At seven-twenty tomorrow, her private jet arrives at Kloten. We'll be there as her welcome party. And we intend to bring her here, to ask her some questions."

"Right. In that case, why don't you leave me and Xavier to get on with this? You have a busy, difficult day tomorrow. I'd like to get something decent to eat and then start some serious work, without distraction. I'm happy to keep at it until I feel I need a break."

Xavier's head bobbed agreement before Beatrice could formulate the question. Kälin's shoulders lifted a centimetre as he met Beatrice's eyes, while Conceição and Sabine looked relieved.

Beatrice sighed. "Yes, Chris is right. Much as I feel guilty about leaving you two on the night shift, it does make sense for the rest of us to take a break now. But the least I can do is order something for you both. What would you like for dinner?"

The two men spoke as one. "Pizza."

"Naturally. That well-known brain food."

"Beatrice? Sabine and I were also thinking of getting a take-away and going back to her apartment. We thought we could discuss the developments over a glass of wine and share any thoughts. Would you like to join us?" Only Conceição's head was visible, as she leant back around the office door.

"How kind of you to include me. And how dedicated you are to continue working. You give me a twinge of guilt, off out to enjoy myself. I'll decline, Conceição, but only because I have a prior arrangement. Thank you for asking me, though."

"No problem. Are you going somewhere nice? It's not a hot date with Kälin, is it?"

Beatrice's head snapped round. "You are getting as lippy as your boyfriend! No, once I have completed all the paperwork here, I am joining an acquaintance for an evening of culture, as a matter of fact."

Conceição appeared to be suppressing a smile. "Well, don't stay in the office too long, you deserve a break. Enjoy your culture and we'll be in for seven in the morning, just in case you need us. Have a nice evening, B."

"You too." The door closed before Conceição's over-familiar address registered. The lack of respect in this team was a disgrace, she thought, picking up her mobile to dial Madeleine. She was still smiling when she left the office.

The handover of Helene Richter's original machine was a solemn occasion. A trolley was delivered by two uniformed officers, the computer loaded onto it and the entire ensemble escorted to the evidence safety vault, under the supervision of Herr Karl Kälin.

"*Schöne Abig mitenand*," called Xavier, folding up the empty pizza boxes into the bin.

With their return wishes dying in the clunk of the closing door, Chris turned to Xavier with a huge sigh.

"We'd better get to work. Another Friday night and I still haven't managed a date with Conceição."

Xavier laughed, settled himself in front of his screen and shook his head. "Perhaps you've missed your chance already."

"No way. It's just a matter of picking the right moment. But I don't have too many moments left. How is it possible that we're closer to cracking the case than I am to cracking that woman?"

Xavier twisted round to look at him. "Probably because you're not her type."

"What do you mean? I'm everyone's type. Tall, good-looking, modest ... Don't tell me you think you're in with a chance?"

Chris faked outrage.

"No, not at all. But that's the difference between us; I know when a case is hopeless. Now the clock is ticking, so where should I start?"

"You're right, let's attack. I'm going underground, you're patrolling the surface. I'll check everything that looks suspicious; deleted, encrypted, odd blanks. You search her 'open' files; documents, emails, website history and build me a picture. And Xav, if anything looks funny to you, it is. Tell me as soon as something doesn't feel right."

Chris had no truck with auras, but right at that moment, Xavier was glowing like a hot coal.

Bullshit. So much bullshit. The clock read 18.27. Chris was already bored and the pizza had made him sleepy. Yawning, stretching and occasional deep breaths were no longer effective. He looked over at his colleague; intense, keen and extremely annoying.

"Pssst."

No response.

"Pssst!"

Xav pressed his fingers to his ears. Chris couldn't believe it. He stood and went over to administer some gentle violence. But before he got close enough to yank on Xavier's ear, he saw what was on the screen.

Art. A depiction of a figure in a chair, maybe an electric chair, with updraughts of air or light or electricity, and a man in purple screaming his head off. Hideous, raw picture of pain. Not nice. Who would ever want to look at that? Using his knee, he nudged Xavier, who lifted his upper arms, threaded his hands behind his head and stretched.

"You already want to take a break, or ...?" Xavier's face bore no traces of weariness.

"Yeah, I'm flagging."

"Did you find anything?"

"Nope, not yet. But I'll be more effective after some coffee. What is that you're looking at? I think it will give me nightmares." Chris couldn't tear his eyes from the screen.

"Images she downloaded from the *may-not-know-much-about-art* forum. She was a busy member on there, but only at specific times. I looked at her web history, you see, and focused on the six months before these deaths. This is what I found. I cannot really see a pattern, but she is active for weeks, sometimes months before one of our guys' deaths, but completely silent in the weeks just after. It feels funny, Chris."

Coffee could wait. "Say that again. She looks at these images from a public forum for months before the guys go down, then doesn't touch it in the weeks just after a death? In all cases?"

"No, there's a strange slip in 2011. She's consistent until early January and then goes quiet. After that, early March to April, which was when Ryman died, she's almost constantly online. I just wondered if this site could be a way of passing information. Encrypted, or coded, or ..."

Chris's mind cleared and a possibility smacked his forehead.

"This activity you describe – is she just posting, or uploading, downloading, what?"

Xavier looked at a printout. "Mostly downloading, but a lot of commenting too. Endless thank-yous. Very few uploads."

"Uh-huh. It could be. What's she downloading? Art images, digital photos, JPEGs, documents, what is it, Xav?"

"The site is for amateur art lovers. Pretty small. Around 60 members and they seem to work like a book club. Discuss an artist, share your images, have a chat. It doesn't seem to be anything exciting, just people talking art. I only noticed the activity records and matched them to the dates."

"She chats and what else? What else does she do on this site?"

"As I said, she downloads. She and another user are fans of this artist," Xavier spread a palm toward the screen. "And they share pictures, talk about them, and that's about it."

Chris kept his voice cool. "Richter downloaded what exactly?"

"JPEGs of fine art... I am still counting how many painting files she has from the same artist. But she uploads very little. An article on him, a story she heard, but no images."

"Articles and paintings of which artist?"

"Francis Bacon. British. He died in 1992. He did a lot of triptychs. Like this one. The first thing she downloaded."

Xavier clicked on the icon and Chris craned in to study the three rectangles. The title below the image read, *Three Portraits: Posthumous Portrait of George Dyer, Self Portrait, Portrait of Lucien Freud*. The figures were strangely twisted and deformed, features like gargoyles, and pools of black seeped from them, like oil-slick shadows. The space in which each figure sat had a marbled floor, and yellow and blue walls, empty but for the photographs in the background of the left and right panels. A photograph within a painting; it made for an odd contrast.

Chris's mind whirred up like a drill. Images within images. Hiding something by not hiding. Something else, there was something else. Receiving large amounts of coded information. He looked again at the smudged faces.

"Xavier, you ever heard of steganography?"

Chapter 33

Zürich 2012

Kälin's BMW pulled onto Kasernenstrasse, nosing its familiar route towards Adliswil. The Mondeo swung out soon afterwards, remaining a good distance behind, as if it knew its destination. Friday evening traffic made for heavy going until they hit Manesse, when the motorway opened up the flow.

As usual, Kälin took Route 4, heading south. The figure at the wheel of the Mondeo relaxed. *Alles in Ordnung.* All going like clockwork. Kälin's dull routine was unchanged. No supermarket stop tonight; it appeared he was going straight home. Which was exactly as it should be.

While Kälin remained inside his apartment, the figure remained in the car, checking the paperwork, memorising every detail so that nothing would be unexpected. Sure enough, the detective, wearing jeans and a casual jacket, left home at six-thirty and turned left along Austrasse. The figure gave it a few moments before following on foot. Kälin turned right onto Bahnweg, checked for oncoming trains and crossed the railway tracks.

There was no need to check. Trains ran this line at ten minute intervals during rush hour, and the last one had gone through five minutes ago. The figure knew the timetable by heart. As they progressed further into the industrial estate, it became increasingly difficult to keep the target in sight without being seen. But there was no need for concern. Kälin never deviated from his routine.

He made for the working man's bar tucked away behind the paint factory. As the figure passed and glanced in, Kälin was shaking hands with three men at the back. Sitting at the bar to observe was not an option. So the figure sat at an outside table, ordered a coffee, engaged the waitress in conversation regarding the menu and watched. None of Kälin's companions looked familiar. One older man began dealing cards. It was *Jassen* night, which could take several hours.

Perfect timing. Some other chores needed completing. The figure paid for the coffee and headed back to Austrasse. Nothing to worry about. The routine was always the same. Kälin would drink three beers, eat two sausages, play a few hands and walk home alone.

Across the railway tracks.

Chapter 34

Zürich 2012

Heat rose from the street, people slung jackets over their shoulders and pavement cafes filled with sunlit smiles. Beatrice found herself approving of the world in general, spreading the late afternoon warmth. She trotted along the river side of the street, water sparkling in her peripheral vision. One of Ken's crumpets would have gone down a treat, but there simply was no time. She would have to call him in the morning.

Madeleine was due at seven. Culture and companionship tonight, coupled with the prospect of unearthing the truth tomorrow made Beatrice almost giddy. Her pinkish blouse would do, with a pair of navy slacks. She stopped, realising she had left her jacket in the office. Never mind, the blue pashmina, her birthday present from Tanya, would suffice instead. Rather a colourful ensemble for a change.

Approaching the turn-off to her street, she saw Madeleine crossing the road, looking for all the world like Lee Miller. Her blonde waves bounced off her white shirt, her khaki trousers were fastened with a leather belt and she carried an enormous designer bag. She noticed Beatrice, waved and hurried to meet her.

"I'm so happy you could make it. Your evil employers released you for the evening?"

Beatrice grinned. "Just. You look wonderful! Can I have five minutes to change?"

"Sure, go ahead. I'm way early but I thought we could have an aperitif before we go. I just need to hit a store to get a couple ingredients. We got plenty of time. The concert starts at eight, so we can wander up and peek at the church windows with a half hour to spare. Shall I come up in about ten minutes?"

"Ideal. See you then. Just tap on the door, room 305 and come on in."

Dumping her bag on the sofa, Beatrice picked up her mobile and dialled as she began to disrobe.

"Matthew, it's me."

"Hello, Old Thing. You're early tonight. I've just come through the door. You checking up on me?"

"Yes. And it seems with good reason. I hear voices."

"You should see someone about that."

"There, I mean. In the background. You have someone with you. No, there's more than one and they're both female. A pair of Swedish masseuses?"

"Tarnation. I've been rumbled. Ingrid, Greta, I'm afraid you'll have to pack up the birch twigs. My other half disapproves."

Beatrice heard Tanya and Marianne laughing and calling their greetings.

"Hello Beatrice!" Both added a comment, but Beatrice only caught '... eye on him', and 'cuckoo clock', amid some strangely simian grunts, which may have been Luke.

"Hello back and give them all a hug from me. You have your hands full this evening, then?"

"Rather. Luke's teething, Marianne is furious with someone at work, and Tanya's computer has a virus. Or maybe Marianne has a virus and Tanya is furious with her computer at work?"

"Good luck, Pops. Now listen, I won't add to your burdens. My day has been most successful and I think tomorrow will be our breakthrough."

"Tally-ho! So we might have you home soon?"

"It certainly looks that way. I'm so glad the girls are there with you. I feel less guilty now. I was only calling to say I couldn't call this evening. I'm going out with my friend – I told you about Madeleine – to see some stained glass and hear some yodelling."

His amusement was audible. "Yodelling?"

"Yes, yodelling. As a matter of fact, I'm thinking of taking it up. James said I could do with a hobby."

His smile became a laugh. "How charming! I'm all for it. It will certainly enliven a Sunday morning in Brampford Speke."

"I have to go. Call you tomorrow."

"Until then. Have fun."

As she replaced the receiver, she thought she heard him singing '*High on a hill stood a lonely goatherd …*' Chuckling, she headed for the bathroom.

She might even attempt to style her hair. It wasn't every night that she had fun.

"Are you decent?"

"I'm never anything else. Come in, Madeleine, take a seat. I'll be two minutes." Beatrice gestured to the sofa and returned to the bathroom. Her hair refused point blank to return its previous sleek and shiny incarnation. Tonight, it was especially troublesome.

Madeleine's voice wafted through the door. "No hurry at all. I'll pour us a drink. We should celebrate."

"Good idea. Oh!" She came back to the living-room to face her guest. "Have you had some good news?"

Madeleine's blue eyes scrunched up and a huge smile lit up her wan cheeks. "You got it! Michael got promoted and we're going back to New York! Permission to leave – as of next month!"

"Oh Madeleine, that is wonderful news. I am so pleased for you. I know you found life in Zürich awfully tough. Have you booked a flight yet?"

"Hey, I'll get one tomorrow. But finally I can go home and start rebuilding my career, you know? So let's drink to our successes, eh? These are Kir Royales – I think we deserve it. To us!"

The glass of blush bubbles looked elegant, appropriate and even matched Beatrice's blouse. She tinked her glass against Madeleine's and smiled. "To us!"

As she sipped, a flush of warmth filled her. Even a dispassionate observer could see the change in Madeleine's demeanour. The woman vibrated with energy and good cheer.

Madeleine waved her glass. "Don't let me hold up your preparations. Take your glass with you, and I'll tell all when you're ready."

"Right. I'll just finish my hair. And tell me anyway, I can hear you from the bathroom. When did you get the news?"

Madeleine raised her voice over the hairdryer. "Just after lunch. Which was so annoying, I can't tell you. I had a pretzel and a Coke on the run, then found out I could have been at Brasserie Lipp, popping champagne corks and shucking oysters. Ah well, it's almost over now."

"You must be so relieved. Mmm, this Kir Royale is hitting the spot."

"My own recipe. Say, how was your day?"

Beatrice despaired of trying to recreate her salon hair, gave it a pat and returned to the living room.

"My day was very pleasing. I have high hopes of soon being able to return home too. So, let's have a toast."

Madeleine stood and lifted her glass. "So let's toast. To my ticket out of here, your breakthrough and future happiness for both of us! To going home!"

"To going home!"

The sweet blackcurrant and dry champagne was most appealing. One of those drinks that tasted dangerously innocent.

Beatrice smacked her lips. "But before we leave, we're going to sample some genuine Swiss culture. I'm very excited about this."

"Me too. To be honest, it's not likely that I'll ever be back, so I should see as much as I can before I ship out." Madeleine drained the last of her cocktail. "So! Shall we go local?" She picked up her oversized handbag.

"Let's." Beatrice gathered her accoutrements from the coffee table. "Key card, mobile, handbag and my shawl. It's a lovely evening, but might be chilly later. Right, I'm ready to go."

As she pulled the apartment door closed behind them, Madeleine started to sing.

"I love Zürich in the springtime, I love Zürich in the fall ..."

"Hush, now!" Beatrice assumed her schoolmarm voice, summoning the lift with a grin. "One Kir Royale and she's anybody's."

But the truth was that she was twice as high-spirited and gigglesome as her companion. Must have been the champagne.

Keep calm. There could be nothing in it.

Chris tried to ignore the adrenalin rush that charged his body.

"Steganography is a way of hiding data within data," he began, before drawing a long breath and trying to focus his thoughts. Xavier waited, full of concentration.

"It's been around since, oh I don't know, the Greeks? It's an old art. But now you can apply the ancient principle to technology. To the casual observer, the piece of music, the photo, the video file looks completely innocent. But it has been altered to include information. Text, visuals, you name it. And the resulting image looks almost exactly the same as the original. Only with the right key; like change every third pixel to 25% darker and so on, can you uncover what's really in there."

"I know a little about that. It is the method of data transmission used by terrorists and military spies, that sort of thing? But even if we have the images, or think we do, we can achieve nothing without the key. Can we?" Xavier's voice sounded hopeful.

"There are two ways of going about this. We can try a universal application, taking this image and analysing it for embedded material. Depends on what's in there, if anything. If the payload is small, we may find nothing. But if there's significant data hidden behind this picture, there are lots of ways of slicing it up to see what's inside. That should give us enough information to see if the image needs investigating. We have the tools to find out where to dig; but unearthing whatever is hidden could be more of a challenge."

"And the other approach?"

"We find the key. This is not a simple 'two steps left, one back' code. This is a complex instruction for this algorithm which she must have recorded somewhere. Maybe it's encrypted, coded ... goddam it to hell!" He slammed his palm onto the table.

"Chris? Is everything fine?"

"Sorry, Xav. Really. It's just that there's something ... I don't know. An idea, a hint of something keeps bubbling just under the surface. But every time I try to grab it, it's gone. There's a clue here, I just know I haven't picked up on a vital point. Maybe coffee would help. You want some?"

"Yes. Would it be intelligent for me to look for the key? While you try the applications to open these pictures, and maybe with luck, one of us will find out what is interred there?"

"Coffee. Come. Give your eyes a break."

Xavier followed Chris to the rest area. Two brains whirred, clunked, hissed and fizzed in an echo of the coffee machine.

"Xav, are we wasting our time? Should we keep analysing the rest of this data and not run off after a wild card?"

Xavier stirred his coffee thoroughly, despite the fact he'd added no sugar.

"If you really feel we are gambling on a wild card, let's call Sabine and Conceição back. They can make sure there's nothing significant somewhere else on the hard drive. My gut tells me we have something, but you're right. We shouldn't run in only one direction and forget the rest. Shall I call them?"

Chris felt a buzzing between the joints of his fingers. He threw back his espresso and tossed the cup into the recycling bin.

"My gut is with your gut. We've found our way in and now we have to crack it. You explore anywhere she might have hidden the key, while I'll apply every steganalysis technique I can access. We'll pull this bastard out of there and present B with a *fait accompli* by the morning. Come on, this has just started to get interesting."

Xavier threw his cup after Chris's and dabbed his mouth with a napkin. Chris filled a paper cup with water and looked at the younger man.

"It's a lot to ask of you, working through like this. Do you need anything?"

Xavier shook his head and met Chris's eyes. "It is nothing to ask of a member of the team. And no, I want no more food. The only hunger I feel is for knowledge."

Chris burst into laughter and wrapped his arm around his colleague's shoulders. "Sometimes, Xav, you are so bloody French."

Bahnhofstrasse was busy. Couples strolled along the wide pavements, groups of businessmen left their offices to continue talking shop in one of the many discreet bars, and a gaggle of shrieking teenagers ran for the No. 7 tram. Crossing the street, Madeleine led the way up Rennweg. No trams, no vehicles of any sort, just cobblestones and wandering pedestrians.

"That's the hotel we're going to later," Madeleine indicated to their right. The white building sported blue shutters and the image of a mountain goat. Beatrice nodded. Hard to imagine yodelling in such an enclosed space. But she supposed yodellers must practise somewhere. As the street narrowed and descended toward the River Limmat, both women were absorbed by the variety of shop windows, intriguing alleyways, courtyards with murals and, the first time for Beatrice, a display of cuckoo clocks.

"Madeleine, look! I haven't seen a single one since arriving in Switzerland. But here they all are. There is something so kitsch and charming about them. Someone wants me to bring one back."

Madeleine wrinkled her nose. "Not my sort of thing. I love the Swiss railway clock. Clean, functional and precise. These things are for tourists."

"True. For people like us." She peered closer. "But as I told her, not at those prices. I'll buy her some chocolate and be done with it."

Before entering the church, Madeleine suggested walking to the Stadthausquai to see the famous windows from the outside. Turning their backs to the river and the sound of swans quarrelling over scraps, they looked up. Passers-by paid them no attention. Madeleine leaned toward Beatrice.

"I thought about buying a camera. But you know what? I am going away with all these pictures in my mind. My skills in photography couldn't do justice to this, anyhow. You wait there a second and I'll just check it's still open."

Beatrice wasn't really listening. The windows must have been 30 foot tall, such fabulously dense works of art. She stepped back to the riverbank railing, leaning back to take in the whole wall. She had no idea what the pictures signified, but they were undoubtedly uplifting.

Madeleine came back and tweaked her sleeve. "Yes, we have another hour before they close. Shall we go in?"

"This is where the bodies are buried, I'm sure of it." Chris called over his shoulder. "The only compressed files which seem to have a data irregularity are those posted by 'Mother-of-Pearl.'"

Xavier tapped at his keyboard. "I'll look back at the conversations between the two of them, and see if anything comes up. 'Mother-of-Pearl' is definitely her favourite poster; they have a whole series of private messages to each another."

"Print them out, and let's take a look. Do they discuss any

other artists?"

"A little. There are some comments on Paula Rego and on Freud."

"Freud?"

"Yes, Lucien Freud. He was in that Portrait triptych. Oh, you were thinking of *that* Freud. No, it's the other one."

Chris's head jerked up and he stared at Xavier. "The other one."

He clasped both hands to his forehead and leant back as the realisation hit him. "Xavier, that's it. That's what I was trying to grasp. The other Bacon. There was another Francis Bacon, a scientist, philosopher and so on. Some people think he wrote Shakespeare's stuff. But what's important is he was one of the earlier print steganographers and he came up with a cipher. Shit! I think we've found the way to decode it."

"Have we? Even if we have, what is it that we decode?"

"It has to be in the early communication between Richter and this 'Mother-of-Pearl'. Did you print those personal messages? Give them to me. We're looking for anything that looks like strange English. Or just strange."

All of it was bloody strange. Chris scanned the bland exchanges with increasing irritation. Then something caught his eye.

Yes, the skin quality was the first thing that drew me. It's like meat.

Is that where you got your name? Mother-of-Pearl?

Yes! I find an agony in his work. Such pain, such tragedy.

He had such pain and tragedy in his life.

Everything about him breaks my heart.

You're right. Bacon seems so sad. There is a sadness about him, poor boy.

I understand his work. It makes sense to me.

I'm happy to hear that. Me too.

"What do you see, Chris?"

"What do *you* see, Xav?"

"The only thing that made me wonder was this bit. *I understand, it makes sense.* I'm probably naïve, but does this communication mean 'message received', do you think?"

"In which case, the previous sentence, or conversation above is our payload. What do you see there?"

"Nothing. I tried everything. First letters, take out vowels, I think I may need some time to work the code."

"We already have the code. It's Bacon's cipher. We need to find some communication which uses a binary combination. For example, a combination of two different size fonts?"

There was a moment's silence. "Yes! It's there! '*You're right. Bacon seems so sad. There is a sadness about him, poor boy.*' That's got two different sizes."

"It has, but they're pretty close. You wouldn't notice unless you were looking for it. Now what we need to do is decode. Let me drag up Bacon's cipher. Shit, it's so true. Keeping it simple always works best. Right, Xavier, copy this into a WORD document, then denote each use of a font with *a* or *b*, starting with *a*. And group them into five."

Xavier nodded, and like a trouper, got down to work. "Twelve, twelve, eleven, twelve ..."

Chris did exactly the same in his head, and reached his conclusion minutes before his colleague. While waiting, he proceeded to do the decryption the other way. Belt and braces.

Xavier's head snapped up. "Finished. You want to hear? I've got aabab, abbab, baaaa ..."

"Hang on. What you have is a series of a/b combinations. Here, look. Each combination of a/b delivers a letter. So now we apply Bacon's cipher. For example, aabab in Bacon's chart represents the letter F. Now we need to decode the rest. God, I hope we got this right. Go, take your text and work it out."

Xavier's eyes flicked from Chris's print-out to his own handwriting, making notes and noises of satisfaction. Chris checked both his versions mentally and forced himself not to crow as he saw it.

Xavier got to the end. "It says 'forty two LSB'. Least Significant Bit! That's pixels, that's the instruction for how to explore it. I think we found it, Chris!"

Chris kept the lid on his elation.

"Well, we found part of it. There must be a whole lot more, but we can get started. Keep looking for more phrases like that in their conversations, and transcribe it the same way. I'm going to begin unpacking some of these images."

Reseated at his workstation, Xavier turned. "Are you going to look at the most recent stuff, in 2012?"

"I think I'll start with 2007. Let's build up a chronological picture. There's no hurry. As B said, she's already got her victim for this year."

The heavy handle banged an echo to announce their entrance, but no other tourists were in sight. Stopping just inside the doorway, Madeleine carefully closed the door, while Beatrice took in the huge vaulted transept. A change in atmosphere drained her frivolity. This was obviously a perfect time to come sight-seeing – not a soul around. Jewel-bright colours up to her right caught her attention. The Giacometti window. Row upon row of men and angels robed in rich shades looked down on her. Feeling under-informed, she picked up a brochure bearing a Union Jack and began to read.

Madeleine bumped her hip up against her. "Beatrice! Come on, we can do the research later. Let's just take a look at the real thing."

Turning the corner, they entered the choir area and stopped in their tracks. Five Chagall windows; one right, one left, and the three they had seen from outside. The late afternoon light, contrasting with the darker interior, enriched the vivid pictures and threw reflections at their feet. Like a patchwork quilt of glass, leaded seams joining squares, triangles and parallelograms of cobalt, daffodil, cyan and turquoise. A raw joy pulsed through Beatrice, elation at experiencing such beauty. Twin impulses rose: to cry and to laugh. She did neither but soaked up the scale of the vision. Such grandeur, such majesty; unsurprising that one should feel a sense of religious awe. Stars adorned the ceiling and the clean, palest grey stone bore engravings of angels' wings. The collusion between Nature and Man achieved its objective – she felt small in the presence of grace.

"What's the time?" asked Chris, returning from the bathroom.

"Twenty past seven." Xavier stood behind Chris's chair, reading the data extracted from *Fragment of a Crucifixion*. Photographs, bank details, company description, financial statements, news reports and medical history, along with a detailed record of the movements and sexual preferences of Jens van der Veld. "It's unbelievable. So much information hidden in one picture."

Chris scanned the bottom of the screen, packed with tiny icons indicating the various documents he had found in the file. "Like the Tardis."

Xavier looked up in enquiry.

"Never mind. OK, so it's taken me over an hour to reveal this. Presuming the steganalysis tool is accurate, we have eight more files to unpack. We can do two at a time. Now, if the key were different for each image, we could be here a long time. However, it seems that the same key is valid for each of these JPEGs, with some slight adjustments. All of which she has communicated through the same channels. So we could, in theory, expose the lot by midnight."

Xavier's expression was puzzled. "Why are there eight, Chris? There's a pattern up to a point. This *Crucifixion* stuff was communicated in 2007, and obviously correlates with the Utrecht killing. There's one image per year, so presumably we'll find Thompson behind *Three Studies from the Human Body*, and *Man in Blue I* contains everything on Belanov, and so on."

"Yeah. And so the only oddity is the number of images for 2011 and 2012. There are two for each. In 2011, *Untitled*

(Marching Figures) was downloaded in January, and *Blood on the Floor* in April. So the latter must contain data on Ryman. Who's behind *Untitled*, then? Did we miss someone?"

Xavier shrugged. "Maybe we did. Two deaths in 2011? But I'm more worried about the extra file for this year. One of them must be Esposito, of course. Probably *Head IV*, downloaded April 2012."

"That was the one you were looking at, right? The purple agony? Oh God."

"Yes, why?"

"Xavier, you do remember how he was killed?"

"Oh." Xavier's expression of disgust seemed less repulsion at the man's demise and more disapproval of the killer's poor taste. "So why is there another image for May 2012?"

Chris shook his head. "I guess it's possible they have a secondary target in mind in case they fail for some reason with the guy in pole position. Maybe Esposito and Ryman were second choices? What do you think?"

"That's possible for Ryman. But this year, the first choice has already been executed. In which case, whoever is in the second picture is probably still alive. Would they try to kill two people so close together?"

"Maybe. Or if there were targets she missed, she may come back for a second try. Let's work on the living first, before digging up the dead."

"Right." Xavier's leg bounced with nervous energy. "Which one do you want?"

"I'll take the *Marching Figures*. Which leaves you with the *Nurse from Battleship Potemkin*. Rather you than me."

Xavier was already back in his seat.

Chris's mind ranged over the possibilities as he applied the codes to the picture on his screen. He was missing something, he could feel it. He shook his head to clear his thoughts and scanned the details below. Cesare Boldoni. Nice-looking guy. Chairman of Aceso, the Lombardy pharma giant. Lots of accusations against the company centred on one particular drug: *Ristorex*, the anti-depressant. Wealthy guy, married with a kid. Some powerful allies in Milan, but few in Rome. Apparently faithful, Catholic and hard-working. What happened, Helene, did you change your mind? Why did you let Boldoni go? Or did D'Arcy make that decision?

Pressing his palms against his eyelids, he ran through it. If Antonella D'Arcy is on the other end of Richter's leash, then why these men? An avenger in the form of struck-off doctor he could understand. But a woman whose lifestyle is funded by working hand-in-glove with these profiteers?

"Chris."

He lifted his head from his hands, the soft sound of skin parting. His eyes refocused on Xavier's stricken face and all the hairs on his arms rose. In one stride, he was at Xavier's screen.

"The other target for this year."

With her typical preoccupied expression, wayward hair and familiar grey suit, the image Xavier had extracted from behind the screaming *Nurse in Battleship Potemkin* was unmistakeable.

"Beatrice. Oh Christ."

"Giacometti has something special. But then I always tend to favour the underdog."

Beatrice agreed. "Poor devil is rather overshadowed here, but I agree, he certainly has something."

Madeleine glanced at her watch. "We should get out of here pretty soon, but I so want to take a look at the crypt. Wouldn't it be the coolest place for a Halloween party?"

Madeleine's laughter jarred in the wood and stone, stained-glass peace.

"I can't imagine the crypt would be open to the public."

"Sure it is. There used to be a convent on this site, which is why it's called Fraumünster. The original abbesses built the crypt to house the relics of the martyred saints. And we should take a peek before we leave, we owe it to the girls. But we need to be quick; the concert starts in a half hour."

"Very well, let's have a look. Always best to get in a martyred saint before a batch of yodelling. Come along then, you ghoul."

Madeleine laughed again and made a sweeping gesture. "After you."

Beatrice led the way down the steps. "Take care, Madeleine. There's not much light down here."

As she descended, a stone chill wound around her like a musty hound. Spores of chalky damp clung to her hair, her clothes, her skin. She was turning into a mushroom. She stopped at the bottom of the steps, with no inclination to go further. Madeleine slipped past her and into the murky interior. Candle-shaped bulbs in brass sconces reflected a weak glow up the stone walls, so that the central area, containing the tombs, remained in half shadow.

"I am surprised they let the public in here. It doesn't feel at all healthy."

"Don't worry. I just want a quick look at these, and we're gone." Madeleine studied the ancient remnants of an altar. Beatrice moved a few paces into the room, which had none of the spruce of upstairs. A damp dust lay on the floor and the graven images of the stone centrepiece, settling in the corners on some spiders' webs, giving them an appearance of old frayed cloth.

"What an eerie place." The final, funereal atmosphere punctured Beatrice's mood. Optimism here was unimaginable.

"Damn right. But you know what's weird? Like I say, I have no plans to return here, but this cathedral will always stay with me."

"I'm pleased to hear that. At least, you'll walk away with some happy memories of Zürich." Beatrice joined Madeleine and they looked down at the faded representations of the long-deceased.

"Yeah. I saw some fun sights, I learned a bit about Switzerland and I met you. Those things are all mine. Thanks to you, not all my memories of Zürich are shopping, surfing and the absence of Matthew."

"Michael."

"Michael, yes. That's what I meant."

An icy wave broke over Beatrice and her scalp contracted. Frozen, she stared down at the stone, as a series of images blew through her mind like playing cards on the wind.

Matthew.

"My day has been most successful, and I think tomorrow could be our breakthrough."

"Tally-ho! So we might have you home soon?"

She'd told Matthew it was a breakthrough. No one else.

"My day was very pleasing. I have high hopes of soon being able to return home soon."

"Kir Royales. Let's toast your breakthrough."

Matthew. Michael.

"Be careful of anyone with an interest in this case."

The empty church.

"I'll just see if it's still open."

Good God, she'd fallen into the most obvious of traps. Her quarry was standing beside her. And both of them knew the veil had dropped. Beatrice raised her head. Madeleine lifted her gaze.

"Beatrice ..." she reached out a placatory hand to catch Beatrice's arm. Beatrice recoiled, her forearm pulling through Madeleine's palm. The syringe caught her wrist, a needle slipped through cherry silk and a piercing pain arrived simultaneously in her arm and the pit of her stomach. She wrenched her arm away, tearing open a wound, and backed toward the steps. The syringe fell to the floor.

Madeleine watched her with a resigned expression. Her voice changed, the accent flatter, and the permanent expressive sparkle in her eyes turned dull and cold.

"Beatrice, I'm actually sorry about this. You have many fine qualities I admire. But fundamentally, you're on the wrong side. You know, we could have been friends, in another life."

Shot through with fear and adrenalin, Beatrice lunged up the stone stairs, ears straining for the sounds of pursuit. None came and she knew before she pushed at the door that it would be locked.

After you.

Madeleine had not moved, obviously trusting the drugs to disable her. Whatever it was would probably take effect in seconds. If she was quick, she could call for help. Scrabbling for her mobile, she sensed a shadow blocking the light.

"Come down, Beatrice. I don't want you to fall and hurt yourself. I doubt you'll get a signal down here, but just in case, I removed the SIM card from your phone while we were having our Kir Royales. It's now floating somewhere in the Limmat. Come down, please, we're going to have another little cocktail."

Beatrice's descended on unsteady legs. This was not over. She would fight this bitch, this vigilante, this dispenser-of-misguided-justice till her last breath. Madeleine smiled at her, before glancing back at the altar, bearing her huge handbag. Two things occurred to Beatrice. Whatever Madeleine's chosen method of disposal might be, it was in that bag. And albeit smaller, but still carrying substantial weight, her own handbag rested in her left hand.

With enormous effort, she swung it at Madeleine's head. It connected with a weak clout.

"*Gott verdammt*!" Madeleine's voice seemed to come from the other end of a long corridor. Beatrice's legs gave way and she collapsed onto her knees. As Madeleine eased her onto her side, Beatrice's eyes closed against her will and her last conscious thought was what a shame they were going to miss the yodelling.

Chapter 35

Zürich 2012

Chris snatched up the desk phone before realising he didn't know her number. Xavier was a step ahead and had already dialled on his mobile. Chris listened as he reached for his own handset to call Kälin.

"Her mobile is unobtainable."

"Shit! Call the hotel. And Xav, let's get round there. Find the address while I call Kälin."

His fingers clumsy, he found Kälin's number. His hands shook as he listened to the spaces between long ringing tones.

"*Kälin?*"

"Herr Kälin, it's Chris Keese. We found data on Richter's computer on all of the victims, one every year, downloaded shortly before the murders. She's recently downloaded two more. Giuseppe Esposito and Beatrice Stubbs."

Kälin drew a breath. "*Where is Frau Stubbs now?*"

"We don't know. We called her mobile and her hotel room ..." he took in the shake of Xavier's head, "but there's no answer. We're going there now."

"*Call me if you find anything. I'll meet you back at Zeughausstrasse in twenty minutes. And get the others.*"

Chris dialled the girls as he ran down the stairs after Xavier, the long lens photograph of DI Stubbs burned onto his retina.

Kälin's black hair and thick moustache sharpened the contrast with his white face, as he entered the fluorescent-lit workroom.

Chris walked to meet him, leaving Sabine and Xavier to continue their calls. He dispensed with greetings.

"Not at the hotel. The staff didn't see her leave. Her room is clean and tidy with no sign of any problems. They have no CCTV. Conceição is still there, looking around."

Sabine and Xavier joined them. Kälin acknowledged them with a nod.

"What do we know?"

Sabine appeared pale and tired without her make-up. But her energy was undimmed. "The receptionist has no idea where she might be. But tonight she had a visitor. An American, blonde hair. They left together, apparently happy and laughing."

"And we have no trace on Frau Stubbs' mobile phone?"

Chris shook his head. "Nothing."

The door opened, and for an instant, Chris expected Beatrice to walk in, with a look of surprise and irritation to find them all there.

For the first time since they'd met, he was disappointed to see Conceição.

"Good evening, everyone. Forensic officers have examined B's room. Her stuff is still there, but there's no sign of anything untoward. Apart from two glasses on the draining board. One clean, one dirty. It's already gone to the lab, but we've seen this before."

The skin of Chris's buttocks and thighs chilled into gooseflesh.

Kälin clasped his hands together and looked from one face to the next. Chris observed the thin line of his lips before he spat out his words.

"So Richter has attached herself to Frau Stubbs and the murder of Esposito threw us off the track. Frau Tikkenen, with your knowledge of this woman's mode of operation, what is her plan? As quickly as you can, please."

Sabine's complexion was startling. Chris had never seen such a bluish pallor on something living.

Her voice was quiet. "It makes no sense. The deaths have always been merited, in the killer's eyes. So why Beatrice? And in orchestrating their end, she uses something that she sees as just in her method. I don't see what 'sin' Beatrice has committed and therefore I can't imagine how she plans to kill her. But one thing we do know is that Richter always has sufficient information to find a way in."

Conceição drew in a breath. "Well, we now have the same information. It's all on that computer. We don't have the luxury of time, but we could know as much about Beatrice as Richter does. Let's look at those details and see if there's something which can help us."

"Chris and I have already looked. It wasn't only her photograph hidden in there. She even had Beatrice's bank details, transcripts of telephone conversations and her police personnel file." Xavier seemed despondent, and with an inclination of his head, handed the baton to his colleague.

Chris hated this. It was like rooting through her diary. But he had no choice.

"Beatrice suffers from bipolar disorder. According to this information, she has done since her early twenties. She's been managing it with a combination of mood stabilisers and anti-depressants for a long time. But it seems she had a pretty serious episode about a year ago and is just getting back on track. This is her first major case since."

"Can you elaborate on 'a pretty serious episode', Herr Keese?" By the look on his face, Kälin had guessed. Or already knew.

Chris rested his mouth on his fist and took a deep breath, unable to look at the misery on Xavier's face. He straightened.

"She tried to kill herself, Herr Kälin. She took an overdose."

Conceição's hand rose to her throat. "And Richter knows."

Kälin broke the silence. "Think! Richter has somehow got Frau Stubbs's confidence and has taken her somewhere to stage a suicide. They are not at her hotel, so where are they? Where did they go?

Conceição spoke. "She had plans for tonight. Sabine and I invited her for dinner, but she had plans. She said she was going out with an acquaintance to get some culture."

"Culture? That narrows it down," observed Chris.

Kälin looked up. "Swiss culture. That's also what she told me. Religious art and yodelling."

"You could kill someone at a yodelling concert, I suppose. But faking a suicide? I don't think so." Conceição shook her head.

Silence can take many forms, thought Chris. Calm, comfortable and soothing. Or charged with the electricity of five frantic minds.

Sabine took a sharp breath. "The Kunsthaus! She was going to see some art tonight! We were talking about the Kunsthaus, and she was going to see some more."

"That's a possibility," said Kälin, reaching for his mobile. "Was there a particular exhibition, Frau Tikkenen, involving religious art?"

"She mentioned the Expressionists, and Matisse, and Chagall. She liked Chagall and said she was going to see some more tonight."

Xavier grimaced as if he were in pain. "How can I be so stupid? She asked me this morning which church was which. Herr Kälin – religious art, Chagall, it must be Fraumünster!"

Chris saw Kälin's face change, each taut muscle relaxing. "*Genau!* Exactly! The Chagall windows. The perfect place, it's closed at night. Herr Racine, find a number for the church management. The rest of us will go there. Come!"

On such occasions, Chris's long legs gave him an advantage. Running down the steps as fast as he could safely manage, he left his colleagues behind. Except for Kälin, who was right on his heels. As they reached the door to the car park, Kälin turned and shouted something back to Xavier in German. Shoving open the door, Chris couldn't be sure, but it sounded like '... *die Hunde*.'

The dogs?

The church sexton, despite radiating disapproval, was punctual. Kälin's brief explanation received no queries and the man opened the door. He led the way, turning on the lights, Kälin at his shoulder, Chris, Sabine and Conceição close behind. The church was huge. Chris grew despondent at the plethora of nooks and crannies, chapels, alcoves and tombs. Kälin instructed them to search a section each and proceeded towards the other end of the building.

Some sense of place held Chris back from calling out Beatrice's name. Instead, he investigated the nave, checked behind curtains and explored the pulpit. He lifted his head occasionally to check with his colleagues. Nothing. What if Richter had taken Beatrice some other place? That maniac could be slitting B's wrists elsewhere while he knelt on the floor, looking under pews. Frustration and impotence built into anger. Kälin was wrong, she wasn't here. It couldn't happen here. Tourists would be swarming through the very next day. There must be a vestry, or a separate chamber you could use for storage. There had to be a hiding place. Just like a computer; some data visible, some encrypted. But how do you hide a human being? A door banged open and Chris's hair stood on end as he heard panting.

Xavier led the way down the aisle, followed by two armed officers with police dogs and caught Chris's eye with a hopeful look. Chris shook his head. Kälin marched towards them, but said nothing and watched as Xavier knelt to offer the dogs a piece of cloth. Only then did Chris notice the traditional Alsatian was accompanied by a bloodhound. Without lifting his head, Xavier explained. "Her jacket."

The handlers spoke gentle motivating words and the dogs responded, tails wagging as they inhaled essence of Stubbs. Along with the team, the sexton was fascinated and on request, gave his permission with enthusiasm. Unleashed, the dogs went to work. Beginning in small circles, like metal detectors, they sniffed, stopped and started; sudden runs interrupted by a slow study of a particular spot. The handlers followed, muttering encouragement.

Sabine descended from the balcony to watch, standing close to Conceição. The quiet tension built as they all watched. A bark made everyone jump.

The bloodhound took off, followed by its colleague. Without lifting its snout from the ground, it ran in a direct line to the door in the south transept, where it stopped, barking, scraping and wagging.

Kälin turned to the sexton. "*Was ist dahinter?*"

"*Die Gruft.*"

Conceição looked to Chris for a translation.

Why had he not listened to his subconscious? *Just like a computer; some data visible, some encrypted.*

"The crypt."

The police team formed a reception line, as if they were at a wedding, allowing the sexton to come forward with the keys. The poor old guy shook, a combination of nerves and the spotlight of attention.

Door opened, the two dogs hared down the stairs, stopped and began a relay of barking. As Chris stumbled down, he recognised there was no aggression in that sound. It simply said, 'We found it.'

And they had.

Chapter 36

Zürich 2012

Fluorescent lighting at Kloten Airport's Jet Aviation terminal did Kälin's grim features no favours. Catching his own reflection in the tiny arrivals area, Chris realised he looked even worse. Each absorbed in his own thoughts, neither man spoke, but occasionally checked his watch or mobile phone. D'Arcy Roth's Gulfstream G550 touched down twenty minutes late. Two police cars were already stationed on the tarmac and airport security escorted Chris and Kälin to the aircraft.

Chris couldn't help but be impressed by the performance as she descended the steps. Hair swept up, she wore crisp white trousers, brown loafers, a gold silk shirt and over her shoulders, a suede jacket. She carried a brown leather briefcase and her gold jewellery caught the morning sunlight. Her make-up was light and she looked fresh, as if she were leaving her apartment for work, rather than coming off a sixteen-hour flight. With an artificial smile, she walked up to them. Her bodyguard and her daughter stopped at the bottom of the steps.

"Hello again, Herr Kälin. It seems I just can't get rid of you. And Frau Stubbs?"

Kälin held her gaze. Neither blinked.

"We have a few more questions, Frau D'Arcy. Will you come with us, please?"

"Oh God. This has gone beyond a joke. I have work to do. I cannot sit around waiting while you people try to find some way of making me your scapegoat." She shook her head in exasperation. "Wait, I must instruct my staff."

"Frau D'Arcy? You may not remember me, but I'm Chris Keese, a member of Frau Stubbs's team. Your staff will need to accompany us to the police station. You can take the first car. Would you like your daughter to travel with you?"

Without even registering his question, she barked over her shoulder.

"Dina!"

The girl jumped and hurried towards them. D'Arcy stalked straight to the waiting police vehicle and stopped. As he suspected, a first-class bitch who can't even open a door. Chris yanked the handle and swung the door open as if it were a limousine. D'Arcy slid into the back seat without acknowledging Chris. Again. The girl dropped her head and ducked into the car as if she hoped she'd gone unnoticed.

Seemed like Kälin had no intention of helping out, so turning to the bodyguard, Chris indicated the second patrol car. The man obeyed with a worried frown. Closing the door behind him, Chris instructed the officers to take them back to Zeughausstrasse. Kälin stood watching the cars pull away as Chris joined him.

"Shouldn't we head back to the station?"

Kälin did not reply. Chris saw the tiredness in the detective's expression had been replaced by something else. A commercial jet took off from the main airfield, the roar of engines making speech impossible for a moment.

"Herr Keese. Please tell me exactly what you saw just then. In detail."

Chris needed coffee. And sleep. Not mind games with Kälin.

"A very glamorous, very fresh 24-carat bitch just got off the plane, got mad with us for taking her into custody and showed her true colours by treating me and her daughter like non-humans. Did I miss something?"

"I did. Surprise. Her reaction was rehearsed. She was expecting us. This whole scene was prepared." He began walking back to the tiny terminal.

"And?"

"And I don't know. But for some reason, she thinks she's invincible."

"D'Arcy refuses to talk without legal representation. The company's lawyer is coming. Should we get coffee?" Chris rubbed his eyes.

Kälin lifted his chin abruptly in acknowledgement. "Get that warrant. We'll need it."

"Warrant?"

"Herr Keese, we need permission to take samples from all D'Arcy's female employees."

"Why do you want to do that now? We can't take samples until Monday. The only females we could test today would be D'Arcy's daughter and her cleaner. One of whom is too young and the other too old."

"We leave no stone unturned. Get the warrant and test them, please. Out of respect to Frau Stubbs. Call me when that lawyer arrives, I'll be in my office."

Chris chose not to be offended; the man's stress hummed like a piano wire. He delivered the warrant to Conceição, insisted she took samples from the daughter and the housekeeper, before excusing himself and returning to the computer room. He switched off the light and his mind, rolled up his jacket and lay on the floor.

"I repeat, Herr Kälin, I have no idea what happened to the doctor who made that mistake. That was the last I heard of her. I decided to take the matter no further as the hospital had already begun an investigation." D'Arcy voice was controlled and patient, as if talking to a child.

"You had no contact with her at all after she was struck off?" Chris demanded.

The deep blue eyes flicked in his direction, but she addressed her question back to Kälin. "Are all policemen this slow?"

Chris was used to this; her hostility was a good sign. Her lawyer – grey hair, navy suit, forgettable face – barely looked up from his note-taking.

Chris pressed on. "I repeat. You had no contact with her at all after she was struck off? This question is not restricted to Switzerland. Did you have any further contact with this woman – real or virtual?"

Her focus remained on the wall. "I repeat. No. I had no contact with her. Real or virtual, whatever that means."

"You never communicated with her via the Internet, for example?"

"Why would I do that? What on earth would we have to discuss?"

"Modern art, perhaps? Did you ever participate in an art forum?"

Her full focus returned to him. "Modern art? I am the CEO of a major financial services provider. We have a turnover of 16 billion Swiss francs, and we employ 50,000 people worldwide. In my free time, I am a highly regarded polo player, which demands several training hours a week. I have an active social calendar and spend 90 minutes every day in the gym. I have better things to do with my time than an art forum."

Kälin sighed. "Repeating your position in society will not work as a smokescreen here. Until you can prove you did not orchestrate these killings through Helene Richter, we will continue to believe you are involved."

D'Arcy gave a patient, pitying smile. "I am not one to teach a man his job, Herr Kälin, but I think you'll find that the burden of proof lies with you."

Chris spoke. "Don't worry about that, Frau D'Arcy, we are

very confident we have the right woman."

"I do hope so, Herr Keese. Because from here, it looks like you are wasting both my time and yours."

So she had taken note of his name. Chris could feel the balance of power tilting. And he wasn't the only one. He saw her direct a cold glare at her brief.

"Ahem." The lawyer, Herr Wortmann, prepared to speak, but a knock at the door prevented his response.

Xavier entered the room and bent down to whisper in Kälin's ear. The older man's brow creased into incredulity and he turned to face Xavier, with a shake of his head.

Xavier nodded. Kälin, expressionless, looked at Chris, and with a minute eyebrow movement, indicated the door.

Once outside the interrogation room, Kälin voiced his question. "Are you sure?"

Xavier's head bobbed up and down again. "The laboratory says 100%. The DNA is the same and Conceição agrees. A complete match on all points."

Chris looked from one to the other. "Who?"

Xavier jerked his head towards the cells. "The daughter. I put her under arrest."

"And does her DNA match what we found in Frau Stubbs's hotel room?" asked Kälin.

Xavier nodded again.

Chris shook his head. "How is that possible? Not only is she clearly a woman, but she can only have been a kid in 2007. And she was in Argentina last night. It makes no sense. What does she say?"

Xavier shrugged. "Nothing. She won't talk."

The three men stood in silence, until Kälin exhaled a sharp breath.

"I've had enough of this. That smart-mouthed female is going to tell us what's going on. Herr Keese, where are her weak spots, from your observation?"

Chris forced himself to think. "She thinks she's cleverer

than she is. She overestimates her own intelligence. And underestimates ours."

"Good idea. Herr Racine?"

The request clearly came as a surprise and Xavier's face went blank, before his eyes sharpened. "Her principles. We know she's behind this, so we have to get at what drives her."

"Thank you. Let's go."

"Herr Wortmann, more water? Frau D'Arcy? So, perhaps we can go back to my point. The connection with Frau Richter."

"It does not exist."

Kälin's voice changed from amenable to icy. "Here's the theory, Frau D'Arcy. We know you lost your father, Robert Wolf from Seattle, in 1976, and your mother remarried, rather quickly, in '78. You were eleven, correct?"

Satisfaction warmed Chris as D'Arcy sat frozen, unresponsive. They were getting to her, without a doubt. He used the side of his foot to nudge Kälin's, whose face twitched in acknowledgement.

"Jean-Baptiste D'Arcy. Your stepfather. A large personality, by all accounts. He must have entirely eclipsed your father; being so successful, genial, popular and rich. Your mother finally hit the jackpot. The American was a bit of a dud, wasn't he? Still, she struck gold with D'Arcy. The provenance of his wealth is shadowy, true, but on the surface, he was the perfect humanitarian. Sadly, your mother had only a short time to enjoy such good fortune. Six years of living the high life and she succumbed to cancer. That must have been very hard on you. Your stepfather, on his death, was worth some seventeen million Swiss francs, is that right?"

D'Arcy rested her chin on her hands. "And this is your theory? Despite the fact I was his only heir, I killed him for the money. You are of course aware, thanks to your impeccable research, that I had already inherited my mother's property, been headhunted by Hoffmann-Roth, and earned an impressively high salary. At the age of twenty-two. I had no need of his money."

"Need and want are two different things. After your mother died, you lived with D'Arcy for another five years. You were a high-flying businesswoman. You had more than enough money for a place of your own. A palace of your own. What possible reason would a young, successful woman like yourself have to spend five years in the same house as an older man, with whom you had no blood ties whatsoever? You say you had no need of his money. Maybe you stayed because of *his* needs."

Chris forced his expression to remain cool. Kälin's tactics surprised him, but he delighted in the result. The lawyer seemed to wake up. "Herr Kälin, that is unacceptable! I cannot allow my client ..."

D'Arcy snapped her head toward Wortmann and he petered out. She took a breath and returned her eyes to Kälin's.

"You are a small-minded little pervert. My stepfather was the most wonderful man I have ever known. My father taught me ethics, but when it came to practical applications, he was weak. Jean-Baptiste showed me that ethics and business are not divorced. Not even separated. It's a question of perspective. After you make difficult decisions, you have to compensate by being a force for the good. A lesson I learned well and have applied ever since. Jean-Baptiste was one of the greatest men I have ever known."

"So why did you have him killed?"

She locked onto Kälin's eyes. "I did not 'have him killed', as you put it. I gave him the one gift I could. I had already buried two parents and faced the loss of the single most influential person in my life. He was my guiding light, my star. I loved him more than anything. I would have taken his place if I could. When my parents died, I was too young to influence their suffering. But Jean-Baptiste knew he was dying. The only question was how long it would take. For the first time in my life, I was able to act. I talked to the anaesthetist and found a sympathetic mind."

She stopped, aware she had been provoked. Her brief leaned

in to speak to her, but she ignored him. "An act of supreme humanity on that doctor's part, not to mention her bravery, for which she was richly rewarded. End of story."

"But that was only the beginning for Helene Richter. Seems she had a taste for wiping out influential men and your stepfather was only the first. Or were they also 'mercy killings'?"

"Jean-Baptiste's death has nothing to do with this. And why would you suspect Richter? You're making ridiculous assumptions."

D'Arcy fixed her eyes on Kälin and blinked. But Chris knew the calm gaze obscured a maelstrom of thought. He tapped his foot to Kälin's. The response was immediate.

"So you're telling me Helene Richter had nothing to with the deaths in question?"

"I cannot imagine why you think she would."

"You're sure?"

She lifted her chin with an expression of boredom.

Kälin inhaled. "In which case, the prime suspect is clear. We have evidence that indicates the involvement of a woman, despite the DNA discovered. I am sorry to inform you that we have arrested your daughter, Frau Dina D'Arcy. She is now in police custody."

Chris didn't need to nudge Kälin for this one.

The pale face lost all colour. In the harsh light of the police interview room, she looked sickly, although her dark pupils shone.

"That is impossible. You have made yet another huge mistake."

"No. The male DNA planted at the site of each murder is a perfect match for that of your daughter."

The tension dropped from her jaw. "You took a sample of her DNA? Surreptitious gathering of samples can be challenged in law." With a slow turn of her head, she faced her lawyer.

"That is correct. We would certainly question the validity of ..."

Kälin interrupted. "There would be no question about the authorisation and technical accuracy of these samples."

D'Arcy shook her head. "You only tested the men yesterday."

"That is true, we did. But Frau Stubbs decided that we should also test your female employees. A wise move."

D'Arcy stared at Kälin for so long that Chris began to shift in his seat. She suddenly switched her attention to her brief and dismissed him. He hesitated, but not for long. As the door closed behind him, she exhaled a long, controlled breath.

"How ironic. When this was to be the last one." Closing her eyes, she took several slow breaths, before returning her gaze to Kälin.

"If you can assure me that you will not question Dina, or treat her as a suspect in any way, I will tell you what you need to know. You must be careful with my daughter. She is very fragile; her life has always been sheltered. She doesn't really understand the outside world. She is special."

"So her DNA seems to show." Kälin observed. "I give you my word we will proceed no further with Frau Dina D'Arcy until we have heard what you have to say."

Chris watched D'Arcy compose herself. His fatigue gave way to fascination; she was going to spill.

"Everything I said about Jean-Baptiste is true. I loved him. I persuaded Helene to help me end his suffering, because I could not bear to see his pain. It was an act of kindness. He never hurt me, or treated me as anything other than an adored child."

"What happened to Richter?" asked Kälin.

"Helene continued her studies. First in Brazil, and later in Canada. I had to pull more strings to get her a place there than I did to adopt my daughter. But she performed very well and exceeded expectations. I'd say my investment was repaid."

"Why did you pay for her education?" asked Chris.

"Because she should never have lost her place in Switzerland. Our plan, at the time of Jean-Baptiste's death, was for Helene to study anaesthesia and euthanasia, and for us to open a clinic where people could choose to end their lives, without pain and with dignity. We both agreed on that as a basic human right."

"A noble concept. I am curious as to how you made the leap from assisted suicide to serial murder." Kälin's tone sounded calm, but Chris sensed a seismic anger building.

D'Arcy frowned. "There was no leap. In fact, we saw our work as exactly that. Assisted suicides, where the individuals concerned required some help."

Chris paused to take that in. "Where does Dina fit into your 'work'?"

"She doesn't. She had nothing to do with it."

"So how do you explain ..."

"Herr Keese, your interrogation techniques appear to come from American television programmes. Please, let me speak."

Chris did not react, but watched her take a sip of water. There was not one sign that she was feeling the pressure. He admired her, in the same way he would admire a scorpion.

"After Jean-Baptiste died and Helene left for Brazil, I felt more alone than ever in my life. I had no one, nothing apart from my work. I wanted to be with someone, to have someone of my own. I considered an adoption and discussed the idea with Helene. She was a good friend to me. Then she had a stroke of luck. A small boy from one of the favelas got badly burned and Helene treated him. The family could not pay her; they had more children than they could afford and the woman was pregnant again. So Helene arranged a payment in kind. I paid her a large amount for her unborn child and prepared to embrace a baby into my life. In September 1994, she had a boy, Nino. I was desperately disappointed. I wanted a little girl."

"Did you sue her?" asked Chris, with heavy sarcasm.

D'Arcy gave a dismissive shake of the head. "No. Everything was arranged, and I intended to adopt a baby. A baby girl. Helene signed the certificate, confirming the age and gender as I instructed, and I took Nino back to Switzerland. I bought him dresses, I plaited his hair, I gave him dolls, and told him how beautiful she was. Nino became Nina."

Chris gaped, unable to think of a thing to say. Kälin seemed equally stunned for a moment, before recovering himself.

"What about when he went to school?"

"There is no 'he' anymore. We began gender reassignment operations before puberty. As for school, Nina was home educated until the age of fourteen, and very successfully, in fact. She has an impressive IQ, despite her parentage and may take up a place at a major university. This is why I insist you must be careful with her. She rarely leaves our house alone. Talking to strangers is hard for her."

Chris shook his head, his belief stretched. "Did Nino want to become a girl?"

"There was no question. To all intents and purposes, she was a girl. A sweet girl who has grown up into a lovely young woman. I am very proud of her." Her taut jaw indicated genuine emotion.

Kälin nodded. "It's no surprise the girl is so shy. You control her whole life. Most people would prefer their child to grow up with a little more worldly wisdom."

"Oh she *is* worldly wise. These days you don't have to go out there, Herr Kälin, the world can come to you. Her knowledge of the Internet allows her a whole online life. You know, sometimes even I don't know what she does out there. Her own mother!"

Her light laugh, with the confidential tone of parents at the school gate, caused Chris to hunch his shoulders against a sudden creeping thought.

He asked the question. "Did you change the child's gender in order to help you effect these fake suicides?"

D'Arcy glanced away and back in irritation. "Please try and keep up, Herr Keese. I explained that I wanted a daughter and that is what I achieved. Yes, there were barriers to reaching that goal, but I overcame. My choice to take some action against malevolent elements of society came much later."

Kälin's brows formed one continuous shadow over his eyes.

"Yes, let's talk about that choice."

She sat back in her chair, as if being interviewed on a popular chat show. Chris had to admit, the woman had balls.

"By 2006, the strategy I learned from my brilliant stepfather had turned Hoffmann-Roth into one of the Big Five. I was made Senior Partner and when Hoffmann retired, the company became D'Arcy Roth. My personal wealth exceeded the one billion mark. It was time, as Jean-Baptiste had always taught me, to give something back. The difficulty was that I was surrounded by 'takers' who never paid their dues. True, it was entirely my idea to drop Hoffmann's ethical standpoint and the decision proved profitable for the company. But the downside was that I spent years of my life smiling and shaking the hands with the foulest beings on the planet."

"So the next logical step was to get rid of them?" asked Kälin, head tilted.

"It had occurred to me. Planning the demises of certain individuals occupied much of my thoughts. Nevertheless, I believed they should do the honourable thing and make the world a better place by leaving it voluntarily. Only when Helene returned from Sault Sainte Marie did I realise the two things could be combined. We talked about it for almost two years, solving practical problems theoretically. The idea of leaving DNA to muddy the waters arose long before we realised we had the perfect source." She laughed, as if recalling a happy memory. "So that's when we changed Nina's name. It was our little joke."

Chris stared at her, aghast. Kälin looked down at the table, pressing his fingers to his forehead. When he looked up again, there were four white pressure points above his eyebrows.

"I think a break would be beneficial. I will send someone to see you have everything you need." His chair scraped back and he reached for the recorder. Chris stood and made for the door. D'Arcy's voice halted them.

"Herr Kälin. Dina submitted to the DNA sampling as she had done the operations. She thought it was part of her life and never asked questions. She had no idea what we used it for. She's entirely innocent."

Kälin turned, his eyes dangerously dark.

"All the men you targeted ... you believed that killing them was for the greater good. So why Frau Stubbs?"

D'Arcy leant back in her chair. "A combination of reasons. I dislike people passing judgement on me. I take it personally. We were, in fact, on the same side, if only she could have seen it. We both wanted to take out the bad guys. But her perspective was so narrow, bound by petty legal constraints. I shouldn't speak ill of the dead, but it's no wonder she was an unhappy woman. She fought a constant battle against bureaucracy. In another life, she might have joined us in making the world a better place."

Kälin's growled. "You think the world is a better place without Frau Stubbs?"

D'Arcy thought for a second, before offering them a smile.

"My world is."

Seconds ticked by and no one moved. Kälin froze, his finger poised above the recorder. Chris trained his eyes on D'Arcy, mentally hurling every curse he knew in her direction. Finally, Kälin spoke, directly into the recorder, without looking at either D'Arcy or Chris.

"So, you hunted down men who broke the law for their own selfish needs. You removed individuals who profited from the misery of the poor and disadvantaged. You took out those people who treated others like puppets for their own ends. You decided you were above all the systems and moral codes others adhere to and nominated yourself as judge, jury and executioner. And finally, you chose to kill someone who quite simply disagreed with you. In short, Frau D'Arcy, you became one of *them*. For your information, Frau Stubbs is recovering in hospital and quite determined to be fully fit to testify at your trial. Interview terminated, twelve forty-three."

Chapter 37

Zürich 2012

Klinik im Park was much quieter than the University Hospital. Out of the window, there was a glorious, blossom-filled park, and beyond, the Lake of Zürich. Nordic walkers, cyclists, joggers and a varied group of bathers revelled in the sunshine. A light knock sounded and the door opened. About time; she was starving.

"Beatrice! You're up!"

The sight of Sabine and Conceição's familiar, bright faces brought tears to her eyes.

"Beatrice?" They rushed to her side.

"No, no, it's silly, I'm fine. I'm just awfully pleased to see you."

Sabine leant down to give her a hug. Conceição's hand squeezed her shoulder. These wonderful girls.

Dabbing at her nose, Beatrice turned her attention to their bags. "I hope you've brought me something to eat. I don't think I've ever been so hungry in my life."

Smiling, the two women sat on the bed. Sabine unwrapped flowers and Conceição unpacked the contents of her paper bag.

"Food, yes, but the nurse says you must take it slowly. We also brought flowers, some books and magazines, all best wishes and the latest news. Number one topic? Your doctor says you can go home tomorrow, if all is well with the tests," Conceição announced.

Beatrice's heart leapt. Hospital was not all that dissimilar to prison, in her view, so when a reprieve was in sight, her hopes soared.

"Really? Oh, that's wonderful."

Sabine arranged the yellow bouquet in a water jug. "You don't really need to stay in hospital another night. The main reason they moved you here was to avoid the Apart'hotel. Kälin thought it would be best."

"That's very kind of him. But I'll have to go back there to pack, anyway."

Conceição shook her head. "It's all done. Your cases are at Sabine's, ready to go when you are. We did it this morning."

"Oh you are marvellous. Right, I need food, immediately followed by an update. Sabine, those flowers are delightful."

"Courtesy of the boys. They're coming in later."

"Potato salad, pasta with pesto and tomatoes, or a blueberry yoghurt?" Conceição held up three plastic tubs.

"All of them and in that order."

Sabine brought Beatrice's tray from the bed to the window chair, and Conceição opened the lids for her.

"The nurse did say that you had already eaten lunch," Sabine said, with an air of innocence.

Beatrice put down her fork. "I was given some thin soup, around elevenses time, for your information. And the doctor at University Hospital emphasised the importance of keeping my strength up. So allow me a light snack, while you bring me up to speed with the case. News, please."

Conceição kicked off her shoes with a laugh and tucked one long leg underneath her.

"*Bon appétit.* D'Arcy has confessed to organising all the murders, including one that didn't happen. A pharmaceutical boss slipped the noose, after having met Richter. They couldn't risk his recognising her on her second attempt, so they chose Ryman as the substitute ..."

Sabine interrupted. "So we've got D'Arcy, but still no sign of Richter. All border police have been alerted."

Beatrice shook her head. "She's long gone. After thirty-six hours? We've lost her, I'm afraid. What about the girl, Dina?"

"Under psychiatric observation." Sabine responded with enthusiasm. "She's a fascinating mix. I observed a few interviews. One minute, brilliantly intelligent; the next, you would think she had some significant learning disability. She was the person who kept the art forum active, logging in as all the different members, raising discussions, having arguments, and creating an entire imaginary world for Richter and D'Arcy to use for their own purposes. I have asked Dr Thiel, the psychologist in charge, if I can follow this case. I want to know what happens to this girl."

Beatrice nodded. "So do I. I feel for that poor child. Did D'Arcy confess to the press leak?"

Adding sliced gherkin to a potato salad was a sublime idea. A top tip she intended to use to impress Matthew. Beatrice tore the lid off the green and red pasta fracas and tucked in.

Sabine bit her lip. "B, the police team checked your room and belongings for any forensic evidence. They found a bug in your mobile phone."

Beatrice closed her mouth. "No. So *I* was the leak? Oh how awful!"

"We think D'Arcy probably organised that after the first time you locked horns."

An uncomfortable heat crawled up Beatrice's neck, making it harder to swallow.

"How's your throat, B?" Conceição asked.

Beatrice waved her fork in an indiscriminate gesture to communicate the fact that she was fine and they were to get on with it.

"So the case is finished. We have the woman behind these killings, and you led your team to a successful conclusion. Everyone's happy and tomorrow we go home!"

Sabine's comforting words stuck in Beatrice's throat and tears tickled her nose. Conceição knelt beside her, offering a tissue.

Beatrice grimaced. "I'm sorry. I seem to cry at the daftest things. Please ignore me. There's really nothing wrong with this pasta."

Conceição gave her shoulder another squeeze. "B, you're bound to be a bit raw. We've been just the same, haven't we?" She glanced at Sabine.

"Yes, and none of us went through what you did."

"Thank you, girls. You've both been wonderful to me. Visiting with food, news, a super pair of pyjamas, and more food. Worth your weight in coal. I shall miss you, you know. And I suppose I'll miss the boys, too. Are things still running smoothly with you and Chris, Conceição?"

Scooping up a cherry tomato, it took Beatrice a second to catch up. But the look between the pair was unmistakeable. She stared for a second, her mind processing what she saw.

"Oh, I see."

She really should get her radar re-tuned; she'd made the classic sexual jealousy assumption. "Well, congratulations! Oh dear, how did Chris take it?"

Conceição gave a resigned smile. "He's a cool guy, actually. He took it in his stride. Look, B, it's not common knowledge, okay?"

"I am the soul of discretion. Can I have my yoghurt now?"

Halfway through a BBC Prime episode of Doctor Who, Beatrice was lying on the bed when three light raps announced the arrival of Xavier and Chris. She felt a slight blush, hopefully imperceptible in the light of the television screen. The last time she'd seen these two was just after her stomach pump. But a civilised veil should be drawn over that.

"B! You look so much better than the last time we saw you! After they pumped you out at *Universitätspital*, you were grey. Like more dead than alive?"

"Chris, you are always such a joy. Xavier, I am thrilled to see you again. Have you brought cakes?"

Xavier beamed. "Sabine mentioned you are hungry, but all food must be soft. I brought you a *Birchermuesli*. How are you feeling?"

"Better. Hungry. Emotional. Sore. Curious."

Chris laughed and stretched out on the window chair. "We can satisfy the 'hungry' and 'curious'. I got you a tiramisu. Where do you want to start?"

"With the tiramisu, please. Oh, I see what you mean. What happens to D'Arcy now? And how's Dina coping?"

"D'Arcy will be charged tomorrow, but Dina will spend at least two weeks under observation before a decision is made. We have written up all our reports, Lyon's handing out gold stars, and tomorrow we can leave. Although I was thinking of staying on for a couple of days." Chris had a certain light in his eye.

"For work or pleasure?" Beatrice swallowed a large mouthful of coffee cream to disguise her curiosity.

"Could be both. I've got an opportunity to see how the extreme left works. I'm hoping to achieve some undercover anarchist penetration."

Xavier's face was a mixture of embarrassment, amusement and concern. "Can you also go home, B?"

"Pending the test results on my liver, yes. As you obviously know, this isn't the first time I've taken an overdose. My liver can't tell the difference between voluntary and not. So the damage is likely to be similar."

Meeting two pairs of sympathetic eyes was unbearable. "What about you two? I hope you received a glowing report from Kälin at the end of this."

"He's not writing our reports. He says it's your job," Chris replied.

Xavier hurried to add his comment. "But this time, B, he means it in a good way."

After taking note of her flight wish-list for the next day, the two men said their goodbyes. Beatrice remained professional throughout, only admitting gloom after the door closed. Switching off the light to allow her to watch them unseen, she stood at the window until their dear familiar forms crossed the road and got into their vehicle. With a sad smile, she gazed out at the lights across the lake on the Gold Coast. That beautiful empty villa. What would happen to that mosaic floor? What would happen to that mixed-up young girl? The tail-lights of Xavier's car disappeared around the bend. Goodbye, Chris, goodbye Xavier. What were the chances she would ever see them again? And since when had she started talking like Ingrid Bergman? An age-old ache cracked her chest, and a chasm began to open. Then a movement below drew her eyes. A few spaces back from Xavier's slot, a car's interior light glowed as the driver's door opened. It looked like a Ford Mondeo. A figure exited and made its way across the road to the clinic. Beatrice was ready.

"Ken! I am so pleased to see you."

"Thank Gawd you're still in one piece. Me and Noemi have been worried sick. What the hell was all that about? Kälin didn't have nothing to do with it, I'm sure of that. I was watching him all evening. I don't think he's your man."

"I know, I know. Rather embarrassingly, it seems I was the leak. I found out this afternoon my phone was bugged. Probably by the same person who tried to do away with me."

Ken folded his arms. "Well, I'll be blowed. And old Kälin was clean as a choirboy all along."

Beatrice agreed. "He was. He is. I was being over-cautious. I'm so sorry to have sent you off after a dead herring when it was my own indiscretions that let us all down."

"But you are all right, eh?"

"Right as rain. Now you're here, you may as well deliver your report."

"If you like. But that's not all I'm delivering. I got you some grapes. I wanted to bring you a Bakewell tart, but Noemi said it might be too much for you."

For once, Beatrice wasn't interested in food. "Thank you, that's most considerate. So, Karl Kälin? What did you find?"

"Here you go. Typed and everything. But there's nothing much there. I followed him for over a fortnight and found sweet Fanny Adams. Never seen him with any journos, apart from the official stuff. Divorced, lives alone, creature of habit, never breaks the law, a few close friends and he plays cards on a Friday. I could get to like this geezer."

"Thank you, Ken. And I'm sorry for dragging you out of retirement."

"None of that, mate. I had a right laugh getting back in the saddle. Tell you what, B, I wish you was staying longer."

The strangest thing was, so did she.

The sun sank, leaving both coasts illuminated by the thousand individual twinkles from streets, homes and cars. Beatrice had tucked herself in for the night and found Bergerac on TV when the knock came at the door.

Kälin's bear-like shape filled the doorway.

"Good evening, Frau Stubbs. I hear you are recovering."

Beatrice killed John Nettles with the remote. "What a nice surprise, Herr Kälin. Please come in, take a seat."

He sat on the window chair, his expression uncomfortable. His empty hands showed he had brought her nothing to eat.

"Does the Clinic suit you?"

"Apart from their appallingly tiny rations, yes. It's comfortable, private and most attentive."

"And professional. They check everything your guests bring and adjust your diet accordingly. They know what they are doing."

"I am going home tomorrow," she blurted.

"Congratulations. I know that makes you very happy."

Beatrice opened her mouth to correct him, but had no idea what to say.

Kälin cleared his throat. "Frau Stubbs, I came to say I am glad we had an opportunity to work together. I learned from you and that is my definition of a good collaboration. I leave you now, and wish you every success in your future career and the very best of health." He stood up to shake her hand.

Beatrice swallowed down her unreliable emotions, shook his hand and forced a professional, chirpy smile.

"Thank you, Herr Kälin. It was an experience I shall never forget, especially as it is likely to be my last case. But I will take many happy memories away. I wish you all the best for your future and I have one small request. I see a great deal of potential in Xavier Racine. Should you ever find yourself in a position to help his career, I would consider it a personal favour if you did so."

"You have a good eye."

"I used to have. None of us escapes time, Herr Kälin."

Kälin stepped back. "As you told me once before, you are stronger than you look. You led this investigation to its conclusion through sound leadership and good judgement. Perhaps your dreams of retirement are premature."

"Lyon may take an alternative view of what constitutes good judgement."

Kälin walked to the door, the corridor illumination silhouetting his form and hiding his expression. "It was a tough task. Under the circumstances, your performance was not too bad. All the best, Frau B."

The door closed.

Beatrice's brow creased and more infuriating tears seeped out. Sniffing and stemming the flow, she barely heard the knock. The bossy nurse.

"Frau Stubbs, you have eaten far too much today. But as this is a special request, you can have one more thing before bed. Now, after you have eaten this, you must drink a herbal tea and I will check you every hour. It is not recommended for this situation."

The smell was delicious; garlic, cheese, a hint of alcohol ... the woman placed a small plastic pot in front of her, beside a tiny plate of cubed bread. She handed Beatrice a fork.

"It is only microwaved, I'm afraid. But Herr Kälin said no one should leave Switzerland without eating a fondue. Not even in May."

Chapter 38

London 2012

As the five-note melody announced her phone restored to life, the baggage carousel in London City Airport cranked up. Intolerably excited by the knowledge that Matthew was waiting the other side of one of those bland grey panels, she fidgeted from foot to foot. Would he have thought to get milk? They could always stop on the way home. What did it matter, he was staying for the rest of the week. Such luxury. There would be time enough to do all the galleries, to loiter in Borough Market, to while away afternoons in the second-hand bookshops, to cook, to eat, to talk. Impatience swelled and she paced around to the other side. Her suitcase, naturally, was nowhere to be seen.

Vibrations from her mobile made her jump before she heard the ringtone. She checked the screen.

"Herr Kälin?"

"No, I am Herr Kälin. You are Frau Stubbs."

"I am aware of that, thank you. It was a question. What can I do for you?"

"It is really only a courtesy call. I thought you would be interested to know that Frau Dina D'Arcy managed to leave the psychiatric facility last night. As yet, she has not been located."

The bloody suitcase appeared exactly at the wrong time.

"What do you mean, 'leave the facility'? Wait a minute."

Beatrice shoved forward to drag her case off the conveyor belt. "How did she get out?"

"She was not a high-risk patient, so she was permitted to go out in the grounds. This afternoon, when someone went to find her for an appointment, she had gone missing."

"She can't go far. She has no money, and no idea of how to get around. Surely she'll be picked up in a matter of hours."

"A visitor's handbag is also missing, containing cash, ID, a mobile telephone. I think she might get further than we think."

"So the case is not closed at all. Do you think I should come back?"

"That's not necessary, Frau Stubbs. The case has been assigned to another team. But they have an excellent consultant."

"You."

"No, they don't need me either. They already have an expert in the form of Herr Racine."

Beatrice beamed. "Wish him all the best from me. And Herr Kälin, if you wouldn't mind, I'd appreciate the occasional email. Just to let me know what's going on."

"From Herr Racine, or me?"

"Both."

"I'll see if I have time. I must go now. I wish you a nice afternoon."

"Same to you. Goodbye, Herr Kälin."

He rang off and Beatrice dragged her case through the automatic door and into Matthew's embrace. He looked down at her, concern showing behind his smile.

"Nice hairdo. How are you feeling, Old Thing?"

"Surprisingly full of bees. Did you get milk?"

Chapter 39

Lake Konstanz 2012

The sun sat low over Lake Konstanz; pink, purple and silver flashed in the subsiding wake of a departing ferry, like the rippling flank of a rainbow trout. The white boat churned white water, confetti after the bride, as it passed its sister ship on the opposite journey. A figure rose from the bench outside the Zeppelin Museum and walked along the lakefront to the harbour to meet it. Shadows crept across the lake as the sun faded, yet it seemed as if the boat would beat the darkness to the shore.

Passengers gathered on deck, eager to step into another country. Docking, the engines' grinding ceased and the silence filled with the lively voices of tourists. Loud colours and opinions flickered past as the figure waited. Eventually, as the final few pensioners descended, she saw a slight, nondescript shape come along the deck, scanning the shore. Helene raised her hand, as if identifying herself for roll call. Dina lifted a palm and splayed five fingers in recognition.

Helene waited where she was. With great care, the girl stepped off the boat, almost as if it were her first time, and with similar caution, walked over to greet her. Three kisses.

Always three.

But now only two.

Acknowledgements

Beatrice and I owe a huge debt of thanks to:

You Write On and *The Bookshed* for early encouragement; Lorraine Mace, Jo Reed, Anne Stormont, Michelle Romaine and Barbara Scott-Emmett of *The Writing Asylum* for expert guidance; Klaus Böhni, Fulvia Staub-Mastellone and family, Martin and Nicole Horler, Julie Lewis and Janet Marsh for their input on first drafts; Catriona Troth for her continuing wisdom and support; Libby O'Loghlin for her friendship and whip-cracking; Sheila Bugler, Gillian Hamer and Liza Perrat for advice, enthusiasm and teamwork; Jane Dixon-Smith and James Lane for their creativity and class; and Florian Bielmann for his invaluable opinions and infinite patience.

Also by JJ Marsh

Raw Material

"I loved JJ Marsh's debut novel Behind Closed Doors, but her second, Raw Material, is even better... the final chapters are heart-stoppingly moving and exciting." Chris Curran, Amazon reviewer.

"Some rather realistic human exchanges reveal honest personal struggles concerning life's bigger questions; the abstruse clues resonate with the covert detective in me; and the suspense is enough to cause me to miss my stop." – Vince Rockston, author

Tread Softly

"The novel oozes atmosphere and JJ Marsh captures the sights, sounds and richness of Spain in all its glory. I literally salivated as I read the descriptions of food and wine. JJ Marsh is an extremely talented author and this is a wonderful novel." – Sheila Bugler, author of *Hunting Shadows*

"There are moments of farce and irony, there are scenes of friendship, tenderness and total exasperation - and underlying it all a story of corruption, brutality, manipulation and oppression with all the elements you'd expect to find in a good thriller, including a truly chilling villain. Highly recommended". – Lorna Fergusson, *FictionFire*

Cold Pressed

Editor's Choice – The Bookseller

This is J J Marsh's fourth, snappily written crime mystery featuring the feisty but vulnerable Stubbs, a most appealing character. It's all highly diverting, and an ideal read for those who like their crime with a lighter, less gruesome touch. – Caroline Sanderson, The Bookseller

Human Rites

"Enthralling! The menace of Du Maurier meets the darkness and intrigue of Nordic Noir. Keep the lights on and your wits about you." – Anne Stormont, author of *Displacement*

"Human Rites has got it all: organised crime, Beatrice Stubbs, nuns, Stollen, wine, Adrian and Expressionist art, with the added delights of a German Christmas, gay men's choirs and a farty Husky. She's back and she's brilliant!" – The Crime Addict

Thank you for reading a Triskele Book

If you loved this book and you'd like to help other readers find Triskele Books, please write a short review on the website where you bought the book. Your help in spreading the word is much appreciated and reviews make a huge difference to helping new readers find good books.

Why not try books by other Triskele authors?
Receive a complimentary ebook when you sign up
to our free newsletter at

www.triskelebooks.co.uk/signup

If you are a writer and would like more information on writing and publishing, visit http://www.triskelebooks.blogspot.com and http://www.wordswithjam.co.uk, which are packed with author and industry professional interviews, links to articles on writing, reading, libraries, the publishing industry and indie-publishing.

Connect with us:
Email admin@triskelebooks.co.uk
Twitter @triskelebooks
Facebook www.facebook.com/triskelebooks

Made in the USA
Coppell, TX
29 December 2020